GENTLE RAIN

Mario Arturo

GENTLE RAIN

© 2020 Mario Arturo Hernández Navarro.

All rights reserved. United States Copyright Office,
under registration number: TXu 2-212-592

ISBN: 978-84-09-24310-5

ONE

JESSE WATCHES THE WAITRESS walk away through the crowded diner after clearing his table. He can't help but to laugh inside at the sight of the tray looking so small next to her big head. It still gets to him to this day, after all these years. Actually, her hair is what creates the effect. At the same time, he's hoping and wishing she doesn't return, but for a whole different reason.

The first time he set foot in the Waffle House marked his initiation to that very chain of restaurants. He was in his mid 30s, he was blonder then and very sad. Also, much out of it, most likely due to the drugs he was taking at the time, he now thinks. He was recently widowed and his mother thought advisable to prescribe him the best sedatives in the market due to his obvious depression. The brand that probably paid for his parents' cruise to the Bermuda Triangle, he reflects. His mouth had a will of its own those days—twelve years ago—and whatever words came to his head would flow out, free and unfiltered.

He now observes the waitress speeding up towards the kitchen, thankful she has not remembered him. But then notices as her steps paced down to a sudden halt, making her lose her composure, not to mention her balance. 'Fuck!' Jesse and the waitress seem to be in total sync with their reactions as the dishware flies in several directions across the floor. The diner is packed with people and quite loud. The once loud atmosphere becomes quiet and still, only the jukebox escapes the sudden silence. 'She remembered,' Jesse accepts. And why wouldn't she, he was so rude back then. Calling her Jolene, commenting on her hair-don't, and making that tasteless comparison between cows and her thick southern accent did not go unnoticed. Plus, the fact that he wrote her in into his most popular series to date—and finding an actor with an uncanny resemblance to her—did not help in the least for her to never forget him. It did help the restaurant though, it is becoming the most successful branch of the franchise in the state of Tennessee and the whole south for that matter. And in the process making this real-life Jolene nearly as famous as the Dolly Parton song with the same title.

Jesse is pretending to be looking at his cell phone, but every few seconds he peeks at her, now kneeled to the floor. She's mumbling something he can't make out to the busboy who is busy helping her. Now they both turn to him, so he quickly goes back to his phone. 'Why the hell did I pick this diner? I should have known better.' For all the short time Jesse lived in Memphis all those years ago, he avoided going there to not face "Jolene" again.

Jesse doesn't remember now, nor did he know then, why that meeting was set at that specific Waffle House. The sky was grey, very much like the sky is today, and it drizzled just as it is doing now. The diner was half empty, unlike today, but the jukebox was probably playing the same song. The circumstances that led him to Memphis then were somehow similar to what brought him back this afternoon. Though he was waiting for someone, just like today, back then his head was in a very different place, a distant place, a dark place.

If he had had a pack of cigarettes, that day would have been the perfect start to the killer habit. His sudden craving for a smoke must have come from staring at a man with a red cap outside smoking. Jesse had been staring at him for a while. He had been doing that a lot in those days: putting a thought into pause mode and getting lost somewhere inside his head, gazing at a random target, only to snap back to reality a few minutes later. He had just finished a half BLT sandwich and a cup of coffee, and he wasn't hungry for anything else, which left him with nothing to do but wander. Before he left LA, his mother warned him about the side effects of the pills she had prescribed for him. It came as a complete surprise how he could blurt out his thoughts as though his mouth had taken control over his brain. Other side effects included a lack of interest in things he normally enjoyed like writing and running. He had lost his ferocious no-pound-gained appetite, not to mention his libido. But at

2

least, he was getting sleep and plenty of it, which helped keep his guilty feelings under the carpet in his mind.

The trucker-looking individual in the red cap outside seemed friendly enough to bum a cigarette from. Jesse could see him standing by the door under the Waffle House's bright yellow marquee, sheltered from the few drops of rain that had been coming down all afternoon. He had a sudden urge to leave his table to go outside, only to be convinced not to by his laziness. 'Too much of a hassle,' he thought. First, he would have to tell the waitress he would be outside. Then he would have to put on his jacket, grab his brown leather backpack with his laptop, go outside, get a little wet, and make small talk before and after bumming a cigarette. Frankly, Jesse was not in the mood for small talk or any talk whatsoever. He remembered that he was waiting for some lawyer's assistant who should be showing up at any moment. Jesse figured, there would be plenty of time to take up smoking later, so he gave up on the idea altogether.

At that very second, a young woman with shoulder-length dirty blonde hair walked in the door. She seemed to be looking for someone, so Jesse figured she was the person he had been waiting for. He waved her over to his table. He glanced at the time on his cell phone on the table and noted she was barely two minutes late. Jesse looked up again and watched her approach. She introduced herself as Sally, shook his hand with a smile, and before sitting offered him her condolences. This caught Jesse off guard because it had been months since anybody had been sorry for the loss of his husband. She turned to the waitress who was on her way to their table and asked for a cup of coffee.

The waitress finally arrived with Sally's coffee and refilled Jesse's cup for the fourth time. Like the previous two times, she didn't even look at him after their little, yet violent incident. By then, the guy and the aspirant lawyer had not had much of a conversation. His attorney had handled all the specifics about the inheritance back in LA, so the meeting was merely about a technicality. She brought him a large manila envelope with the title and legal papers for his newly inherited house. She handed him a set of keys attached to a ring that also held a long metal silhouette map of Tennessee with colorful letters spelling the state's name. Jesse couldn't believe the size of that keyring and stared at it for nearly a minute. As he

3

stared, the silence made Sally uncomfortable.

"Did you know the house is around the corner from Graceland?" Sally asked as she added artificial sweetener to her coffee.

"I know, I've been there a few times," Jesse answered bluntly.

"In Graceland?"

"No! In the house." He finally looked up at her. "On spring break, the first time, about eight years ago, then for a funeral two years . . . no, three years ago."

"The family gardener has been taking care of the property all these years. It is up to you to continue with his services. We asked him to remove the shutters from the windows two days ago. They're all in the garage now."

"Is the power on?" Jesse asked.

"No. Neither is the water. There is power in the house, but you have to switch on the main breaker. It's in the kitchen, on the side, above the refrigerator. The main water valve is outside by the backdoor in the kitchen. It's hard to miss."

"But I specifically asked for the power to be on. Didn't your boss get my email?"

"Yes! That's my bad. I meant to get back to you about it. We haven't for safety reasons. It's standard procedure. If you'd like, I can meet you at the house and lend you a hand with finding it."

"That's not necessary," replied Jesse leaving another long silence for Sally to fill in.

"Do you plan to stay in Memphis long?" she asked, placing her half-empty cup of coffee on the table.

"I have no idea." He looked out the window to see if the smoker with the red cap was still there and he was. "I don't even know why I came here in the first place." Although he said it out loud, it was more for himself, but he couldn't care less if she heard him.

Lucky for Sally, who was searching for what to say next, Jesse's phone began to vibrate. He saw that it read "Lauren" again, but he ignored it. 'That's too bad,' the young woman thought, but she then decided she has had enough of Mr. Jesse Santos. She picked up her cup and quickly finished off her coffee. She raised her wrist, slid her cuff back to check the time, and

4

then said she had to go back to work. She got up, and after another short handshake and a quicker goodbye, Jesse watched her walk to the register. He saw her pointing out their table to the cashier and then waited for the bill. She turned to Jesse and grinned at him politely, but absently. Jesse nodded and saw her get her change. He watched her until she left the restaurant. The man in the red cap was no longer there, 'damn it!'

A few blocks away, there was a dark, empty living room, unvisited for nearly ten months. Flowered wallpaper from another era with fat multicolor pastel flowers bloomed all over the four walls. White wooden frames on bare windows and closed doorways loomed over bright green wall-to-wall carpet. The oversized fake renaissance furniture was too big and too far apart to hold a conversation. The sound of the key turning in the lock broke the room's reverie. Jesse slowly swung the door open and entered the home. He dropped his backpack on the nearest chair, then turned around and walked out the door, returning a few seconds later with two navy blue suitcases, one smaller than the other. He sat them by the doorway, just in case he decided at the last minute to stay elsewhere instead. He nearly opted for that idea when he closed the door, and the smell of a forgotten home penetrated his nostrils. He immediately opened the front door again to let some air in, then walked to the other end of the house and entered the kitchen to do the same thing to let the house breathe for a while. Finally, he switched on the main breaker, then went into the hallway and turned on the light. He went into every room of the house, except for the one, and opened all necessary windows; that's when he realized he had been walking on that green carpet that spread throughout the whole house. He recalled joking with his husband, Steven, on how the bright version of that color made the home like an indoor mini-golf course. Only the bathrooms and kitchen were spared from such a hideous invasion. Jesse always thought the house came from a 1972 *Sears Roebuck* catalogue, so the green carpet was very becoming.

Nearly an hour had passed when Jesse felt the house was getting too cold. He went through every room again to close the windows, but with the lights on; this time feeling a sense of peace. Though he hadn't had special feelings for this house in the past, he had the odd sensation that the house was now welcoming him. He wandered around again, trying to decide where he would sleep for the next few days or months, or whatever time it took to make up his mind about what to do with the place or his life. He found himself stopping at a closed door, the one he had previously and purposely avoided. It belonged to the bedroom where his husband stayed every time he came to see his grandparents. While Jesse and Steven were in college, they visited Memphis a few times and stayed in that very room. They had just started dating the first time Steven invited him to his grandparents' home for Thanksgiving.

After standing in front of the room with his right hand on the knob, Jesse finally found the strength to open the door. He hit the light switch, but it didn't work. He went to a window and opened it to let in the fresh air. This one was harder to crack than the others in the house, so the guy struggled to get it to slide up. He began exploring the room; he browsed the titles on the small bookcase by the window, just as he did the first time he was there. He moved on to the desk and picked up a writing contest trophy Steven had won in high school. He looked at it for a bit, just as he did the back in the day. He could almost feel those arms coming from behind surrounding him in an embrace.

"Whatcha doing, Whiskers?" he remembered Steven saying.

"Sorry, I didn't mean to pry." Jesse turned around gently to face him.

"That's fine. That means you feel at home and that what's mine is yours."

"I wouldn't put it that way, but . . . Where are your grandparents?" He put back the trophy, without leaving Steven's arms.

"Actually, they left for the supermarket."

"Well, what did they say?"

"About what? You mean, about you?"

"Yes, I'm spending the weekend here. I wanna be prepared . . . what to expect."

"They like you just fine." Steven kissed Jesse once on the lips, "Just like all my old boyfriends."

"You asshole," he pushed Steven away in a joking manner. "You told me they hated all of them, why would it be any different now?"

"Cause you're different."

"You sure know what to say to a guy, don't you?"

"Did you hear what I said? We're all alone." Steven said, with a look on his face Jesse could not say no to.

"No, no, no. We're not doing it in your grandparents' bed."

Jesse threw his head back as though he was going to laugh, but he didn't. He remembered he was all alone in the room. All alone in the house. That big lonely house he just inherited all for himself.

TWO

JESSE WAS RETURNED TO THE PRESENT by the horns from the cars behind his. And there it was: the green light in front of him. He hit the accelerator and turned left just as the traffic light turned yellow, which made his escorts even angrier. He drove into a strip mall on Elvis Presley Boulevard, a few blocks away from his house, to go to the Piggly Wiggly supermarket. He had been in Memphis for two days and had been eating out for every meal; too numb to cook for himself and too sad to eat in alone. Dining out by himself was way easier to bear. Earlier, he had forced himself to go out and buy food for a few days, plus some basic things needed for the house. A long night was ahead of him: two broken TV sets, no Wi-Fi signal in the house, and sleeping on a queen-size bed dead people have slept on; the perfect ingredients for another sleepless disaster. So why not go shopping and to try to put together a meal to make the night a little less depressing?

'Where was I? Back there?' he wondered to himself as he looked for a parking space. 'Should I even be driving?' As he parked the car, he thought, 'Oh, yeah! That dark and sad place I am getting so accustomed to. I should call Mom to ask her about laying off these pills. I hate spacing out like that. Oh, shit! I need to call Lauren, she must be going crazy, I'll do it now.' But he forgot to call her. Instead, there he was, many minutes later, absent in front of a freezer door staring at a dozen and a half versions of chocolate chip cookie dough ice cream.

"Son, you look like you are in urgent need of assistance." A very deep voice brought Jesse back again. He blinked a few times before realizing that he had returned from wherever he'd gone. He turned his head to find the source of that baritone. He had to raise his head a bit to meet the pair

9

of honey-brown eyes, both owned by a tall 60-something-year-old black man with very dark skin, wide shoulders, and a soft grin. He was wearing a white polo shirt, khakis, and a black apron with an embroidered Piggly Wiggly logo.

"Man!" Jesse scanned the man from head to toe. "You sure are big!" escaped from his mouth, "Shit! I'm sorry!"

The man just smiled, trying to hold his laughter, purposely ignoring what the guy blurted out. "Nowadays, you need a bachelor's degree to get through the varieties of chocolate chip ice cream."

"The funny thing is, I don't care much for ice cream. I was just passing by when I spotted . . . I don't remember . . . I dazed off again."

"Yeah, you seemed a bit lost for a second there."

"Right, a second."

"Wasn't that you at the stop light earlier?

"You were there?" Jesse asked with eyes wide open. "You saw me?"

"Kind of, I was in the parking lot bringing back carts when I heard all the ruckus."

"Ruckus?" Jesse stopped. "I haven't heard that word since 1894."

The man chuckled. It was just then when Jesse noticed the man's gold tooth, the first molar next to his right upper canine. "That's pretty funny," the man continued, "I am the only one I know who says it. I just like the word." The man paused briefly. "You are staring at my gold tooth, son. Didn't your mother teach you it's not polite to stare at strangers?"

"Actually," Jesse grinned, "my mother only warned about talking to strangers."

"Touché!"

At that very moment, Jesse's phone vibrated in his pants back pocket. He pulled it out and saw on the screen that it was Lauren. He raised his eyebrows out of amazement but kept the wild coincidence to himself. He immediately hung up to go back to his conversation.

"I'm sorry, I didn't mean to stare. Lately, I've been acting like a zombie, staring at people. These pills I've been taking . . . I like your gold tooth, though; it has a hipster quality to it."

"I don't know if that is good or not, but coming from you, I'm guessing that's a compliment."

"It is, believe me."

"Sooo, you don't need any ice cream, then."

"No, I'm good."

"Hey, I was on my way back from the bathroom when I saw you were still standing in the same place that I saw you when I was on my way there. I just wanted to make sure you're OK, that's all."

"Thanks, I'm OK." The guy extended out his arm to shake the man's hand. "I'm Jesse, by the way."

"Orson, Orson Davis." The man said, returning the gesture.

"Orson? I wasn't expecting that . . . cool! Good for you, a true gentleman with a very cool name."

Jesse was so distracted by the man's name that he dismissed the handshake. The man stepped back to leave when Jesse realized how small his hand had felt in Orson's.

"You come back soon, you hear?" The man said as he returned to work.

Jesse watched Orson walk away as his phone began to ring. It was Lauren calling again. Jesse didn't realize it at the moment. Still, he was in a better mood, enough that he could pick up the call and update his biological mother on his Memphis retreat.

Jesse was standing in the checkout line when he finished talking to Lauren; that's how he had always addressed her—by her first name. He found himself feeling lighter, in a sense, relieved that he finally got that phone call out of the way. They talked at least once a week, and the 'I am fine and settled in the house' phone call that was long overdue, but basically untrue. He just didn't want to worry her. Texting her, "I'm OK," would have only made things worse. That would have only made her crazy, and she would have booked a flight to Memphis right away.

When it was Jesse's turn to check out, the young cashier did not acknowledge him at all, she just started ringing up his items. He noticed she would slightly smile, not at him, but at her cell phone screen lighting up by the register, as it received messages every other second. The bill came to $258.53, and those were actually her only words to him in a thick southern accent. Amused and too nonchalant to be bothered by her, Jesse pulled out his wallet to pay. He opened it, and his face went pale in an

11

instant when his credit card was nowhere to be found. He reached for every pocket on him and nothing. He felt his skin growing cold, not understanding how that could be possible.

"I can't find my card!" Jesse announced.

"Don't you have cash?" She purposely said it out loud to encourage the shoppers in the queue behind Jesse to move to another line.

"Not that amount." By now, his hands were shaking, and his forehead was moist as he kept looking for his card.

"I'm going to have to call the manager."

"It's got to be . . ."

"Son, you look like you are in urgent need of assistance—again." It was Orson. He had been watching the whole exchange while bagging Jesse's groceries at the end of the checkout line. He walked to Jesse but addressed her; "What seems to be the problem?"

"He doesn't have any money." The obviously irritated cashier said to Orson. "I'm gonna have to call Mr. Hucklebun."

Two of the three customers behind Jesse had already moved to other registers when Orson politely suggested to the remaining lady behind Jesse to move to another line. Then he asked the cashier in a soft tone to keep calm.

"I was certain it was here, it's always here." Jesse turned to tell Orson; his eyes were watery. "I'm sorry."

"Don't worry, son. It's not a big deal. We'll find a . . ."

"Mr. Hucklebun, you're wanted in line one!" The sound system blasted all over the store. The cashier had the phone in her hand next to her mouth.

"Patty, I asked you to please . . ." Orson snapped at her.

"Mr. Hucklebun, we have a situation, please hurry." the cashier kept at it, ignoring Orson.

"Fine!" he went back to help Jesse, who was trying hard not to sob, "OK son, set your wallet here. If you have nothing to hide in there, take out everything, one by one. Remember, there's no rush now. Mr. Hucklebun is out on his break." He lifted his head to eye the cashier and emphasized: "He, himself, told me he'd be back in 5 minutes." He came back to Jesse, who did as the man suggested. By the fifth item out of his wallet, the card in question turned up. Jesse handed it to the Orson, who handed it to the surly cashier, with a look in his eyes that needed no explanation.

Out in the parking lot, Jesse pushed the shopping cart to his rental, Orson walked beside him carrying a bag in each hand. The bags could have easily fit in the cart, but Orson wanted to walk Jesse to his car to make sure the guy was OK.

"Orson, thanks a lot for your help."

"Sure thing, it's part of my job."

"No, I mean with credit card, I don't know how I could have missed it."

"I'm glad to be of help." He paused and looked at how full Jesse's shopping cart was. "You sure bought a lot of stuff. I know you're not throwing a party, so either you have a big family or you are not planning to leave your house for a while."

"No, it's all for me. I just moved to Memphis."

"Is that right? Where from?"

"California."

"Hollywood?"

"As a matter of fact, yes."

"I knew it, you look all Hollywood. Young, blonde hair. Those green eyes, you kind of look like an actor."

"Watch your language!" Jesse joked, "I'm a writer for television, though. And I am not blonde, the LA sun does that to my hair."

"Really, a writer? I'd ask you about a show, but I don't watch TV. My daughter and her husband, on the other hand, are addicted to series."

"Good. Thanks to them, I can buy all this stuff."

"So, how do you like Memphis so far? You must be in culture shock coming from Hollywood."

"It's certainly different, but I only moved here two days ago."

"Where to? If you don't mind me asking."

"Not far from here. In the same block as Graceland."

"No kidding, not the Morrison house. I know it's been unoccupied for a while now."

"Well, yes. You know it?"

"I worked at Graceland. I thought Stevie owned the place, did you buy the house?"

"Stevie?" Jesse stopped the cart, and so did Orson. "Did you know Steven?"

"Not really, we would acknowledge each other from a distance. I worked on Elvis' cars for his automobile museum, so I worked in Graceland on and off. I used to be a mechanic before I retired."

"Did you meet Elvis?"

"Yes, just a couple of times. But my boss used to fix all his cars before I took over the business, he knew the King better than I did."

"But you remembered Steven. How?"

"Well, he would be out in the yard smoking. He was wild, that kid."

"Yeah, I know he used to be pretty racy." Jesse pushed the cart again, and both men continued walking.

"Racy? My buddy, who used to be a guard there, told me that Stevie made Thanksgiving, Christmas, and spring breaks his busiest time." Orson laughed. "He and his friends would stay out in the backyard smoking and drinking until the wee hours. He said that many times Stevie and his friends tried to climb the fence to get into Graceland."

"Well, I was one of those friends. Wait a minute!" Jesse stopped again, "that was your buddy, who called the cops on us that night?"

"Probably." They continued walking. "He said that Stevie was harmless, really, but sometimes he could be a big pain in the neck. But to me, he seemed all right. I do hope he's settled down by now; that he's a little calmer these days."

"Yeah." Jesse released a nervous laughter.

"That's right!" Orson remembered, "he lived in LA, working for TV. Is that how you know him? Is he back here with you?"

"Steven passed away six months ago."

"I'm sorry to hear that." He nearly stopped but kept walking. Instead, he said, "So that's why you seem so sad, are you two related?" He stopped this time. "I'm sorry, I didn't mean to be nosy . . ."

"That's quite all right!" They continued to the car. Jesse hesitated, but thought 'what the fuck?' "He was my husband . . . We were married . . . I'm his widower."

"I hear you, that's cool, you were a couple." Orson tried hard not to laugh about the way Jesse tried to make his point, but it was definitely not the time. It was obvious to him the guy was testing him. "I don't care. I'm a grown man; I've seen it all. Were you together for a long time?"

"Seven years, but we were able to get married only last year." They finally made it to the car. "This is me!" Jesse unlocked the trunk of his rented SUV with the remote. The door opened automatically.

"Hey, hang in there; I know it's tough at first." Orson placed his two bags in first and then moved to the cart to grab a couple more and handed them to Jesse, so the guy could arrange them as he wanted to in the trunk. He paused to make eye contact with Jesse again. "I'm a widower myself, for many years now. It takes a little time, but it does get better, believe me."

Both men finished loading the car—putting the groceries in the trunk and in the back seat. Jesse closed the doors and walked with Orson to the side of the car.

"Thanks a lot. So, to pick up those empty boxes, I should come back tomorrow, you said?"

"Yes, park around back and ask for Charlie, but come before noon and tell him you know me."

"Where is the Salvation Army again?"

"It's on Austin Peay Highway."

"I'd better write this down." Jesse pulled out his cell phone and started typing.

"That's the northeast part of town, my granddaughter goes to school near there."

"How many grandkids do you have?" Jesse asked as he finished writing the address.

"Just one. And one daughter."

"Hey, thanks again." Jesse put his phone back in his pocket he then pulled out his wallet and took out a twenty dollar bill. "I am very grateful for everything."

"I feel bad taking your money. I enjoyed talking to you, plus we're on a first-name basis. Hey, but it is not every day you get a big tip like this one from a TV celebrity." Orson takes the bill and puts it in his apron pocket. "Thanks, son."

"You helped me with a few issues; my ice cream trance, telling me where to find boxes, the mean cashier, and yeah, and you saved me from mister what's-his-face? Mr. Hucklebuns."

"Hucklebun," Orson smiled, "one bun."

"The fact is that you helped me out . . . a lot." Jesse opened the driver's door and stood by it, facing Orson, "Dealing with pressures while on antidepressants can be challenging at times. I don't know if taking that medication is doing me any good."

"I don't believe in taking pills to deal with emotions. I believe in taking it on the chin, as they say. I don't know what your condition is, but facing problems clear-eyed can be good for the spirit. Things happen to learn from them, we must be aware and look for the signs. They are all over the place."

"You're probably right. It was my mom's idea, she's a psychiatrist," said Jesse. But what he really wanted to say was: 'You would love California; a lot of people talk like you.' He kept that to himself.

The conversation lasted longer than both men expected. Jesse realized he was stealing time from Orson's work and didn't want to get him in trouble. He could have easily talked to Orson a little longer. Instead, Jesse forced himself to extend his hand to the man one last time to say good-bye.

On the way back home, Jesse realized he had turned on the radio to play music. He hadn't done that in a long time. The radio was set to a blues station. He thought he'd give this music a shot and listened on for a bit. Shortly, he hit the auto scan button looking for a Top 40s kind of station, hoping to find something he recognized. By the time he did, he was at home. He looked at the house as he pulled into the driveway. It was getting dark, and walking into that empty green-carpeted house did not appeal to him whatsoever. But 'hey!' he thought, 'I'm feeling OK now. I'll make myself some linguini with clam sauce and have a little wine. Shit! Can't have wine. I wish I had some weed. Oh well. Who knows, maybe I'll write a little.'

THREE

THE SECOND TIME I SAW YOU, it was quite a surprise. I was just settling in at my other job at the self-storage facility. Even though the fall season was showing signs of coming, it was a fine night to sit outside. I took out a foldable wooden chair from the office and placed in the middle of the wall around the corner to sit below the one lamp on that side of the building. I liked putting it there, facing the rows of storage spaces in the dark, lit by a light coming from each aisle.

I was feeling a little melancholic, so I put on that mellow blues playlist I put together for just this kind of mood. I remember leaning my chair against the brick wall while music was playing soft and low. I loved the echo bouncing back and forth down the aisles. I knew I wasn't alone, Mike from the earlier shift told me someone was inside their storage unit. Little did I know it was you. Right before he left, he made a suicide joke referring to all the time you had been in there. I did not care to laugh about that.

At some point in the night, the playlist came to an end, and I was just enjoying the silence on this nice breezy night. I recalled the times I had to do guard duty in Vietnam. It was way back then that I started writing my little tunes in small notebooks. First, I did it out of boredom, but later it became a habit that, as you well know, continues to this day. So, I took my little red notepad and pen out of my jacket pocket and wrote for a while.

I was under the spell of inspiration when I remembered I had half a jay concealed in my jacket. I figured what a better way to say goodbye to the summer than with a small buzz and listening to the blues under a starry night. I set aside my notebook, switched the music back on, lit up, and took a drag, and held it in. Right after that, I heard a metal sliding door rolling up, and I froze. I'd completely forgotten I was not alone and grateful I had only taken one hit of that joint. I let go of the smoke and put out the jay when I heard the same sliding door closing down; I wasn't certain which aisle the racket had come from. Soon I heard steps, but my music concealed the direction of where they were coming from. First, I saw a silhouette emerging from the second left lane as it walked towards me. Finally, you were illuminated by the faint light. It couldn't be. My first thought was that all white folks look alike, but the similarity was too uncanny. And then I heard you say:

"Orson?"

'I'll be darned!' I whispered to myself, but out loud I asked, "What in the world are you doing here? Jesse, right?"

"I was just . . ." You got closer, and I could finally make you out clearly.

"What's up, son?" I asked, and then I saw your face up close. "Are you OK?"

"I have been locked inside that room . . ." you sobbed and pointed at the rows behind you, "for nearly four hours looking for . . . fuck! I'm so goddammed angry at myself!"

"Now, now, there's no need to talk like that." I stood up and got a better look at your face. You looked like you'd been crying the whole time you were inside your unit.

"C'mon, sit over here and keep me company."

I let you have my seat and went back to the office and grabbed a desk chair that I rolled over to my spot. I placed it beside you, with its back against the wall.

"Now, can I get you something to drink? Coke, Diet Coke, Sprite, or water? My treat. Sorry, that's all the vending machine has."

"Nothing, thanks, but I'd like some of what you've been smoking. Do you have any left?"

I smiled at your lack of shyness and then sat next to you. Do you remember, Red? I pulled out the joint from behind my ear, lit it up again, and passed it to you. You took a drag, held the smoke for a few seconds, offered it back to me, and released the smoke. I was done, and so were

18

you. You commented on the fact that just a buzz was enough—just like me. But that coincidence was nothing compared to what just hit us. We were blown away by how random it was for us to see each other again. My other job, out of all the places in Memphis we could have met, and exactly one week after our first encounter.

"So, Jesse, what's been troubling you?"

"I lost my wedding band. Actually, both of our wedding bands."

"Oh, I'm sorry to hear that!" I understood completely. "How?"

"I must have . . . well, now I think maybe they could still be back at the house, but I looked everywhere, man."

"Then, why are you here?"

"I thought they could be in one of the boxes I brought this morning . . . twenty-three boxes of camp vintage shit I've decided to keep to sell later."

"Did you unload all twenty-three boxes here all by yourself?"

"No, I hired movers and met them here this morning."

"So, you didn't go to the Salvation Army, after all?" I asked.

"Oh, yeah, I did that three days ago. Twelve boxes of stuff and eighteen large trash bags filled with old clothes. Man, am I glad that's done."

"Boy, you've been busy."

"Yep!" you replied with a note of pride, "Well, I haven't been sleeping much lately." You ran your hand over your face and through your hair. "Dude, you should have seen how I left my storage locker. Now I have to come back tomorrow and repack everything, and I still have 8 boxes to sort through."

You paused for a few seconds, "I was there, sweating away when I heard your music, and that's when I stopped. I realized I had to get out of there for my own sanity. And then, here you are. It's crazy!"

"I still can't believe it."

"Orson!" You said after a few seconds of silence.

"Jesse!" I replied with a smile.

"Orson, who's playing?"

"Oh, that's 'Spike Driver Blues,' by Mississippi John Hurt, his 1963 version. He first recorded it in 1928, and to this day, I still can't decide

19

which one I like best."

"You're a big blues fan, obviously, right?"

"It's the music I live for."

"Really?!" You seemed a bit surprised, in spite of only the blues coming out of my wireless speaker. "Cool, I'm asking because I've always been drawn to it, but I never really spent the time getting to know them."

"You just play them, son, and listen. Not much to it."

"Of course, I hear the blues in movies, or at bars and restaurants . . ." You paused for a few seconds. "What I mean is, I haven't taken them seriously, you know? Understand what's good from what's bad. I really can't tell."

"Well, you either like it, or you don't." I stopped talking. "Oh! I feel you; you should start with the good stuff and take it from there."

"Well, yeah!" You replied, even though you hesitated a bit.

"I can help you with that, Jesse."

"I'd love to have a copy of that playlist." You pointed at the speaker.

"I can do better than that."

"You're not gonna sing the blues to me, are you?" You teased.

"No, you don't want that. I'm thinking I could take you to my friend Ambar's place. It's a hole in the wall not far from here, but the music there . . ."

"Tonight?"

"I wasn't thinking tonight," I said, "but hey, tonight is as good a night as any."

Your face read 'please, take me' in neon lights so I couldn't say no. Plus, cheering you up seemed the right thing to do. So we agreed on me picking you up at home. I still had an hour and a half to go at work. Also, you realized you hadn't had dinner. The weed must have sparked your appetite, so you left to get a quick bite and then went home to clean up.

I made it to your house around 1:30 am. I had no trouble finding it; I remembered exactly where it was. I pulled into the driveway, and as I was parking, you were already walking out the door. Must have been the excitement of your first night out in Memphis. You had changed your clothes; naturally, you even shaved and combed your hair. You had a pair of blue jeans on, a white long sleeve shirt and leather boots. You looked sharp,

I remember, all neat and clean, as I'd never seen you before. You basically looked as if they ironed you out sharp. You got in the car, and off we went.

You also seemed more talkative, like another Jesse had surfaced, but still, with that sad look in your eyes. The first thing you told me was that you found your wedding bands. They were on top of the fridge if I recall correctly. And then you went on and on about how cool my car was. Naturally, hearing a man as young as yourself compliment my pride and joy was music to my ears. My code U, number 1070, medium aqua-colored, metallic 1970 Lincoln Continental.

And you kept talking, all the way to The Grasshopper. The parking lot was pretty packed for a Tuesday night, and it took a bit to find a spot. I said hello to Mick, the bouncer, and introduced you to him. We walked in, and it was instant: you got a few looks. At first, I thought it was because you were basically the only white dude in the joint, but when I saw how the women were fixed on you and smiling at you, I realized I was way off. The music was blasting, and from what I could see from the distance, the dance floor was rocking. It seemed like the perfect night for a crash course on the blues.

It took us some time to get to the bar. I greeted a few people; some I introduced to you. When we finally made it, I found the usual scene: Ambar chatting away behind the bar while Bad Ass Jimbo was busting his butt serving drinks beside her. You remember him, that white dude taller than me?

I spotted a couple of stools at the opposite end of the bar from where Ambar was standing, and we went and sat there. When she saw me, she excused herself and came over to us. She was looking fine that night, wearing red, unusual for her on a weeknight. It was one of those vintage Japanese type outfits cut below the knee with yellow and white ornaments that fit tightly on her dainty figure. It gave the impression that if she ate a bite of anything, her dress would explode. But it looked nice; it matched perfectly with her medium-tanned skin. I could also tell she had been to the hairdresser that day; her hair was perfectly straight, and it curled into her neck at the end. And if I know Ambar, she was probably trying to impress one of the boys from the band that was playing that night. You were flabbergasted by her beauty and shocked when I told you we were the same age.

As she approached us, she took a long look at you and then back at me with an expression on her face I could not make out. I would learn later that you passed her test with flying colors, right at hello. You two seemed to hit it off right away. While we were talking, halfway through our beers, I noticed you would sneak a peek at the dance floor, but would quickly come back to our conversation.

"So, guess who was here the other night asking about you?" Ambar popped out of the blue.

"I don't wanna hear anything about L.C., please," I snapped.

"Elsie? Is that an ex?" you asked me and took a drink of your bottle of beer.

"Sort of," I replied. "L.C. basically ruined my life and nearly exterminated my self-esteem. Talking about that piece of shit makes me wanna vomit, so I'd really rather not talk about it."

"Man, that bad, eh?" you asked.

"Ok, but one last thing," she continued, "That piece of shit was asking me about where to find you, just so you know."

"Ambar, I hope you kept your mouth shut," I said to which she nodded yes.

"How long were you together?" You dared to ask.

"On and off, for about 11 years," Ambar volunteered.

"C'mon, can we please change the subject?"

You quickly picked on it and asked, "Ambar, who's playing tonight?"

"A local band, the Wolf River Boys. They're good, aren't they?"

"They rock!" Then took the last sip of your beer. "Or should I say they blue?"

"Ambar, Jesse is not sure he likes the blues," I teased.

"Dude, don't say that," then turned to Ambar, "I always liked the blues, I just never got around to making friends with it."

"Well, you've come to the right place." She replied.

"Jesse, go on!" I pointed to the dance floor in front of the stage. "it's obvious you're dying to go over there, instead of staying here with us ancients."

"Speak for yourself, old man!" Ambar barked.

"Go on, son. I'll catch up with you later."

"Don't mind if I do." You put your bottle down and got up.

Ambar and I looked at each other and then watched you walk away, catching the rhythm as you disappeared into the crowd.

"Mmmm, where on earth did you find that beautiful thing?"

"He came into the Piggly Wiggly the other day, and then tonight he turned up at my work, by chance." I took a drink from my beer. "Anyway, he's new in town. He's been depressed..."

"And you brought him to this hellhole?"

"Well, he was recently widowed . . ." I stopped talking, looking at my near empty bottle.

"And?" Ambar quickly grabbed two more beers.

"No, I was just thinking about something he said out in the parking lot." I picked up my bottle, clinked Ambar's bottle, and took a drink. "He's been taking all kinds of antidepressants, and the other day I had the dumb audacity to tell him he should face his sorrows without pills. Little did I know, he took it to heart and stopped cold turkey, probably that very day I said that. Now his sleeping patterns are all fucked up."

"And you feel responsible for that?"

"Kind of. But actually, he seemed OK about it. He said he's been getting a lot done since."

"So, what's the big deal. You do that a lot and don't even notice. You say what's on your mind and people listen. You have this power over people; you should use it more to your advantage. It's what leaders are all about."

"All right, all right . . . gimme another beer for Jesse; I'm going to the floor."

"I like Jesse; he's cool." She handed me the bottle. "And dashing. He looks like a movie star."

"That's what I said." I got up and grabbed our beers. "Too bad for you, he doesn't like girls."

"I'll be . . . not again!" Ambar said.

I left her with her mouth half open to go and look for you.

At first, I couldn't find you, Jesse. I scanned the tables around the dance floor and nothing. I confess, I was a bit concerned, but only for a few seconds. Then I saw you in the middle of the dance floor, mingling with the swinging crowd, dancing to the blues as if you've been doing it since birth. The funny thing was, you seemed to be somewhere else, moving with your eyes closed, swaying in rhythm, only aware of yourself and the beat, sweating and tripping out like the rest of them. I was tempted to join you, but instead, I stood against the wall with our two beers to keep me company as I watched you dance in a trance.

It was fun to watch the atmosphere shifting from hotter to steamier one degree at a time. You seemed to be getting higher and higher, moving smoothly through the crowd. Everyone danced with anyone, from time to time you would open your eyes and acknowledged whoever was in front of you, with a wink or a smile, a touch, a caress, a rub, or sliding hands. Man or woman, it didn't matter who you danced with. I was a witness to an orgy of music, sensuality, and ecstasy.

The song that captivated everyone came to an end with a mixture of disappointment, cheers, and applause. The dance floor was clearing out as the band prepared for the next set. It revealed to me a brand-new Jesse, one with a wide smile and bright sparkly eyes. I saw you looking around to find me, so I stood still until you spotted me. I smiled at you and lifted the bottles I had in my hand. I drank your second beer but had already ordered two more. I pointed to an empty table near the stage; I figured you needed the rest. You let your body drop to the chair; your white shirt was now see-through because of the sweat. I handed you your beer, and we air toasted, grinned, and drank without saying a word.

The band started playing again, a slow tempo song this time. As the singer got in front of the mic, we looked at each other as if we made a mutual agreement to continue in silence and just listen to him sing. You turned your chair just a bit to face the band straight on. I just drank my beer and looked at you enjoying the moment. You hardly blinked as if you were studying the band, shifting your eyes from musician to musician. I got a big kick out of watching you.

By our fourth beer, the music from the band seemed to be coming to an end. I can always tell by the tone of the last selection. The place was half empty by then, and the short staff was putting things away. Clearing everything they could get their hands on to be able to go home soon.

When the band finally stopped, you turned to look at me and thanked me with a look from those green eyes of yours. We got up and headed for the bar to pay our bill. On the way there, you forbade me from paying. To make sure of it, you went straight to Jimbo instead of Ambar. While you were at it, she yelled at you to put your wallet away—it was her treat. She then grabbed a bottle of Cuervo and called out.

"Here, guys, you too. Jimbo, Jesse, get over here."

"I couldn't possibly," I said. "Besides, I'm driving, well, not for another hour."

Ambar set four shot glasses on the counter. "C'mon, one more for the road," she insisted.

"When are we? The 1940s, and no one told me?" You joked.

You made me chuckle, "OK, but now I have to wait longer until it wears off to drive."

"Hey, I can call a cab," you pulled out your phone. "I'll drive you here later to get your car."

"Good one. Abe, spending the night in an empty parking lot?" said Jimbo standing by Ambar as she poured the Tequila shots.

"Orson will never leave his beloved Abe alone in this neck of the hoods."

"Who's Abe?" Jesse asked. "Oh, I get it. Cool!"

"That's right; I'm staying here with him." I exclaimed as the four of us lifted our glasses and toasted, "To Abraham Lincoln!" You all repeated after me and swallowed.

"You're serious about not leaving your car here?" You asked.

"You can call a cab if you want to, but I'm staying here. Ambar can take you home even; she only had that one shot."

"No, dude, I don't mind staying and keeping you company."

"Suit yourself."

We all four stayed in the bar talking for a while. By the time Ambar and Jimbo finally left The Grasshopper, it was almost 4:30 in the morning. And you and I tried to get some rest in my car. But you didn't seem very tired at all; in fact, you were kind of hyper. You had suggested we drank lots of water to chase the drunk out of our bodies. I thought it was a good idea, but later I regretted it. With you talking and me going out to pee every 30 minutes, it was everything but a restful wait. You laid down on the back seat with your head behind the passenger seat, and I sat behind the wheel, with my seat reclined. I remember that instead of trying and get some sleep, we couldn't stop talking.

"And you have that nightmare every night?" I asked, probably rubbing my two first fingers onto the top my left ear, it's a little tick I have when something intrigues me.

"Not every night, but often."

"And the party is always the same? Same people doing exactly the same thing?"

"Nothing changes, even though I know I have the power to change the outcome in the dream, but I don't want to. It's fucked up."

"So do you mean to tell me you could make it on time, but you don't want to?"

"Uh-huh."

"I have to think about that one," I said, although I didn't know you enough to make something of it.

"Hey, dude," you started, after being quiet for a while. "Big O, can I call you Big O?"

"No, you may not," I replied, half kidding, half not. "Dude!"

"Are you originally from Memphis?"

"No, I'm from New Orleans"

"I thought so by your accent. For a minute there, I thought you were from Baton Rouge!"

"Do you make up this stuff as you go along? You really should rehearse before you deliver." I teased.

"Ha!" You totally got me. "Paging Mr. Hucklebuns, we have a situation!" You imitated that Patty's tone perfectly.

"Cute. Very cute!" I laughed.

"When did you move here?"

"Do you want the long story or the short one?"

"What do you think? The long one, I'm not going anywhere."

"When I was two," I said after a short pause, "my parents, my older sister, and I moved to Chicago. In those days, there were more and better jobs. But when I was fourteen, my mother sent me back to live with her folks."

"To Memphis?"

"No, back to New Orleans, Memphis came much later. You see, in Chicago, we lived in the projects, and there were a few street gangs, and my parents were concerned I'd get in trouble. I wasn't too happy about leaving the big city at first, but I got used to living back in New Orleans fairly quickly. I hated the weather up north. My parents came down often to visit, and I did the same from time to time."

"What about your sister?"

"She got married. She was much older than me. She had a family of her own, and it was hard for her to come down."

"So, how was living with your grandparents?"

"It was fine. I loved them. My grandmother was a great cook, which is how I got to be so big." Even though you weren't looking at me, I rubbed my belly. "All that southern cooking."

"How about your granddad."

"Papa Joe? He was great; a sweet man. Didn't talk much, but boy did he play the piano. My grandma and I would just sit and listen to him. We didn't own a TV set, you know. On Sundays after church, Papa Joe's friends would come over and play while the wives made lunch. After lunch, they played some more."

"So, when did you move to Memphis?"

"That was later after I got out of the army."

"You were in the army? Tell me about that."

"No, no, no. That's a whole different and long story. Jesse, I want to get some shut-eye."

"OK, but finish the story with Papa Joe."

"There's not that much to tell. I lived with him—I mean them—until I was eighteen and then I joined army. Papa Joe died a few years later, and my grandma ended up moving to Chicago with my folks."

"But you know New Orleans pretty well?"

"Very well. In fact, I go often. I have good friends down there. Why?"

"Nothing, I need to go there one of these days to see my mother-in-law, but I keep putting it off."

"You'll love it there. The music scene is fantastic—probably the best in the country. And don't get me started about the food—it's about the greatest in the world."

We talked a bit more, stepping out to pee from time to time. I frankly don't remember who fell asleep first, but we were out until the sun came up. By then I was just a little hungover; your thing about drinking lots of water actually worked. You weren't all that talkative in the morning. You limited yourself to saying "good morning" before hopping in the passenger seat in front. I drove you home, you got out of the car and shut the door. You then leaned over to look in, placing your folded arms on the open window.

"Big O—sorry!—Orson. I gotta say this: I can't remember the last time I had this much fun dancing. I feel so indebted to you. It was quite a night, and exactly what my head and body needed. In fact, I think tomorrow I'm gonna start jogging again. Dancing last night made me realize how out of shape I am."

"If you say so, I believe you."

"Thank you so much for last night."

"You are welcome, son. Anytime. You get some rest now."

"When I hit that bed . . ." you continued, "do you live far from here?"

"About twenty miles, maybe. I'm not going home. In a couple of hours, I have to pick up my granddaughter to take her to school."

"Dude, you should have told me. I would not have kept you out so late."

"And what, miss all the fun?" I replied. "I'm heading to the Waffle House to get myself some breakfast."

You insisted on joining me even though I wanted some alone time. I wanted to read a little, maybe try and finish that piece I was writing when you interrupted me the night before. You then stretched your arm and shook my hand. I wasn't sure, but you seemed disappointed that I wouldn't let you join me for breakfast. You turned around and walked to your door. I saw how you scratched your head as if to trying and figure me out. I stayed until you went in and closed the door, happy to know you had a good time. And most importantly, glad to discover the Jesse that surfaced from learning about the blues.

28

FOUR

JESSE WAS SITTING ON A STOOL writing away and drinking coffee on a high table by the window at the Java Hut Café. He would have preferred to have coffee anywhere but in that sad little shop, but it was the only place close enough to the Piggly Wiggly, and the coffee was, surprisingly, not bad. He stopped at the supermarket a few minutes earlier to see Orson, not even sure the man would be working that day. They had only met twice before, and it never occurred to either of them to exchange phone numbers. Jesse found him quickly; being the biggest and darkest man in the place, he was hard to miss. Jesse walked up to him and asked him when his next break would be. He needed to talk to Orson.

While waiting for him, Jesse had been busy with his new notebook, one of those black hardcover ones with lineless white pages, normally used for sketching. He particularly liked this type because he felt free to express, write, doodle, and draw all his ideas. He had already filled the first twenty pages or so with scribbles of a new story he had in mind. Out of the corner of his eye, he saw someone passing by the glass window. He looked up, hoping it was Orson, and it was. The big man walked in the door and went straight to him. Jesse stood to greet him, and the men shook hands.

"What can I get you, Orson?"

"Nothing, I've only got 20 minutes."

"Not even an espresso?"

"Sure, why not?" Orson sat on the stool while Jesse went to the main counter to order. The man turned his eyes to the table and took notice of the open notebook. He waited until Jesse came back with his espresso and cappuccino served in paper cups.

"Whatcha got going on there, son?" Orson asked and pointed at their table as Jesse set the coffees and sat next to him.

"That's part of why I wanted to see you." Jesse took his coffee and moved it close to his mouth.

"Is that a cappuccino? I haven't had one since I was in the service."

"Here." Jesse pulled it away from his lips and put it back on the table then switched it for Orson's espresso. "I haven't put sugar in it."

"Are you sure?" He looked Jesse in the eye about the coffee trade.

"Sure, be my guest."

"Thanks, Jesse. So, what did you wanna see me about?" He took a sip of his coffee, painting a white mustache above his mouth, which he immediately wiped off with a napkin. "This is pretty good."

"Well, ever since the other night at The Grasshopper I've been giving the blues a lot of thought," he stopped and took a drink from his coffee. "That's not exactly true. I have been listening to a lot of blues. Some stuff I like and some I don't like . . ."

"Well, the blues has many variations."

"Yes, I found that out these last couple of weeks, and that's why I want your help."

"How?" Orson put his coffee down.

"You see, I have this idea going through my head for a story." The guy placed his hand on the open notebook. "Actually several ideas, and they all revolve around the blues."

"Cool, you're writing again."

"Yes, I've been doing that a lot lately."

"Are you still not able to sleep?"

"No, I'm back to normal, thank God."

"Good for you, son . . . I'd like to read something of yours, I'm curious."

"Sure."

"Do you have any short stories?"

"Yes, I have a few."

"What is your story about, the one you're writing now?"

"Well," he picked up his espresso one last time, "the main character is loosely based on you."

"Say what? I don't like where this is going."

"No, no, wait, buddy! Hear me out." Jesse said, not sure whether Orson was joking or being serious. "It's not about you at all. It's about this musician about your age who hasn't played in years due to something traumatic. I haven't figured that out yet! But the part that is inspired by you is the fact that he worked at Graceland. I took that from when you told me you worked there."

Orson drank from his cappuccino in silence, giving some thought to what Jesse had just told him. He finished and put the empty paper cup down. "I gotta go." He said as he stood up.

"Hey, Orson, wait!" Jesse also got halfway up and held his arm, "I haven't finished, please sit down, I'll be brief. Well, it's not about you. I had the idea when you told me you worked there, that's all. That's how my mind works; you tell me something, and my head runs its course. What you said about working at Graceland triggered the idea for my story. I hope you don't mind."

"In that case, I guess it's OK . . ." He paused and sat back down. "So, how can I be of help?"

"I need your expertise on the blues. I want to know more about them; I want to get them through my heart; feel them if you will. Last Friday night, I went downtown to a couple of blues bars on Beale Street, but it wasn't the same as The Grasshopper. Actually, I didn't care too much for them. Too touristy for my taste and too white. It felt like a bad fraternity party."

"Ha! You'll never find another bar like Ambar's place; I'll tell you that."

"So, I was wondering if you could take me on a tour around Memphis and show me the real blues hot spots."

"Hell, I know quite a few, and some even out of town. But I warn you, some of them are genuine dives that I can't let you go alone to."

"And how about New Orleans?"

"You do know that's six hours away, right?"

"Dude, I know, I looked it up. I have to go see my mother-in-law. Remember?"

"Well, the music there is great, but it's a whole different story down

31

there. I haven't experienced the nightlife there in years. I'm sure it's very different now, but I can find out for you, son. No sweat."

"This research on the blues is work for me, so I am willing to pay you for your time and cover all expenses, gas, food, drinks."

"I don't feel right about that; we gotta talk about it. But now I really have to get going, Jesse." Orson got off his stool.

"Listen, I can go see my mother-in-law whenever I want to, I just need to pick a date, so I'll let you know with plenty of time, so you can ask for the time off. Whatever works for you."

"No big deal, I just have to give some notice. Since I'm retired, they let me do what I want."

"Cool!" Jesse pulled out his phone from his back pocket, touched the screen a few times. "Here, type in your phone number. And put your email in as well, please, so I can mail you my short stories . . . when I find them. In the meantime, I have to go to the bathroom. Could you please watch my stuff? I'll be quick, I swear." The guy handed his phone to Orson, who pulled out his reading glasses and put them on.

"Man, you look cute with glasses." Jesse smiled and said in a low voice, just in case Orson didn't like that sort of talk. "You don't mind me saying that, do you?"

"No, but don't make a habit of it. Remember, this is the South. Now, go take care of your business. I'm in a rush, son!"

As Orson wrote his phone number down, he looked over his glasses and watched Jesse go to the restroom. He smiled and shook his head softly from side to side. He was wondering whether or not he would tell Jesse that he was turning 63 that very day. He didn't feel like having anyone make a fuss about it, and much less that sad white boy he'd just met. 'What would Jesse do if I told him?' Orson wondered. The guy would probably insist on taking him out to lunch to celebrate—Jesse's treat, of course. But Orson would have none of that.

Early that morning, he had gone to his daughter's house to take little Gennie to school. He looked forward to it every Wednesday and Thursday because, in addition to spending time with his granddaughter, he would make a stop at the Denny's nearby and treat himself to their Grand Slam breakfast after dropping her off. But to Orson's surprise, his son-in-law waited a bit longer to go to work to wish his father-in-law a Happy Birthday and then insisted on taking little Gennie to school. So, the drive with Gennie and the big breakfast was suddenly slammed. Instead, he was forced to accept his daughter Angela's invitation to stay for coffee. In his opinion, Angela's coffee was about the worst, and to make matters worse, whatever time they spent together was anything but pleasant. She was no fun to talk to; she would constantly complain about how her life should be. And that's exactly what happened; after talking about herself, she never had the courtesy to ask about him, her own father. The rest of the time, they just drank coffee, or at least he pretended to do so. Luckily, at one point, she had to go through the house to look for her cell phone. Orson took the opportunity to toss the hellish drink down the drain.

After that ordeal was over, it was too late to go to Denny's, so he went off to work. No one there knew it was his birthday. The previous year, he warned Mr. Huckelbun not to tell anyone about the yearly occurrence, so the first part of the day went by without anyone even mentioning it. On top of that, he forgot his cell phone at home, so his buddies couldn't get a hold of him with their birthday wishes. Ambar, his only hope for a fun birthday outing, was in St. Louis with her father, who was ill again. Now he only had to wait for Jesse to come back from the bathroom so he could go back to work to finish the remaining two hours of his shift; to make the day speed along. Orson didn't tell Jesse about his birthday.

That afternoon after work, he went home, took off his shoes, played his favorite Blind Lemon Jefferson LP, and took a long shower. He sat in his chair by the unlit fireplace and listened to side B of the same record. It occurred to him to have a jay. 'Forget it,' he thought. Not if he may be driving later. 'I am getting old.' He then felt he was less impulsive, prudent, even boring.

Orson did end up getting in his Lincoln Continental and driving out of town. It wasn't a spur-of-the-moment kind of thing. In fact, he had been doing this every time he felt melancholic. He arrived at his favorite spot, his secret place to have some alone time. But the truth was, he was always alone most of the time anyway. He walked in the misty woods and found his very own "meditation rock," as he called it. He climbed it effortlessly. 'I am not that old after all.' He stood there looking at the lake surrounded by trees below him. Orson noted the Spanish moss hanging from the trees, all blended in the thick of the mist, and he felt a sense of eeriness that almost embraced him. He then sat down on the cold ground, not caring about the moistness. He rubbed his hands against each other to wipe the dust from his palms and watched the landscape, reminiscing. He thought about those birthdays with his ex, that poor excuse for a human being he never wanted to hear from again. L.C. was an asshole but always went out of the way to make every birthday for Orson truly special. Actually, those were about the best times for Orson, the only moments when L.C. truly shone. This birthday Orson was going to be alone, just like last year and the year before that. He finally lit his jay, put on his headset, and played his mellow blues playlist and reminisced some more—too much even—which took him from the valley of regret. He stayed there at the lake until dusk and then drove down sorrow road to end another lonely night at home.

FIVE

AT THREE MINUTES TO SIX in the morning, Jesse parked his rental in front of his new friend's house. He had dropped Orson off at home many nights before, but he never paid much attention to Orson's house. But that morning, Jesse was happy to discover that Orson lived in one of those small 1920s brick bungalows he liked so much. He got out of his car and walked on the curvy cement path that led to a little covered porch. Jesse rang the bell, and Orson answered right away, but he wasn't ready. He needed a couple of minutes to water the plants in the kitchen. Jesse grabbed Orson's medium-sized suitcase, rolled it to his car, and placed it in the trunk next to his own. When he got back to the house, Orson was already locking his front door. They walked together to the car.

"Toothbrush?" asked Jesse.

"Check!"

"Clean underwear?"

"Check!"

"Passport?"

"Oh shit!" Orson stopped, "Paging Mr. Hucklebuns, we have a situation!"

They were both chuckling as they got in the car. Before starting it, Jesse reached into the back seat and pulled a cardboard carryout tray with two cappuccinos. He asked Orson to open the glove compartment. The man did as requested, only to find a bag of Gibson's donuts: Memphis' finest, and Orson's favorites. The man couldn't help but turn to Jesse with a big smile as he opened the bag. They had gone to Gibson's a few times in the last three weeks. It was one of their after-hours places to wind down after a night out 'in search of the perfect blues,' as they jokingly referred to their outings. Jesse knew that 5:00 in the morning was the best time to get fresh donuts, and he figured what better way to start their trip to New Orleans than to have a quick breakfast in the car with their favorites.

"OK Orson, before we go I want to settle this once and for all because we haven't been able to finish this argument since it started," Jesse said, watching Orson with his mouth full. "Like I said many times, this trip to NOLA is for work, so I don't want any fights about who's paying for what. I know you said that you're showing me around and blah, blah, blah. So how about this? I'll pay for gas, hotel, and meals, and you pay for drinks because I'm afraid there's gonna be some occasional drinking throughout this trip." Jesse got a hold of his coffee from the top of the dashboard and took the lid off. "I do want to apologize for something."

"What?" Orson barely finished swallowing his donut.

"It's about that bag from Gibson's; I only brought it to keep you happy and quiet while I talked. That way, you couldn't argue with me until I got my message across. So, forgive me. Are we cool?"

"Yes, we're cool."

Jesse was excited about this trip; he wanted to find out firsthand the difference between the music scenes in New Orleans and Memphis. Three weeks of intensive dive-hopping in the blues capital had made its mark on Jesse. During those after-hours meals at Gibson's, the Waffle House, or at times in Abe's front seat, Orson would talk about different blues artists and bands. He would also recommend albums the guy should listen to; some that could only be found in library archives—anything that Orson thought was suitable for Jesse's research for his story.

Jesse had been productive working on his manuscript. He had a few possible subplots, but he didn't want to tie the knot with any of them until they got to New Orleans. He was ready for this trip, but he also had mixed feelings about it since arriving in Memphis. The lack of direct flights and trains to New Orleans made it easy to procrastinate going to see his mother-in-law. He always hated driving long distances alone, so it was perfect that Orson agreed to come along. Jesse just had to find the right moment and the words to tell his friend there would be a third passenger on the trip back to Memphis, the main reason for this journey, actually.

That moment came when they were halfway to New Orleans. Woody Guthrie's "Hard Traveling" was playing in the background when the car dash screen was interrupted by an incoming phone call. It read Cruella De Ville. Jesse refused the call, and the music continued.

"Cruella De Ville?" Asked Orson, nearly laughing. "Is that your mother-in-law?"

"Good guess!"

"I know you, son."

"I don't feel like talking to her just now."

"Does she know you're coming?"

"Yes, I talked to her last night. She's just a little bit of a control freak, that's all."

"She's that bad, eh?"

"If you consider manipulative, sneaky, condescending, and overbearing as negative qualities, then the answer is yes, she is."

"Wow! I don't think I wanna meet this woman."

"No, actually, Dottie is pretty nice, but she's not to be trusted. This is all based on stories Steven told me about her." Jesse took a deep breath as if he was about to say something else.

"What?"

"What, what?"

"It seems like you were going to say something else. What's on your mind?"

"OK! You're right. I do want to tell you something." Jesse turned down the volume using buttons on the steering wheel. "Orson, I have to come clean."

"Now, you're scaring me."

"Well, the reason I'm meeting my mother-in-law is because she's giving me Steven's ashes, and I'm bringing them back with me. I wasn't going to tell you 'cause I didn't want to spook you."

"It takes a lot to spook me. I thought you were going to take me to a gay resort or something."

"So, you don't mind going back home with Steven's ashes?"

"Why should I? As long as you don't put the urn here in the front seat between us. Wait . . . you're not planning on talking to him and shit?"

"Fuck off, Orson."

"So how come she has Steven's ashes? Did he pass away in New Orleans?"

"No, he died in LA."

"So she had him air-trayed?"

"What? Is that military lingo?"

"I guess that's what I've always called it."

"I should know that, I'm a writer," said Jesse, making a mental note of it. "When Steven died, I was a wreck. She flew to LA, and I guess she took advantage of the situation because somehow she talked me into having Steven airlifted to New Orleans."

"Trayed. Air-trayed."

"She wanted to have a private family service. They're Baptists, you know. But now I'm sorry I'd agreed to this 'cause it's like it's extending Steven's death much longer than it should have been, dragging on this whole . . ."

Orson noticed Jesse's voice was cracking, so he subtly shifted the conversation.

"How did you meet Steven? You must have a great story."

"Not really. It's pretty boring. We met during our last year at UCLA. We were in the same creative writing class. The fireworks came much later," Jesse slowed down his delivery, getting lost in thought. "Then, it got bumpy, and then it crashed."

"Son, I was trying to help you to lighten up, but it's not working. Let's talk about something else."

"No. Wait. You're right. I wanna tell you."

"Are you sure? I don't want you to get all upset."

"I think it'll do me good to talk about Steven with someone who knew him just a little. Besides, it will keep me on my toes on the drive to New Orleans."

"I like you, Jesse, I feel you," Orson's tone shifted to a humorous one. "But first you drop the bomb on me about Steven's ashes, and now you're telling me I have to listen to your love story for the remaining three hours of this trip? What did I get myself into?"

"Well, do you want to hear the story or not about how I met my lover?"

"Funny!" He said ironically. "Work on that one. You can do better; I've read your stuff. And I thought this trip was going to be fun." Orson looked at his watch-less wrist. "What time did you say we'll get to NOLA?"

"Fine! You win."

Just as Orson could foresee, Jesse seemed at ease talking about Steven, probably because he was recounting the beginning of their story and not the bitter end. The end Orson knew from googling Jesse, but he was puzzled about some facts. Still, he would make sure not to let Jesse get to that point, not that day anyway. The beginning of their relationship was just like the guy had told him about earlier: no sparks when they met. In fact, Jesse hardly noticed Steven in class. He said their teacher divided the class into pairs so that each team could write a piece together. The attraction came much later when he and Steven realized they were finishing each other's thoughts when they were writing; they were creating as a unit. Their teacher was so pleased with the results. She encouraged them and the rest of the teams to work on a bigger project. They had to turn in a chapter each week to be read aloud in class. By this point, the competition among the students was palpable. In spite of this charged atmosphere, everyone waited impatiently for Jesse and Steven's next chapter. Their work was outstanding.

For Jesse, the relationship with Steven developed by default; it simply happened, no flirting, no courtship, and much less romance. One night in Steven's dorm room, they were working on the last chapter that was due the following day. When Jesse finished typing the last sentence, they both felt like they had given birth to something more than that story. Neither could put a finger on it nor remember who made the first move. The fact is they kissed and sealed the deal right then. From then on, they were a fixture in each other's lives.

"Don't mind me saying this," Orson said as Jesse finished his story. "That's pretty romantic if you ask me."

"Dude, really? Our story is dull." Replied Jesse. "You either don't watch many movies, or you haven't been in love."

"I've been in love."

"Yeah, let's talk about that."

"Easy son, you're telling your story, not mine."

"You wanna know something funny?" Jesse continued. "This is actually the first time I get to tell this story without any interruptions from Steven. We always told it together, and we had different versions of how we started. He would say that I hit on him constantly when he was the one nearly drooling over me since day two. But he was bipolar, so he had a twisted way of perceiving some events."

"Bipolar? Shit, that must have been tough," said Orson. "Was he on medication?"

"Yeah, but he never told me about his condition until way after we moved in together."

"That sucks!"

"That was Steven. One minute . . ." Jesse was interrupted by another incoming phone call. The screen displayed "Lauren." Before he hit the answer button, he told Orson it was his mother calling from upstate New York.

"Hi Lauren, I meant to call you last night, but I was busy packing—"

"Don't worry about it," she interrupted. "I fell asleep as soon as I hit the bed at the hotel, plus I left my phone on silent mode, I would have missed your call anyway. Are you on your way to New Orleans now?"

"Yes, we are on our way. When are you going back home?"

"I'm on my way to JFK now. I'll be in San Diego around seven tonight."

"Is your friend Orson with you?"

"Yes, he's right here, so watch what you say."

"No, I just wanted to thank him for getting you off those darn happy pills your mother prescribed."

"Lauren, he didn't." Jesse turned to look at Orson for a couple of seconds. "He simply expressed his opinion about antidepressants. I made the decision to quit. And I am grateful to him for it." Jesse turned to Orson again and grinned at him.

"You know, you're on speakerphone. He can hear you."

"Hi, Orson, nice to meet you."

"Hello, Jesse's Mom. How are you doing today?"

"Please, call me Lauren. Orson, tell Jesse to take a selfie of the two of you. I want to put a face to that fabulous name of yours."

"OK, I'll make sure of it, I promise."

"Anyway, I just wanted to thank you for pointing Jesse in the right direction."

"C'mon Lauren," Jesse added, "you make it sound like I was on meth or something."

"I'm just glad you started writing again." Lauren continued, "Orson, have you read anything of his yet, or watched any of his shows?"

"Yes, I've read a few short stories he emailed me. They are amazing, no wonder he's famous. I haven't seen any of his shows, though. I don't own a TV set."

"Hey! Neither do I." Her voice tone shifted up. "Orson, what sign are you?"

"Virgo."

"I'm a Leo, good. Jesse told me you are very tall. How tall?"

"Six foot five."

"Mmmm, very tall."

"OK, Lauren. Enough." Jesse began to be embarrassed by his mother, so he picked up the phone, taking it off speaker. "Yes, and he's also dark and handsome and way out of your league."

They exchanged a few more words. They had a kind of small argument before Jesse hung up the phone and switched the music back on.

"That was funny." Orson smiled. "She's cute."

"Well . . . she is. You'll like her too. Sorry, she acts funny like that when she has to fly."

"How come you call her Lauren?"

"Well, I met her when I was four."

"Oh, so she's your stepmother? Wait, I'm confused."

"No, she's my biological mother." he explained, "When I was born, Lauren suffered from postpartum depression. She and my dad started going to a psychiatrist together, and that's who I call mom."

"Say what?"

41

"Sorry, scratch that! Reverse it!'"

"And you call yourself a storyteller?"

Jesse stayed quiet for two seconds, "Mr. Hucklebuns, we have a situation."

"Please, Jesse, go on."

"Anyway, after a few therapy sessions, Lauren took off, abandoning my father and me. What dad said is that Lauren refused to take the drugs my mom prescribed for her."

"Why?"

"Wait! Listen to this song." Jesse interrupted and turned up the volume a bit. "Do you know this guy, 'Lazy' Cooper? He's great."

Orson turned the volume down. "Son, finish your story. Why wouldn't she want to take her medication?"

"She's always been into natural healing, so she preferred that over chemicals."

"You mean like alternative medicine?"

"Yes, but obviously that wasn't working, because she just packed up and left us. My father really needed therapy then and kept making appointments with my mom. And I guess that's how they fell in love, they got married soon after, and that's how she became the one I still call 'Mom.'"

"Wow! You should write this in one of your stories."

"Wait, there's more," Jesse said. "Then a few years later Lauren moved back to San Diego, that's where we lived. By then she had overcome her depression and feelings towards my father, and so did he. She apologized to my dad and me and even to my stepmom. Gosh, it's weird calling her that. Anyway, they worked it out. Lauren could visit me and eventually take me out. My mom, being a shrink and all, thought it would be confusing for me to call them both 'Mom,' so Lauren agreed that I should call her by her name. She just wanted to make up for lost time, and my folks were great considering . . ."

"That's so cool that they were able to work that out to your benefit."

"I think it worked great for Lauren too because she's a free spirit. She's always traveling around; she can't be tied down to a family. She's too independent." Jesse went on, "she became a healer herself, working

42

with crystals, Reiki, sound therapy, Aromatherapy, you name it. She subsequently became a writer on a wide variety of subjects. When she's not writing, she gives lectures on New Age subjects around the country."

"Wow! I'd like to meet her one day. I am interested in these subjects. Oprah woke my interest in them, believe it or not."

"It's not my thing, but like I always say: if it works for you…"

"Jesse, I see a diner coming up the road," said Orson, pointing out the window. "Can we stop here? I gotta go to the bathroom, plus I wanna eat something."

"Here? Are you sure? You know we'll be in New Orleans in an hour. Can you wait?"

"I am starving. I've been up since five."

"What about the donuts?"

"What about them? I'm a big guy, I need food."

"Yeah, that's not all you need."

"Hey, what do you mean?"

"Look, there's the diner!" Jesse joked as he pointed at the restaurant, so he wouldn't have to answer. Orson let it slide, not really wanting to find out what his friend meant. He was just happy Jesse had agreed to stop in that small town.

SIX

THE GPS REPEATED, "You've arrived at your destination" for the fourth time. Jesse had yelled at the recording out of impatience before switching it off. Orson hadn't noticed because he was admiring the Victorian mansion in the heart of Garden District, where his friend reserved rooms. It was already past three o'clock in the afternoon, and they were both ready for some rest before going to town.

"Isn't it beautiful?" asked Jesse taking off his seatbelt, "I've only heard good things about this place."

"Looks expensive."

"Dude, we've already talked about this; besides, we're here for work, not enjoyment."

"Yeah, right," Orson said ironically while opening his door.

As they got out of the car, Jesse mentioned he had always wanted to stay at the Bald Cypress Inn. But every time he and Steven came to New Orleans, they had to stay with Ms. Deville. She wouldn't have it any other way.

Jesse rang the bell to the bed and breakfast, and soon after they were greeted by a beautiful woman in her thirties. They were expecting a southern drawl, but she introduced herself with a French accent as Jeanelle. She led them into a wide hallway. At the end of it, a young man about her age came out of a door. He was rubbing his hands together as if he was trying to dry them. Orson figured he just came out of the kitchen. Jesse thought he came out of the bathroom. He walked towards his new guests and introduced himself as Justin, their hostess' husband. He had a strong New Orleans accent. The couple showed them into a small room that served as the office for check-ins. It was a bit cramped, filled with three chairs, one of them behind the antique wooden desk, old portraits on the wall, and plenty of books on the shelves, all hosted by a wall-to-wall-sized Persian rug on the floor.

They had a standard talk about bed and breakfast registration: IDs, keys, breakfast hours, nearby restaurants, shops, tourist attractions, and 'have a nice stay' kind of welcome. After checking-in, Orson and Jesse went up the stairs with their luggage. They walked into the hallway to decide on a room. The doors of their respective rooms were across the hall from each other. They set their bags down next to the one on their left.

"Are you sure you don't want to flip a coin?" Asked Jesse, who knew very well which room Orson would pick.

"It was part of our deal not to, son."

"You got the keys, dude, open up!"

Orson unlocked the door closest to them, expecting a room with traditional decoration. He was surprised to find a trendy space with a few clean and straight-lined pieces of furniture; a combination of country style and contemporary minimalism. The hardwood floor gave the room a homey atmosphere. They walked in, and Jesse went straight to the window, curious about the view from there. His friend chose to look around the room. The guy stood by the curtain, viewing the beautiful Renaissance-style garden displaying signs of autumn in the back of the house. He then turned around to find Orson standing under the bathroom doorframe studying the hot tub that was sitting next to the large window facing the backyard. It was obvious to Jesse his friend was taken by the large-sized bathtub with a view.

"It looks like you've already decided," said Jesse, turning around to leave.

"Wait, let's look at your room now."

"My room? Need I say more?" The guy went out to the hallway, picked up Orson's bag, brought it inside the room, and set it by a chair next to the door. "Excellent choice, I know what mine looks like I saw it on their website, it looks a lot like this one."

"Thanks, Jesse."

"Are you going to call your friends to find out what time we need to be there tomorrow?" said Jesse stepping out the door.

"It'll probably be around noon." Orson picked up his bag from the floor. "What I do know is that it's going to be at my buddy Frank Torres' house."

"Puerto Rican, like me?"

"Cuban. You're not Puerto Rican, your dad is, and neither of you speak the language."

"I can say *Buenos nachos.*"

"Please, don't embarrass yourself or me with your Spanish in front of Frank."

"Remind me later to tell you to go fuck yourself, will you?"

"Listen," Orson couldn't help but smile. "Frank told us to come with an empty stomach, so tomorrow we should have light breakfast.

"I can't wait to try all that soul food."

"Jesse, please don't call it that. You'll definitely embarrass me if you do." He set his bag on the bed. "It's a Pig Pickin' lunch, and it seems Frank and Cynthia are really going out of their way for you. They want to impress you, my Hollywood friend."

"What the hell did you tell them about me?"

"Not much, only that you're famous for your TV shows and movies and that you are rich and handsome. Very handsome."

"I wish you hadn't."

"Relax, son, I'm just kidding, I told them you were writing a piece on me."

"Is that all?"

"Yes."

"Swear?"

"Yes!"

"Good," Jesse headed for the door. "I'm going to my room to call my mother-in-law and then I'm going for a run. I'll take a shower and a nap before dinner. Text me whenever you're ready."

"At what time do you want to have dinner tonight?" Orson asked.

"Eight?"

"Whoever is ready first should knock on the other one's door," said Orson while he stood by the door watching Jesse take his bag from the floor in the hallway. The man waited until his friend went into his room to shut his door.

It was nearly eleven o'clock the following morning when a persistent knock on the door woke Jesse up. Half asleep, he got out of his bed and looked around the room until he spotted his boxers on the floor. He put them on and opened the door.

"Good morning, Orson," Jesse said and turned around. "Please, come in." He went into the bathroom, leaving the door half-open.

"Son, I've been phoning you all morning. I thought something happened to you." Orson walked in and shut the door behind him.

"I switched off my cell, I came in really late last night," Jesse shouted from the bathroom while he urinated.

"You do remember we have that lunch today, right?"

"What happened last night, why didn't you wake me after your nap?"

"I didn't take a nap," Orson sat on the bed. "I took a bath instead."

"Did you fill up the hot tub?" Jesse stepped out of the bathroom.

"Hell yeah!" Orson leaned back, stretching his arms behind himself with his open hands on the bed as support. "I regret not bringing weed, it would have been great for my bath."

"I know. Why didn't you?" Jesse sat on the chair next to the door across from Orson.

"Hey, you said it was work and no play."

"Fair enough. But tell me, what did you do after you didn't wake me? Damn it!" he teased.

"Aren't you getting ready, son?

"Oh, yes, let me take a shower." Jesse got up quickly and went into the bathroom, leaving the door half open again. "So tell me, what did you end up doing last night?" He shouted.

"After my bath, I texted you a few times. I figured you wanted some rest after your run and driving all morning. So I went out and tried to find a place for us to have dinner, killing time until I heard from you, but I didn't, so I stayed and had dinner by myself."

"Did you find a good place?!" Jesse turned on the shower faucet.

"Yes! Creole food. It was pretty good, but I've had better."

"Did you do anything after?" Asked Jesse as he stepped in the shower. "Never mind, tell me later."

Not two minutes had passed when Orson got up and walked to the window, the curtains were half drawn, so he opened them completely to look at the view from that side of the building. He saw the street and the driveway alongside the B&B and felt slightly guilty about his room selection. But he knew Jesse wouldn't have it any other way. He turned to the side when something small and colorful on top of the dresser caught his eye. He moved closer before he realized he was being nosy. By then, it was too late as he saw one of those pocket-sized AIDS prevention condom and lube kits. He heard Jesse turning off the shower and, as if he had committed a crime, quickly walked to the bed. Nearly there, he decided to sit on the chair next to the door instead. Jesse came out of the bathroom with just a white towel around his waist.

"Oh! You changed places," said Jesse.

"Yeah, I had to," replied Orson. "I could see you naked from the bathroom mirror. Quite a show. Congratulations, by the way, nice buns."

"Shit, really? I'm sorry." Jesse nearly turned deep red.

"Relax. I'm just kidding, son," but he wasn't. "I've been in the army, and I've seen it all."

Jesse walked to his open suitcase and grabbed a pair of jeans and a change of underwear.

"So, did you go anywhere after dinner?" The guy asked as he put on his underwear with the towel still around his waist. He dropped the towel to slip into his blue jeans. After he was done, he picked up the towel from the floor.

"After dinner, I walked around to find a place nearby to listen to music, then came back here and read a little." He forgot to tell Jesse he wrote music in his notebook as well. "Then I guess I fell asleep because I don't remember switching off the light."

"That happens to me all the time." Jesse went back to his suitcase to grab a pair of socks and his Nikes and sat on the bed facing Orson. "Well, when I woke up, it must have been ten thirty or so, I went to your door. When I heard you breathing heavily, I decided not to knock. I was starving, so I had to go out. The only place I found open was a pizza joint about four blocks from here. On my way back, I found this gay bar, so I stopped in to have a beer."

"How was it?"

"Same ole, same ole," said Jesse as he finished tying up his shoes. He stood up.

"Did you hook up?"

"Nah! Not interested; not right now." He made a final visit to his suitcase and took out an indigo blue cotton sweater and put it on. "I was just curious about the gay scene in New Orleans, that's all. Shall we?" Jesse tilted his head in a 'let's go' gesture, then grabbed his jacket from the back of the chair where Orson was sitting. He put it on and opened the door and waited for his friend to exit first, then he followed.

On their way downstairs, they figured it was senseless for Jesse to have breakfast at the B&B if they were going to have lunch in less than an hour. Orson had his already a couple of hours earlier. Both men got in the car and went to a drive-thru to get coffee for Jesse, before heading to the Torres' house.

"So Ors," Jesse started as he drove, "can I call you Ors?"

"You just did, and no, you cannot," Orson replied, once more, half kidding, half not.

"I've been meaning to ask you something, and since I've already been telling you so much about me . . ."

"Uh-oh, here we go!"

"Shut up, dude." Jesse smiled and reached for his coffee placed in one of the two small round trays between the front seats, then took a sip before asking: "Who is this Elsie lady who did you so wrong?"

"What lady, who?"

"The night I met Ambar, she said your ex came in asking for you. Elsie, I think that's what she said?"

"Oh, L - C, not Elsie!" Orson explained. "Well, she's no lady."

"You made that clear that night. What in the hell did she do to you, if I may ask?"

"Jesse, you don't understand . . . L.C. is a guy."

"Oh! I understand, she's now a man." Jesse turned to Orson. "What the hell did you do to her?" He joked.

"No. L.C. has always been a man."

Jesse was puzzled and stayed silent for a few seconds. He drank a little more coffee while thinking of what to say next. "Were you two, like, lovers then?"

"Lovers? I don't think that word ever described us." Orson opened the glove compartment for no reason at all and then closed it. Right after, his right leg started shaking up and down, uncontrollably and unconsciously. "L.C. and I were certainly more than friends, intimate friends if we have to call it something."

"How long were you not lovers, then?"

"Way too many years." He paused for a few seconds. "I wasted half my life with that motherfucker."

"You sure kept it a secret."

"I don't like talking about L.C."

"I don't mean L.C. I mean why didn't tell me you were gay."

"You never asked, son. I'm very private about this." The man started readjusting his seatbelt as if something was wrong with it. "I was going to, but I didn't see the point. Besides, I didn't want you to remotely think I was into you. You're cool, Jesse. I like you as a friend, and I wanna keep it that way. But, I don't dig white men, just to be clear."

"I get it." Jesse saw what he was doing out of the corner of his eye. "Dude, are you OK there? You seem a little restless."

"I'm fine." He left his seatbelt alone. "You see, I'm from a whole different generation, son. Young kids nowadays got it easy compared to us, thank God." Orson continued, "In my day, it was complicated as I'm sure you know. And for us black men, to be gay was a whole different ball game, within our race and out, and especially down here in the south."

"I just can't believe you waited this long to tell me."

"I don't go around telling people." He explained, "I don't call myself gay, I just happen to like men. What is it with you and labels, anyway?"

Jesse didn't answer, he drank more of his coffee instead. Then he continued, "Does your family know?"

"Hell no, they don't, and I plan to keep it that way."

"Did your wife know?"

"Genna? No . . . well, she did; that's actually what killed her. Only Ambar knows and L.C., of course."

"So I take it that your friends, where we're going now, don't know anything either."

"That's right, no one knows."

"Except for the guys you've been with." Jesse pressed.

"There haven't been other guys."

"Not even the occasional trick?"

"Oh, that! Yeah! I've gone cruising, but only in emergencies." Orson opened and closed the glove compartment again. "Listen, Jesse, can we talk about something else?"

They stayed quiet for a while, with only the voice of the GPS occasionally breaking the silence. Jesse got annoyed by it, so he switched on the radio. He asked his friend to search for good music to try and make him feel more at ease. It was obvious that Orson was uncomfortable, and Jesse didn't want to make it worse by asking him why. Was he asking him too many personal questions, Jesse wondered? It shouldn't be that because Orson does that all the time. Or could it be that Orson didn't like talking about his sexuality or about L.C.? And what was that about being gay what killed his wife? It was definitely too late to ask, Jesse thought. Orson did find a local blues station, and sure enough, he started feeling his normal self again, chatting away while Jesse finished his coffee and drove to their destination.

SEVEN

I NOW LOOK BACK on our trip to New Orleans, when you first asked me about L.C., and I feel bad about being so evasive, especially after I insisted that you tell me how you met Steven. Jesse, you know how secretive I tend to be, and as I said, I still feel bad about parts of my past, but here it goes:

I met L.C. during my tour of duty in the Vietnam War. I'm talking about 1973. I didn't really meet him, but I noticed him walking around the base camp with a guitar hanging from his shoulder. One day I got word that he was putting together a blues band, so I thought I'd give it a shot and auditioned.

As you already know, my grandfather was a musician, and he taught me how to play when I moved with them from Chicago. Papa Joe was under the weird impression that I wasted too much time reading, which he referred to as doing nothing. He played a mean piano, and damn, did he live for the blues! Who better to pass on his love of the genre than to his lazy grandson. He developed a schedule for me to practice. At first, I had no interest in the piano, and lessons felt more like obligations. But on weekends, I watched and listened to him play with his friends all the time. They would come over after church every Sunday, and while the women were in the kitchen making lunch, they would jam a bit. But it was later, way past lunchtime, when they really jammed. And that's when I finally developed a taste and love for the blues. From then on, I would practice during whatever free time I had. I would beg Papa Joe to let me play with his friends on Sundays. It wasn't until I turned sixteen that he finally let me play with them, but never for too long. It was his time with the boys, and I wasn't part of the group.

Anyway, I did get into L.C.'s band along with two other privates. L.C. was the lead singer and guitarist. There was a drummer, Tim from Dallas, and Bill from Sacramento on bass—the only white boy in the band—and then myself. We liked to call ourselves the Out of the Blues Band. We usually played at night, whenever possible, down at the Officer's Club, that's where the piano was. I was told that on a previous USO event, the entertainers had to flee in a hurry and left a few instruments behind. I thought we were pretty good, at least that's what everyone said.

You could say that L.C. and I were just army buddies, not close friends. We basically only hung out together when we rehearsed. However, all that changed the afternoon that I was assigned to a mission to help evacuate wounded troops from a very hot LZ—that's what we called the landing zone. Some members of L.C.'s platoon were taking heavy casualties in a firefight. They were pinned down and needed all the help that we could give them. Two Huey helicopters were dispatched to pick up the wounded and the dead to take them to the closest MASH unit.

When we flew there, we could see the yellow smoke that our troops had popped to mark their location. It was clearly evident that the Vietcong was overrunning the LZ and that those on the ground needed reinforcements. The choppers hit the ground fast and hard, and I jumped out to help get the wounded on board my Huey as quickly as possible.

I saw someone—it turned out to be L.C.—but I did not recognize him at first, as he was standing in the middle of a firestorm of bullets and yellow smoke that was swirling in the air because of the rotating chopper blades. He was frantically waving his arms to come help him with an extremely bloody soldier lying on a canvas tarp they were using as a stretcher. I ran as fast as I could towards him, hoping that none of the bullets whizzing by me had my name on them. That's when I realized it was my brother L.C. There was no time to talk or even think.

The young guy we were carrying was screaming in terrible pain as we carried and dragged him at full gallop to the side of the Huey. We dumped his body inside on the floor to join several more that were already loaded by others. The metal floor of the chopper had large pools of blood that were already flowing out onto the ground. Then we ran back to get another wounded man who was lying on the ground waiting.

By this time, the Vietcong finally got their sights fixed on the Hueys, and they began exploding rounds of mortars closer to the two choppers that were sitting targets in the LZ. A mortar exploded behind us as we were running to get that other solider; our Huey had taken a direct hit. We fell to the ground only to look back at the burning remains of the chopper with its cargo of wounded soldiers and the flight crew. The other Huey immediately pulled up off the ground and made its way out of the LZ. It moved across the ground as fast as it could, gathering as much transitional lift as it could so it could clear the tree line. Red tracers followed its path out of there as it raced away at treetop level over the thick forest. They had no choice but to pull out of the LZ to save those they had on board. That, however, left the remaining few of us to survive on our own. I looked up, in the direction of that wounded soldier, and in its place there was part of the burning wreckage.

We knew the Huey would certainly not be coming back for us that afternoon. The LZ had been lost to the enemy, and it would soon be dark so they could not risk more lives to find us that day. It was now up to L.C. and myself to find someplace to hide and evade capture or worse until morning.

We looked around and realized that we might have been the only two remaining soldiers left in the LZ alive. We could no longer hear the sounds of the Huey. It was long gone, and we were really on our own. We could still hear the Vietcong around us, and if it were not for all the smoke and haze from the explosions and gunfire, they would have seen us. So, we got down low and began to run for some close place to hide.

We managed to conceal ourselves in the thick bushes next to the river. The darkness soon came, and we hoped that this would afford us more invisibility and allow us to move away from the LZ. The enemy had total control of the place, and they were checking the dead bodies of our comrades left on the ground. Every once in a while, we would hear a few shots from their AK-47s as they killed any wounded who might still be alive that we were not aware of. In almost total darkness, the sound of their automatic weapons being fired was truly frightening, and we were both unsure if we should move or just stay still and hope for the best.

That decision was soon made for us when L.C. lost his footing and made a lot of noise when he tumbled down a riverbank into the river, making a loud splash. A group of Charlies came running our way, so I immediately dropped to the soil. They opened fire on the banks and the river itself. It was totally dark, so their firing was random and not focused as they sprayed their rounds in the direction where L.C. fell. After a long silence the Charlies left, assuming that they had taken care of whatever made the noise. However, they did not go far, and several dozen of them occupied an encampment just a short distance from where I was.

I decided that I needed to check on L.C. Slowly, and as quietly as I could, I inched down the side of the riverbank in the darkness until I could touch the water itself. I felt around for any evidence of L.C. I took a chance, and in a very hushed voice called out for him. It felt like hours what in reality might have been just a few minutes, but I eventually heard his voice telling me to quiet down and that he was hiding over to my right.

I crawled towards his voice. He was hiding inside a hollow space under an old log that washed up when the river ran high, overrunning its banks during the recent monsoon. This old log topped a cave created when the river washed away the earth from under its resting spot. This cave-like space could not be seen from above the riverbank and had just enough room to hide both of our bodies inside it. The only concern about these kinds of hiding places was that they were great places for snakes to live in as well. The moment I was inside, L.C. immediately hugged me; to my surprise, he wouldn't let go.

"We made it!" he said as he pressed against me.

"Have we? We're in deep . . ." I pulled away, "Brotha, you are soaked!"

"I fell in the river."

"I can see that. Man, look at you. You are trembling." I started unbuttoning my shirt, keeping my tank top on, realizing just then he was actually scared shitless but trying to play it cool. "Here, take that off and put this on. And take off your boots," I demanded as I gave him my socks as well.

"Thanks." He did as he was told.

"It's going to be a long night," I added.

56

And indeed it was. We were too on edge because of enemies and snakes to get any shut-eye. We whispered our life stories to each other until our throats could take it no more.

Once in a while, we would hear the Charlies in their camp, carrying on and getting louder. We must have fallen asleep at some point because the next thing I remember was L.C., with his arms wrapped around me, still trembling all over. He said he just had a nightmare that we were caught by the Charlies. He was clinging to me like a baby, helpless and afraid. I felt sorry for him and hugged him back.

The fact is that L.C. never let go of me. I let him be because it felt so nice to comfort him. I could feel his quivering diminishing slowly. I felt a strong urge to caress the back of his neck. Just then, something shifted in me. It was as if his trembling was transferred into me, followed by the feeling of surrendering. Soon after, I felt his erection pressing against my crotch. He then pulled his head away from my shoulder to face me. He completely caught me off guard when he kissed me on the lips. Right then I was gone, so to speak, and it felt right. A side of me I never knew existed emerged from nowhere. I never experienced kissing with such intensity and pleasure, never with Genna, for sure. I did not recognize myself. I went along with it and continued kissing him back as if I'd done this all my life. At that point, there was no stopping either of us. It was the most delicious sensation I had till then. We did not speak a word and then moved away from each other—as much as we could in such a tight space. We just looked at each other as we started removing the rest of our clothes. Soon I had my hands and my lips all over him. I kept tossing and turning him the way I could to discover what another man's body felt like.

My heart—our hearts—must have been beating a mile a minute, and our breaths were muting any sound from the outside. At some point, I realized I could see the color of his skin in the soft orange glow on its surface. I glanced out the hole for a second, and it was no longer dark outside. The sunlight was softly filtering through the trees. Apart from the sound of our breaths, I began hearing the morning birds waking up from the night. Somehow, we completely forgot we were in any kind of danger. We kissed and explored our bodies in any way we could. Jesse, forgive me, I got carried away. It was not my intention to get so graphic, much less while you're here silent next to me. But that's what happened.

That was our peak, for L.C. and me. It never got any better than that for us. Perhaps it came close that month we were stationed in West Germany before heading back home. And boy, did we try, or at least I tried. Attempting to relive that moment, that loving moment and that passion was exhausting. This went on for years until I ran out of whatever it was that drove me to him.

In that early morning, we made love until the sun was finally out. We got dressed quietly and got out of that hole. We did not speak; we would look into each other's eyes and smiled inside like we had something special only the two of us knew about. We climbed up the riverbank and got back to the forest and snuck our way to the edge of the LZ. We waited and waited some more. Eventually, we heard a Huey approaching, and we immediately popped smoke for them to spot us. It was a surprisingly quick pickup without any mishaps this time. We finally got the hell out of there.

For a very long time, I kept telling myself that that night with L.C. was meant to happen. That all the events that conspired to get us to be together were meant to be. Boy, was I wrong!

EIGHT

THEY WERE HALF A BLOCK AWAY From Frank and Cynthia's house when Orson made sure to remind Jesse not to mention anything regarding their earlier conversation in front of his friends. Although he was annoyed by Orson's request, Jesse agreed but warned him he would not censor his own sexuality if anyone happened to mention it. They parked the car in front of the house, an old midsize brick house with white framed windows and dark gray shingles.

By the time Orson and Jesse opened their doors, the Torres' were standing on their porch, waving at them. The couple was in their early sixties. Cynthia was darker than Frank, wearing her grey hair natural. By contrast, his hair was black with a few white hairs near his sideburns. Both guests walked to their hosts—greeting them as they approached. Frank gave Orson a long hug, and Cynthia shook Jesse's hand with both of hers. Before going into the house, Jesse went back to the car to get the bottles of white wine they had forgotten in the back seat. The men had stopped at a liquor store. Jesse Google searched for one that had a great selection of Spanish wines. The guy insisted on getting that for the Torres', wanting to impress Orson's friends. They all walked inside the house into the living room. It was a modest home decorated with early American furniture, a black stone fireplace, and lots of family pictures on the mantel. They went through the dining room to reach the kitchen. The dining room had a large table for twelve with a centerpiece of fresh flowers in a crystal vase. They entered the kitchen, and Jesse saw that it was filled with plenty of dishes; he thought it would be rude to stare. They were greeted by a hefty woman in her early forties wearing an apron; she was mixing coleslaw in a large bowl in the counter. She was introduced to Jesse and

Orson as Tracy, Mark's not-so-new girlfriend. After some small talk, they left their wine bottles in the refrigerator and then walked out to the backyard to meet the rest of the guests.

As they walked outside, Jesse was surprised to find out he was the only white person at the cookout. Not that he had a problem with it, but he didn't expect it, and this made him a bit more self-conscious. Before arriving, he was already feeling like an outcast because he had never gone to a party where every guest had something to do with the army. Also, he learned earlier that he would be the youngest guest of the group. On top of that, Orson had told all his friends that he was bringing some big shot writer/producer from Hollywood. Once there, they all seemed OK, and he figured if they were friends of Orson, they should be just as cool as his new friend.

Everyone outside was sitting at a large table chatting away except for Pete, a stocky, round fellow with a contagious smile. He was standing by the barbecue, concentrated on the large hog spread open over the fire, holding a grilling fork in one hand and a beer in the other. Two veterans at the table got up the moment they saw Orson and went over to him to say their hellos. Jesse shook hands with Mark, a skinny, short man with a serious expression on his face. He was nothing like Jesse had imagined when he was mentioned in the kitchen. Then came Jimmy and his wife Dolores, who looked like brother and sister, mainly because they wore similar eyeglasses. They were one of those couples that seemed to resemble each other more and more as the years went by. And finally, Sherisse, a beautiful woman with flawless skin and beautiful dark hair. Jesse learned she was married to the designated cook, Pete, who briefly left the grill to greet them. Jesse was impressed by the way everyone received Orson; their love for this man was undeniable. A flash of envy rushed over him briefly as he watched the displays of affection towards his friend. Envy notwithstanding, Jesse certainly felt welcomed by every one of Orson's friends.

"Your friends weren't kidding," Jesse remarked to Orson in private, referring to the amount of food on the table. Orson walked to the blue plastic cooler by the back door, grabbed a couple of beers, returned to Jesse, and gave him one. The man gestured with his head for Jesse to accompany him to the grill to talk to Pete. They talked for a while about places they could go in town for good live blues. Pete expressed an interest in Jesse's idea for the story he was putting together and wanted to know how their friend Orson became the source of his inspiration. Orson explained that Jesse's idea was loosely based on him because of the time he worked at Graceland. The rest was all made up by Jesse's "ingenious brain," as the man put it. Jesse enjoyed listening to his buddy's version of the project.

Jesse was finishing his second beer when he saw the food being brought from the kitchen through the back door of the house. Every guest was required to help bring dishes out, except for Jesse, who was exempt from it because he was the guest of honor. "Maliboo" was the new nickname that was given to him as everyone helped set up the feast. Even though Jesse explained in vain that Malibu was not that close to Hollywood and that he didn't live in either place, he found it amusing nonetheless. The dining table overflowed with hushpuppies, fried okra, coleslaw, baked beans, baked ham, cornbread, string beans, and macaroni and cheese. Orson made a point of secretly telling Jesse his mac and cheese was out of this world and that he would make it for him one day. Jesse took his word for it.

Before everyone was seated on the table when Cynthia announced, mainly for Jesse's benefit, that the Pig Pickin' tradition was for each guest to go and pick their own meat from the grill and then help themselves to plenty from the side dishes on the table. Overeating was clearly encouraged. Jimmy opened two of the bottles of Spanish wine and served it around. Jesse declined and mentioned he would switch to good old Southern sweetened iced tea. He was concerned about driving later to meet Dottie, his mother-in-law. Orson, who was sitting three seats over, on the opposite side of the table, assured him that a glass of good white wine might make it easier for him to face her. Jesse agreed and went for it; a couple of times.

Everything Jesse heard about authentic New Orleans food lived up to his expectations. His previous visits to the Big Easy consisted of family dinners and fast-food chains, but never the Creole food he had always longed for. He had never tried pork with so much flavor and texture, a tender and crispy combination, nor had he ever had fried okra before. That was not his favorite, but the baked beans were the best he'd ever had in his life.

Over lunch, Jesse learned a bit more about Orson's past in the army in Vietnam. He was fascinated by the stories his buddies told; it made the guy realize how little he knew about his friend. Every so often, one of Orson's buddies would say something along the lines of "this would make a good movie," before launching another anecdote. Then the conversation drifted to Maliboo's life in Hollywood. Everyone wanted to hear about the celebrities Jesse had met or worked with. Although Jesse never really liked bragging about living in Tinseltown, he told a few stories he thought they would find amusing. Orson was delighted watching his young buddy so relaxed among some of the people he loved the most.

By dessert time, Orson's friends felt even more at ease with Jesse. The few that felt intimidated by his semi-celebrity status felt comfortable enough to ask more.

"So, Maliboo, if you don't mind me asking," said Jimmy as he poured himself some wine. "What is your next series going to be about?"

Jesse was in the middle of a bite of his dessert. "What is this called again? Banana what?" Pointing at it with his fork and with his mouth nearly empty.

"Banana Frost." Orson volunteered.

"Wow!" He finished chewing. "And who is the blessed talent that created this?"

"That would be me!" said Cynthia proudly.

"Mmm. Anyway," said Jesse putting his fork back on the table. "My idea is not fully developed yet, and I don't even know how I am going to pitch it as a film, series, or documentary. I was actually leaning towards a fake documentary."

"What's that?" asked Sherisse. "Is that one of those conspiracy theory things you see on YouTube?"

"No. It's like a real documentary," Tracy volunteered, looking at Jesse from time to time for reassurance, "but everything in it, or parts of it, are made up. The thing is to make it seem like the real thing."

"I've never heard of such a thing," said Sherisse.

"You haven't told me about this change of format," Orson said to Jesse.

"I just thought about it; I know Netflix is mad about stuff like this."

"What is it about?" Frank asked. "All we know is that it has to do with Orson."

"Well, I first got this idea when Orson told me he worked at Graceland. But then when he took me out and about in Memphis to listen to true blues, I came up with the concept of a retired musician who stopped playing because of a traumatic experience. He eventually gets a job as a security guard in Graceland during the last few weeks of Elvis' life. I haven't figured out how yet, but they end up recording something together."

"He's like Orson, all right. He's also retired from music."

"C'mon Jimmy," Orson said. "Don't start with that again."

"I'm just sayin' it's a shame." Jimmy finished.

"Wait, Orson? A musician?" Jesse asked and then turned to his friend, "You told me you were a mechanic."

"That too, by profession," Orson replied, "but it's true, I used to play the piano."

"Dude! I didn't know you played."

"You never asked."

"I'll make my character a piano player then, it's decided." Jesse said "How come you stopped playing?"

"Like you said in your story, son," Orson replied as he got up, "because of a traumatic experience. I'm getting another bottle of wine if you'll all excuse me . . ." The man walked away and went inside the house, leaving Jesse speechless, wondering about the coincidence between life and fiction. He wasn't about to ask Orson's friends what tragic event had led Orson to stop playing the piano.

"I'm not surprised he hadn't told you," Frank remarked. "Orson has always been very secretive."

"I'm beginning to see that now," said Jesse, pleased to find out Orson was reserved with everyone and not only with him.

"He tells you eventually, but he takes his time." Frank continued.

"Yeah, we're still waiting for him to tell us a thing or two," Pete added.

"But man, he was good at the piano, you should have heard him play." Jimmy turned to Jesse, "Back in Nam, your friend and I and a couple of boys had ourselves a little blues quartet."

"That's right, with L.C., and what was his name?" added Pete, "Yes, Bill McDonald."

"Yeah, Bill. Didn't he become a priest or a reverend or something?" asked Frank.

"Yes. He's back in Sacramento." Pete continued. "He keeps busy, traveling around, writing books, posting videos on YouTube and shit . . . really cool stuff."

"Anyway, after the war, we all went our separate ways." Jimmy finished.

"But didn't Orson and L.C. move to Memphis together?" Dolores asked.

"Yes, after we all came back to New Orleans," Frank continued, "Orson left and lived with him for a while. Orson looked for a job, but it took him a while to find one. Then he finally found one as a mechanic. That's how good he is with his hands."

"Working in that shop, he became friends with practically every cop in Shelby county. Remember that, guys?" Mark mentioned. "Every time we went up to see Orson in Memphis, we partied hard and never got in trouble with the cops, thanks to him."

"Anyway, when he got that job, he finally sent for Genna to join him, and eventually they got married." Jimmy finished. "He ended up buying the shop from the owner a few years later."

"Yes, I remember that. Genna waited almost two years for Orson." Said Dolores, "I remember telling her she should find herself another man, but she hung in there, poor child."

"Can we change the subject? Orson's back," said Jesse as he stood up and reach out for Orson's empty glass of wine, "and with more wine!"

Jesse smiled as the man poured the wine in the glass, feeling a bit guilty for finding out more about his buddy's past behind his back.

Orson's friends redirected the conversation back to Jesse and his work on all the shows he had written and produced. Orson learned that

Jesse was very humble about his success and was particularly shy about talking about the more than a few awards he and Steven had won for their talent. The man was amused to see Jesse trying in vain to talk about something other than himself, wanting to find out more for his research about the veterans in front of him and their days in Vietnam.

After lunch and a few selfies, the party divided into groups: the veterans in the backyard and the wives in the living room. Jesse and Tracy were in the kitchen, putting away glassware, dishes, and silverware. Tracy was not a stranger to the Torres' household. In fact, they introduced her to Mark despite their age difference. Tracy and Jesse were standing by the window, drying the last few plates and glasses from the sink while looking out to the backyard, watching the old war veterans laughing away as they talked about the misadventures of their youth.

"I'll bet they're talking about their army days," said Tracy.

"How can you tell?" Asked Jesse with a towel in one hand and an empty wine glass in the other.

"Because I can literally see Mark turning younger. Every time he talks about his army buddies, and especially now, that he's talking to them in person and laughing like that, I see him shine."

"How long have you been together?"

"For more than a year now."

"Wow! You two seem like you've been married forever."

"Jesse, I've never laughed so much in my life since I met Mark," she added as she finished drying a large serving dish.

"That is so cool." He smiled. "Good for you."

"And how about you, how long have you and Orson been together?"

"Pardon?" Jesse asked with enlarged eyes.

"Oh shit!" Tracy saw the look on Jesse's face. "I'm so sorry. I didn't . . ."

"Orson and I are not . . . wait, why do you ask?"

"I assumed . . . well, it's the way you guys interact with one another. When you first came in the kitchen earlier, I thought you two were an item."

"Really?"

"But also, I've noticed the way Orson was looking at you when you

65

were talking about your life in LA."

"How? Never mind! Don't tell Mark or anyone, please. Orson would be mortified if . . ."

"Mark already knows about Orson. They all know, but they won't say anything unless he brings it up. It seems like they've known for years."

"Fuck! . . . really?" Jesse said, putting down a glass and picking up the last one. "You thought we were an item, really?"

"You two look good together."

"I love Orson, he's my friend, but I never even thought of him . . . Well, I just found out he's gay on our way here. He's too old for me, and besides, he's not into white men, he told me that himself."

"Hey Jesse, I simply made an observation, I really didn't mean to freak you out."

"Freak out? Me? You haven't," he said, pulling out his phone from his jeans' back pocket and read the time on the screen. "Shit! I gotta go."

"Not because of what I said."

"No, no, no, I really have to go. I gotta meet someone."

"Oh, yeah, we're supposed to give Orson a ride back to your hotel."

"Please, Tracy, don't say a word about our conversation. We came to New Orleans to work; I don't want him to be upset about who knows what. If I know Orson, he will find amusing that you thought we were a couple, but not if all of his friends know he's gay."

"Don't worry, Jesse; I won't."

"I'd better say goodbye to the gang."

Driving to the New Orleans Country Club to meet Dottie, Jesse tried not to give too much thought to the conversation he had earlier with Tracy. He certainly loved Orson, but as a friend. 'I don't want to spoil something as solid as we have,' he thought, 'Orson is certainly very good-looking, but I don't see him that way. Besides, I've never been with anyone so old, or older than me for that matter. Maybe that guy, that time at our party,' Jesse's mind kept wandering off. Orson's friends certainly knew who L.C. was, but did they know he and Orson were involved? Jesse asked himself. He figured they all knew there was bad blood between Orson and L.C., and that's why probably he was mentioned only once. Maybe out of concern for Orson or they simply didn't care for him. Jesse thought he would ask Orson later that night, but would he comment on what Tracy said? Unlike his friend, Jesse liked to bring things out in the open, so he might as well tell him tonight, he suddenly decided. Would Orson find it amusing or just get all paranoid about his friends knowing he liked men?

"Stop!" Jesse snapped out loud.

The sun was going down, and the sky, partially behind the trees, was colored in red, purple, and indigo blue. Jesse realized he wasn't enjoying any of it. And that's one thing he learned from Lauren: the ability to clear his mind to enjoy the here and now, even though he didn't believe in most of her nonsense. He looked out the window, realizing he had never seen colors like that in the California skies. He decided then to enjoy the drive down that beautiful, empty, country road not giving a damn about the recent past or the near future. He focused on the road and loving the amazing landscape surrounding him. And as he had learned, he stuck to it all the way, not concerned about what lay ahead at his destination.

NINE

I OFTEN THINK ABOUT our second night in New Orleans and how it became a turning point in our story. Mark and Tracy had just dropped me off at our bed and breakfast. Do you remember I told you they live off Treme? I looked up at your window and saw the light on in your room. I was surprised you were already back, and I got all excited 'cause I figured we could go out and hang out like we wanted to the night before. Besides, my brothers helped me make out a list of the best places in town for music, and Jimmy had given us some weed for the weekend.

As I was going up the upstairs to knock on your door, I thought about something Tracy said right before I got out of the car. She and Mark had been going off on how much they liked you, and right before I opened the car door, Stacey said, "He's a keeper, you know?" I didn't understand it then. I do now.

I stood in front of your door and took the joints that Jimmy had given me out of my pocket to show you once you opened the door. I did my "shave and haircut knock," but you didn't answer. I did hear a bit of noise from inside your room, so I figured maybe you had company. I pulled out my phone to text you, and that's when you finally opened up. I was expecting to see your smiling face, but what I saw was the opposite. In fact, I had never seen you like that. I don't know if you remember, but you didn't even say a word, you just opened the door and let me in. I put the joints you didn't notice back in my pocket.

Your eyes were fire red; I could see water on the rims, but I couldn't really read your face. Is he angry? Is he sad? I wondered. I asked what was wrong or something of the sort, but you just stared at me for a few seconds. "What is it?" I insisted. The next instant, I must have read your mind or something 'cause I felt compelled to open my arms wide and said, "C' mere." You moved fast towards me and embraced me tightly. I held on to you. I felt how you physically surrendered and cried inconsolably. It overwhelmed me and nearly broke my heart to the point that I doubted I would ever be able to comfort you. I let you be to take all the time and tears you needed. I didn't speak; I just snuggled you 'til you couldn't cry anymore. I found myself scanning the room with my eyes looking to find the urn with Steven's ashes, but the only thing I saw that could remotely resemble it was a brown paper bag on top of the dresser. Knowing you, that couldn't be the urn.

You finally stopped crying and slowly let go of me. I just looked at you, waiting for an explanation of what got you in such a state.

"I am so goddamned angry." You snapped; tears still in your eyes. "How could I have been so stupid?"

My thoughts ran a mile a minute: 'Did you miss your appointment with Dottie? Did you leave the urn on top of the car and drive off? Did you flush his ashes?'

"Now, now. No need to speak the name of God that way." I replied.

"I can't believe I went for it," the more you talked, the more confused I got. "That conniving, manipulative cunt!"

"Your mother-in-law!" Finally, I thought. "What happened, what did she do?"

"I'm gonna sue her! I swear to . . . I swear it, man!" You jumped up and started to pace in front of me. "I don't care how much it costs."

"Jesse, son, you're not making any sense," I said, but you weren't listening.

"She buried him!" You stopped to look at me; then, your eyes started tearing up. "She buried Steven without my consent."

"What?! She didn't have him cremated?"

"No, she didn't!"

"Fuck me! Now I'm the one who's pissed off."

"We were sitting at the restaurant, at the country club . . . Man, she's so slick."

You explained as you continued pacing again, "She went on about how the country club had changed for the worst in recent years. I kept wishing to get that over with . . ."

"Son, please, you're losing me again." I said as I sat on the bed, I then pulled you by the arm to sit beside me, then I said softly, "Sit down and tell me what happened, from the beginning."

"When I walked into the restaurant, she was already at the table. She was having a cocktail or a glass of wine or something. As I sat down, I discretely looked around the table to see if she had the urn with her. When I didn't see it, I thought it was inside her bag, or maybe she had left it in her car. Oh yes! That's right; she was having wine."

"Jesse, that's not the issue here."

"Sorry, like I said, I wasn't hungry because of the cookout, but I ordered a salad anyway. She ordered a chicken something; she then went on and on about how miserable her life was, especially after Steven died." You snapped all of a sudden, "God! I'm so fucking pissed at myself for letting her fool me . . ." You tried to get up, and I grabbed your arm again.

"Easy, son. C'mon, finish your story."

"Well, basically she went through her meal bitching about everything that came through her mind. Then finally, while we waited for her dessert, I found the courage to ask her about the ashes." you paused.

"What did she say?"

"It's more the way she said it, very nonchalantly with that drilling Southern accent of hers. She went on like, Hon, didn't you get my email? We buried Steven. He's resting at Saint Vincent Cemet . . ." You could not finish. You got up and paced in front of me again, and I let you be this time. I was probably sitting there with my mouth hanging open, trying to understand why anyone would do that to you.

"Then we'll go see Steven tomorrow," I said all of a sudden, "I know where Saint Vincent Cemetery is."

"You don't understand, Orson," you stood still in front of me, it broke my heart to see the look in your eyes. "I was supposed to take him back with me."

I couldn't differ more with you. To me, Steven was only dust and far from Earth; but this wasn't the time for a lecture on my beliefs.

"I swear, tomorrow morning I'm calling my lawyer to see what I can do. You know what? I'm going to call him right now. What time is it in

71

California? I have all the legal rights; I was married to him."

"Stop right there, Jesse." I got up, held you by your arms, and sat you on the bed again. I then grabbed the chair between the bathroom door and the dresser and placed it in front of you and sat down. "I feel you, son, I do, but you'll do nothing of the sort. Tomorrow we are going to stick with our plan and go to the jazz museum that I booked for you, we'll have lunch at a Creole place my boys suggested. After lunch, we're going down to the cemetery and visit Steven's grave. I'm gonna leave you to be alone with him, and you'll talk your ass off with him. Tell him everything you always wanted to tell him, the good, the bad, and whatever occurs to you. You let it all out, out of your system, you feel me? When Genna died, I was a mess. I didn't leave the house for days, stoned out of my mind half the time. One of these days I'll tell you the whole story. Ambar's the one who suggested I go down to where Genna was buried and talk it all out." I stopped for a couple of breaths. "When I did, I saw everything with a whole different light." I paused once more. "Then, after you've done that, if you still want to call your lawyer, go ahead, but do this for me, Jesse. Do this for yourself." My voice began to crack. "Trust me on this one, son. I know what I'm saying"

You looked into my eyes and hardly blinked. You began to tear up, but not like before. Not out of anger or frustration. Somehow, I could see into your soul through those beautiful green eyes of yours. Without giving it a thought, I got up and took off my jacket, put it on the back of my chair, then lifted it back in its place. That's when I noticed the brown paper bag on the dresser again; it had a bottle in it. I recognized the brand; it was a new bottle of Jack Daniels you didn't get a chance to open. I then went back to you, but you weren't sobbing anymore, although you had tears streaming down your face. I kneeled before you and untied your Nikes, took them off, and set them aside next to the night table. I then pulled off your sweater, leaving the t-shirt you had on. I asked you to stand up and take off your pants and you did as you were told, keeping your boxers on. I partially pulled out the blankets from the bed and helped you get under them. I sat on the bed and pushed out my shoes with the help of my feet and got in the bed with you. I turned and switched off the lights, then carefully rolled over to you to be behind you. I wrapped you with my arms and held you inside.

As my eyes got accustomed to the gloom, I watched the glow from the street light permeating softly to everything in the room through the large window. I stared out, not looking at anything in particular. I lifted my head a bit for a second to check on you, and your eyes were wide open, looking into space, just like I was. There was no need to talk, just a need to be. The moment I rested my head behind yours, I began to hear what I suspected to be drops of rain outside the window. I would later find out it is your favorite sound.

I figured I would stay until you had fallen asleep to go back to my room. I was so used to sleeping alone and all, but I guess the hypnotic sound of the rain got a hold of me. Next thing I remember, I was opening my eyes, and everything was the same, except it was dawn, and the room was tinted in blue. Next time I blinked my eyes open again, I heard the birds outside. I gently released you from my arms. Boy, you were gone! I moved slowly to get out of bed. I then gathered my things in silence and stepped out of the room. I wanted to give you, or maybe give myself some time alone.

TEN

HI SWEETS!

Wow, I didn't realize how difficult it would be to call you that since who knows when.

I don't really know how to start talking to you. Actually, it's all Orson's idea. He's the big black guy with a yellow umbrella that was here a second ago. We got these cheap things on our way here; they only had yellow and orange. Guess which one I picked?

Man, I feel so foolish doing this, really. If it is true that you are still around, you must be laughing your ass off just watching me talk to a grave. I must respect Orson an awful lot to be doing this. It is true that every time I take his advice, I seem to land in a better place. You see? Thanks to him, I surfaced back from the abyss when I zombied out on the meds I was taking. It's still weird to me how this casual, seemingly insignificant encounter turned into what he and I have.

How am I doing so far? This actually reminds me of that scene we wrote for *Creepy Encounters*. Remember? The funeral scene when Jake talked to his dead girlfriend, angry for leaving him behind? Well, I'm angry all right, but not at you. I'm actually furious at Dottie. Yes, your mother. Man, I take back all those times I defended her for every time you bitched about her pulling a fast one on you. Well, guess what? She pulled one on me.

You see, dude, I don't know what the hell I'm doing here on this shit day. You were supposed to be in that bed-and-breakfast we always wanted to stay in, resting peacefully in an urn on a table. Nice and warm. It is actually a little creepy now that I think about it.

I'm beginning to see Orson's point. But in any case, Dottie screwed me over. The main purpose of this trip down here was to bring you back home with me, and she stole that! It was like whatever was left of you was physically snatched away from me.

Steven, I miss you so much. The way you looked at me, our long writing sessions in bed, those weekend road trips. It seemed like so long ago. Well, it was! That was our beginning, and that's exactly where it stayed. I barely miss the rest, maybe just the laughs and the high points. But man, did we fight or what? Mmmm, but that make up sex was amazing, and we agreed it was worth every fight . . .

I'm getting off track here.

Steven, I have been so confused by what happened to you. When you died, everyone disappeared. All our friends, the ones we had all those parties for, gone! Some surfaced: Jennifer, Pedro, Lisa, Jake, and Anthony, the ones we didn't invite to those goddammed parties. Most of them probably are still pissed at me 'cause I haven't called in weeks. I didn't even tell anyone I was coming to Memphis, only Denise. I couldn't possibly go to them for support. It seemed unfair, considering we shut them out during our crisis. You know me, I don't like to bother people with my little problems. When you passed, my family came through as always. Lauren stayed with me for a couple of weeks. But then Mom and Dad also came and stayed at the house, and at first, it was OK. They were concerned I was spending too much time in our room, and they were being overly attentive. At some point, I had both my moms trying their particular therapy methods on me. It was a good thing when your lawyer called to tell me about your grandparent's house. It was the perfect time and the perfect excuse to leave LA and be alone for a while.

I tell you, it was rough at the beginning, but then I met Orson. Talk about southern hospitality; we've become good friends. He's about 30 years older than me, but we're able to ignore that because we see many things eye to eye. He's been great, driving me around Memphis to show me the blues music scene for this idea I got for a story. I've been in some dives you would have never been caught dead in.

Last night things between us may have shifted. It is too early to tell, at least from my end. Dude, I was such a mess last night after I met with your mom. When she told me I couldn't take your ashes and that she buried you here, I was so close to striking her or stabbing her with the fork I had in my left hand . . . Anyway, I stormed out of that stupid country club, where she basically lives, and went and bought myself a bottle of Jack Daniels with the intention of drinking it all. It was a good thing Orson came back when he did because I would probably be unconscious now instead of here talking to you. Orson tried consoling me the best he could. I remember being literally exhausted from crying. I guess at some point he was either tired or really felt sorry for me because he ended up hugging me to sleep.

There was nothing sexual about it. But the truth is that the imprint he left in me has been haunting me all morning through lunch. And I have been longing for that sensation ever since. I don't know how to put it, but I am seeing him in a whole different light. He caught me grinning like an idiot as he talked to me—this was during lunch today. Now I am all confused, and I'm trying hard not to show it. And we still have the rest of the weekend to go, so I'd better get a grip on myself.

I guess I have you to thank for that.

Dude, a year and a half ago, I thought we had it made. We overcame the biggest crisis we'd had. We were done with rehab, no more wild parties, no more drugs, a new contract with Netflix, two nominations, and we were looking for a new home, even. Fuck, dude! When I think about how you quit on us, not giving it your 100%, the lying, the deceit . . . I was so angry at you, Steven. I made this clear to you many times, but it has taken me a long time to come to terms with it. Sometimes I wonder if all is forgiven because I can't seem to shake off the feeling of disappointment.

Come to think of it; I am still mad at you.

You tried, I give you credit for that, but I tried too, and I kept my word. I thought you were as strong as I was. I thought we were the same. Now here we are; you as dead as yesterday and I, all alone, living in Memphis of all places, feeling like I'm starting from zero. Making friends with this odd bird I'm beginning to grow fond of, and now a little more than I could have anticipated. Well then . . .

I didn't want to end this on a sour note. I wanted this talk to feel like redemption instead of resentment. So, I'd better stop now and maybe give myself a little more time. I'm sorry, Steven, I'll come to terms with it sooner or later. I swear to you. Now, I'd better go.

Goodbye Sweets!

Jesse had to be careful pulling out his phone, trying not to get it wet as he juggled with his orange umbrella. He texted Orson as he walked down the cemetery aisle between the old tombstones. He looked around and realized they were mostly Christian, and although they were from different periods, they all had the same tone of grey—very much like the sky that day. 'Is it the weather or just the way I feel, that everything seems monotone?' Jesse asked himself, but before he could explore the endless possibilities in his mind, he spotted Orson. The man was coming from the opposite direction, breaking up the dull colors with his yellow umbrella. Jesse couldn't help but smile. He wrote a mental post-it in his head to include that image in a future story.

"You're laughing at me, aren't you?" Orson asked as he met his friend. "You look pretty funny yourself, but we're swapping umbrellas now."

"Sorry, Dude." Jesse put out his arm to make the trade. "Here."

"How did it go?" asked Orson as he reached into his inside jacket to pull out a package of tissue, handing it to Jesse.

"Thanks." Jesse blew his nose and, muffled by the tissue, said, "I think it went well; I definitely feel different. Lighter, even." The men started walking to the direction Orson came from. "I'm still pissed at that woman. Other things surfaced I wasn't aware of, but let's get the hell out of here."

"Jesse, I wish you didn't talk like that here in the cemetery. Man! Who raised you? Wolves?"

"I'm sorry, Mr. Om, can I call you Mr. Om?" Jesse turned to look at Orson's face in time to see a single head swing, meaning no.

"I swear, if I ever run into Cruella, I'm gonna let her have it . . ." said Orson. "All that 'beloved' nonsense, excluding you in that manner."

"What do you mean?" Jesse stopped and turned to Orson.

"Shoot!" Orson said with big eyes, "I thought that's why you mumbled 'bitch' when we stood before Steven's grave."

Jesse dropped his now yellow umbrella and rushed to the spot where he talked out his soul a few minutes before. Orson stayed put, puzzled for a few seconds. He closed his umbrella, got a hold of Jesse's, did the same, and then went after him. When he got to the guy, he couldn't tell if Jesse was crying or simply just wet because of the rain. He opened the orange umbrella to shelter them both. Jesse kept looking left and right, reading and comparing the tombstones of Steven and his father. They were nearly identical, same lettering, same spacing and text distribution. One read, "the II," and the next one, "the III," at the end of each name. Underneath, it nearly said the same.

One noted: DEAR AND BELOVED FATHER AND HUSBAND.

Steven's read: DEAR AND BELOVED SON AND FRIEND.

Jesse sensed his fists tightening, but he also felt a soft shade of orange surround him and keeping him from the rain. Then the tension in his hands finally dissolved as a familiar arm made it around his shoulder, making him feel at home. Home! That's it! Jesse realized at that instant but kept it to himself.

"I'm sorry, son," Orson broke the silence. "I should have kept quiet. I was convinced you noticed it before."

"I feel like I've been hit by a bus." Jesse briefly leaned his head against Orson's shoulder.

"Let's get out of here."

"Dude, please." Jesse lifted his head to meet Orson's eyes to his. "It's a shit d—an awful day and I don't really feel like walking around and getting any wetter."

"What do you wanna do?"

"Remember that bottle of Jack Daniels I bought last night?"

"I sure do."

"I want to get drunk," Jesse paused for a second. "Very drunk indeed."

"It's two in the afternoon. You're kidding, right?" Orson looked at Jesse in the eye, expecting him to break and laugh, but he didn't. "So, I take it you're not going for a run today."

Keeping his arm around Jesse's shoulder, Orson gently turned them around. Under a mist-like rain, they walked down the cemetery aisle as close together as the night before.

Orson flicked his lighter to light a joint he got from his army buddies the day before. He took a long drag and passed it to Jesse across the hot tub. He was glad his pal had suggested going back to the B&B and staying in. It was drizzly and cold outside, and now they were both cozy, warm, and very naked under the bubbling water. The large windows were steamed, so the light entering from the outside was slightly dimmed, enough to keep the bathroom lights turned off. Each man had a glass of whiskey on the rocks. Jesse had his in his hand while Orson had his resting on the edge of the tub.

"So, did you used to be a redhead as a child?" Orson asked right after he released the smoke from his lungs.

"Yes, my hair used to be red," Jesse replied before his turn to smoke, "but then it turned auburn when I reached . . . Wait! Did you sneak a peek?"

"Sorry I couldn't help it. It was there, flashing at me, as red as can be. It was a complete surprise."

"I know, it happens. I must confess, though," he lowered his head, pretending to be ashamed, "I sneaked a peek too."

"Say what?!"

"You didn't see me."

"And that makes it OK?"

Jesse handed the jay back to Orson. "Congratulations, by the way. It must be nice to be big all over."

Orson just laughed, deciding whether to be uncomfortable or to take it as usual with Jesse, just as it is. He tried to remember if he had ever had this kind of camaraderie with any of his male friends: all cards on the table, no filters, direct, clean, and honest. He had his army buddies, but those relationships never got too intimate—mainly because of him—trying to play it cool, intending to play it straight. The closest was with L.C., but even then, there were too many things left unsaid between them.

"I never would have suspected it," Orson continued, before taking one more drag, "your beard seems to grow blonde, but your chest hair is like your head."

"I like it. Some guys are surprised by my pubes, I'm sure you get a

80

similar response from your size."

"Here," Orson wanted to dismiss Jesse's remark. "Have another hit."

"Mr. Big, may I call you Mr. Big?"

"What the fuck, Jesse! Why do you keep insisting on nicknaming me?"

"Sorry, dude, I guess I hit a nerve." Jesse smiled as he took hold of Orson's offering. "Anyway, I wanted to talk about the blues. I've been thinking of my story, and I feel like it needs some spirit."

"Let's talk about the blues, then. What do you wanna know?"

"Not much about the history, I've looked that up, but I want to understand what makes it tick, I wanna hear it from a true blues lover. And with the new information I learned about you at the cookout; I can now say, I wanna hear it from an expert." He lifted his arm, making a toast with his drink.

"As far as I know," Jesse continued, "there are three recurring themes: love, sex, and money—or more accurately, about the lack of them. Mostly: heartbreak, being broke, and just plain being horny."

"I feel you, and that's one way to look at the blues. But it's deeper than that. To me, it is mainly about oneness. One's reflections on longing, sorrow, or misery over one of those subjects you mentioned. In some cases two, or maybe all of them." Orson took back the joint and put it out on an improvised cardboard ashtray next to his drink. He picked up the glass and had a sip. "By the way, I just hope you remember all of this."

"You're right! Let me get this on digital," Jesse said as he lifted his body to get out of the tub. "No more peeking!" He warned, playfully, while stepping out of the tub. "I'll be right back."

Jesse walked to the bathroom door and unhooked a towel robe behind it and put it on. Orson could not help but look at the amusing sight of his friend's fit physique dripping water all over the bathroom floor. A flash of the previous night cuddling came to his mind and thought about how good it felt having his arms around Jesse. In fact, there had been several brief episodes in his head like it throughout the day. Orson was glad his friend had not been all weirded out about it and that things between them were still the same. When in fact, he had been pretending all day that things hadn't changed between them. Without prompting, the flashback took on a life of its own, and this time, he was spooning Jesse without any clothes on. He became aware of it when his penis had a slight reaction to his daydream. 'Dream on,' he said to himself and quickly took another drink. Jesse came back from the next room, and Orson chose to look at the ceiling this time around. Jesse had his cell phone in hand, switched on the recording app, and then placed it on top of the toilet lid.

"I like your nipples," Jesse said out of the blue as he submerged himself back in the tub.

"Pardon?"

"They're like Frankenstein's nipples."

"What the fuck, man?!"

"I like the way the tips are so fat and stick out. I don't think I've ever had . . ." Jesse noticed the startled look on Orson's face. "I'm sorry dude, I'm talking too much, aren't I?"

"Yes, you are," The man put his drink back at the edge of the tub. "No more pot for you today."

"Too bad I can't tell if you're blushing, the same thing happens with my mom."

"Can we continue, please? You're distracting me."

"Yes, but let me switch this off," Jesse turned to the tub control panel next to him.

Orson agreed it would be better for the recording and that he had had about enough of the water moving about. Both of them stayed silent for a few seconds until the water settled, and the only sound was the rain outside. Jesse asked Orson to repeat what he had said before for the recording. The big guy had forgotten most of it, but with the help of his friend filling in the blanks and a few chuckles in between, they got it all on record.

"I can understand what you're saying about oneness," Jesse continued, "and I'm sure it can be the main source of creativity, but doesn't it lose that intimate spirit when you share it with the audience?"

"Well, let's just say you make the pain less yours," Orson remarked. "People in the crowd feel you; they identify with you. We've all been there, feeling miserable at some point in our lives."

"Do you mean, like, a getting it out of your system kind of thing?"

"Well, it's like when you tell a friend about your problems. You actually feel better; you have a sense of release, even."

"Well, yeah, but only for a little while."

"It is like that. You set it free out to the audience," added Orson. "But then it hits you right back like a boomerang."

Jesse stayed quiet for a while, trying to digest what his friend just said. Thankful he had been recording the whole thing, because from time to time, he got distracted. He was enthralled by the sensation of Orson's voice under water; Jesse felt its vibration in his very soul. Though Jesse tried to stay on focus to what his friend was saying, the tickling sensation from under the water made it difficult at times.

"Some people relate the blues to jazz," Jesse went on. "I guess because, from what I read, they come from the same source. But they have two completely different sounds—and saying two is an understatement because both genres have many variations." As he finished his thoughts, Jesse grabbed his glass of Jack Daniels for a taste. "For the purpose of my story, can you elaborate on this, please?"

"We should be listening to the blues for this," Orson suggested. "But do you mind if we continue this later? I'm too high now, and you are making me talk more than I care to while I'm stoned. I'm more of a quiet type when I smoke weed. I would much prefer it if you tell me about this show you are writing about me."

Jesse was about to step out of the bathtub to stop the recording, but Orson insisted it was his turn to get out of the tub. He was feeling lustful enough to write a full blues symphony in his notebook. Weed always had that effect on him, and having Jesse walking around naked in front of him was making it difficult for him to keep his cool. He got out of the water feeling carefree and careless, then walked to the nearest hand towel, and to dry off his hands, he took it with him not concerned about covering himself. He wanted Jesse to look at him again, daring him, provoking him. He picked up the cell phone and handed Jesse the towel first and then the phone. Jesse's heartbeat moved faster as his friend moved near him, but made sure not to look at Orson flashing before him, realizing that was the very first time there was sexual tension between them. He unsuccessfully focused on the phone, trying to ignore whether or not Orson was enticing him. The man retrieved Jesse's phone and settled back in the tub. Jesse, at last, found another list, one he had put together for the trip that began with Jimmy Witherspoon's "I've Been Treated Wrong." He placed the phone on the floor as far from the tub as he could, not wanting to get up and expose himself again. He got back to his spot and looked at Orson, who had his head leaned back and eyes closed with his arms spread open, resting on the edge of the tub holding the glass of whiskey in his hand. 'I'm being paranoid,' Jesse thought. 'I'll just sit here watch him for a while.'

When the song stopped playing, Orson opened his eyes and smiled at Jesse. Like in the movies, Jesse almost heard a small bell tinkling as his friend's gold tooth briefly revealed itself. The man made a point to tell him he loved the selection, that Witherspoon was the man. Then politely asked Jesse again to tell him more about the story he was writing. He knew Jesse summarized it when he described it to his friends the day before. Orson knew Jesse had so much more in store. The guy went on to tell him he had already decided he would sell it as a miniseries. The setting: Memphis in the mid nineteen-seventies, although the first scene takes place in the present with the random finding of a set of reel-to-reel tapes containing unreleased material from Elvis. There were eleven blues tracks on the tapes, all unknown and performed in one voice and a single piano. There was a list of songs glued to the inside of the box printed by a typewriter. On top of it read:

Vocals: Elvis Presley
Piano and Compositions: Otis Danson

The main premise of the series would be to find who this Otis Danson was. Where did he come from? What became of him? And why were these tapes hidden away for so long? Jesse did not have an ending for the story yet, but he did have a title for it that Orson liked very much: *Amazing Graceland.*

ELEVEN

THE ORANGE LIGHTS REFLECTED wide across the wet pavement as the lamp posts stood tall, guarding the empty street. The Garden District rested quietly while the autumn leaves danced in the dark, late-night air. A disturbance from a distance pierced the tranquility of the morning. Two voices, singing in out loud but disharmonized, filled the street where the Bald Cypress Bed and Breakfast stood. Orson and Jesse were singing "That Evening Train," an old classic they both knew and had just heard at the Wild Boar Canteen. An out-of-town dive that was on the must-go-to list of places Jimmy had put together for them. The taxi driver that picked them up after the bar closed was fed up with their drunken antics and asked them to leave the car. Luckily for the boys, it was just a few blocks away from their B&B. For the last block, they'd been changing the lyrics of the song to amuse one another. As they were getting closer to the bed-and-breakfast, they spotted a police car in the distance, moving closer to them. As if they'd read each other's minds, they continued singing in whispers while the car drove by. Once it was gone, Jesse could not contain his laughter, Orson was just grateful the cops were gone and even more thankful they had smoked all their pot and had nothing on them.

They finally made it to their inn and went in quietly, giggling their way upstairs. When they got to the hallway, Orson reached for his key as he moved closer to his door. When he was about to say goodnight, Jesse almost voiced what had been on his heart all day, but his mind took over.

"What a day!" The guy said, "We've done a lot of stuff."

"Indeed, jazz museum, cemetery, lunch, bathtub, weed, dinner, more weed, a hell of a lot of drinking, and a bunch of barhopping."

"And plenty of blues . . . don't forget the blues."

"I hear you."

"How about a nightcap?" Asked Jesse, heading in the right direction.

"A nightcap?" Asked Orson. "Do people still say that?"

"Hey, I work in the film industry, of course they do."

"I couldn't possibly drink any more."

"How about coming in anyway?" He finally made his move. He reached for the key in his pocket, grabbed Orson by his wrist, and pulled him to his door on the other side of the hallway. "I don't want to go to bed just yet." Jesse unlocked his door.

"Neither do I." Orson followed Jesse as he opened his door. "I don't want this day to end."

Orson went straight for the bed and sat on it, letting himself fall backward on it. Jesse took off his jacket and began removing his shoes and encouraged Orson to do the same.

"I actually wanted to talk to you." Jesse pulled out the chair and placed it in front of Orson, who then sat up. "I've had this one thing in mind all day."

"Shoot, son."

"Actually, it is two things now."

"Oh, no."

"Orson . . . buddy! Would you mind it terribly to stop calling me, son?

"That's it?"

"That's the second thing. Orson, I see you more like an equal, like my friend, my pal, and lately, when you call me son, it feels weird. It's like a reminder that there's a sort of hierarchy between us, or a chain of command if you will. Like I should regard you with more than the respect I already have for you."

"I feel you . . . bro."

"No, bro won't work either."

Orson laughed, "You're right, I'll come up with something. Now, what's the first thing you wanted to tell me?"

Jesse stood up and walked to the dresser and grabbed the bottle of Jack Daniels by its neck. Then he remembered they had just agreed there wouldn't be any more drinking, so he put the bottle back.

"What is it, son? Sorry, force of habit." Orson watched him. "Jesse, come back here, it's me, you can talk to me."

"You're right." Jesse sat back. "Well, it has to do with last night . . ."

"Hey, Jesse," Orson interrupted. "It was not my intention to spend the night, I was waiting for you to fall asleep," Orson got up the bed to take off his leather jacket and laid it on the bed, then stood still looking at his friend. "But I fell asleep, and when I woke up, it was nearly daylight; and I was surprised you'd slept at all." He then started pacing. "I've been known to be a loud snorer."

"Well, I slept like a baby . . ." Jesse smiled, realizing his friend was as nervous as he was. "Orson, come back here, I loved that you spent the night here."

Orson sat back on the bed and looked at Jesse without blinking.

"When I woke up in the middle of the night, all wrapped up in your arms, I didn't realize it then," Jesse paused briefly, "but in your arms, I felt at home. And that's a first for me."

Orson's eyebrows grew apart as he tried hard to keep his mouth closed. The only sound that came out was a whispering, "Man!"

"And I wonder," Jesse continued, "if you could do the same tonight; hug me to sleep."

Orson was still speechless. No one had ever come close to opening themselves up to him in such a manner. If he had ever felt any emotions for anyone before, they all seemed hazy and distant. What he was feeling for Jesse at that very moment was totally foreign to him, yet compelling. He didn't want Jesse to read his eyes, so he stood up again and went straight to consult with Jack Daniels.

"Hey, dude," Jesse said. "I've said too much; I didn't mean . . ."

"No, I'm OK." Orson poured himself a glass of whiskey. "Give me a minute here."

"Listen, I need to take a leak. We can talk when I come out." He walked to the restroom and stopped by the door while he switched the light before going in. "Or feel free to leave, and we can talk about it tomorrow—by the light of day. I'll be OK, I'll understand."

Jesse stepped into the bathroom, concerned about the future of his friendship with Orson. He stood in front of the mirror to look at himself in the eyes. He raised his eyebrows briefly and went on to unzip his pants in front of the toilet to urinate. He tilted his head as he lifted his left arm and smelled too much dancing and booze in his clothes, though glad to discover what the New Orleans music scene was all about. All the previous visits to the Big Easy had never been this intense. He took his clothes off, turned on the shower faucet, and then stepped into the shower stall under a waterfall-like showerhead. He figured he would give Orson a chance to leave without being heard. In any case, he would shower quickly, not to be rude.

After rinsing the shampoo out of his hair, he opened his eyes to discover the bathroom was much darker than before. He turned to look at the lamp on top of the mirror, but his eyes were drawn to the doorway where Orson was standing. The man had turned off the light and had left the door open to let in the dim glow from the next room. Orson shyly began to undress without taking his eyes off Jesse, as if expecting some kind of reaction from his friend. Jesse ran his hands on the surface of his hair to finish rinsing. He then moved a few steps backward to make room for Orson, who was getting closer by the second. The man got under the shower stream to be face to face with Jesse. He raised his big hands gently and reached behind Jesse's head, who found himself being magnetized to the man's mouth. When Orson's lips enclosed his, Jesse totally surrendered, which nearly made him lose the strength of his own legs. He quickly stretched his arms and embraced Orson and held tight to keep himself from slipping. Orson began breathing into him, blending each other's breaths. Jesse had never experienced anything like it. He felt like he was melting into Orson's arms, relinquishing his defenses. The warm water running down their bodies occasionally reminded Jesse he was still whole. Orson finally let him catch his breath only to plant his thick dark lips down the side of Jesse's neck, running eventually down to his left shoulder. The guy felt so overwhelmed by Orson's affection that tears began to form in his eyes.

Suddenly Orson stopped kissing Jesse. He wanted to look into his young man's eyes with the intention to read his thoughts. He finally realized Jesse was shaking, although warm water kept flowing over their skin. He also noticed the guy could hardly keep his legs still. Orson proposed, whispering into Jesse's ear, to continue their lovemaking in bed in the next room. Jesse couldn't speak, he simply nodded, puzzled by the effect Orson had over him.

Orson turned off the water and guided Jesse, who had his arms wrapped around himself, out of the shower. The man covered Jesse with the terry cloth robe and nearly wrapped him dry with it, he then took the only towel left and did the same to himself. They moved into the bedroom and split. Jesse got on the bed, and under the covers, Orson switched off all lamps and opened the curtains to let the light from the outside be their witness. Jesse awaited in bed, anxious to hold the man back in his arms.

Orson's eyes grew accustomed to the gloom as he approached the bed. That's when he realized Jesse had his arm stretched, reaching out for him, the man complied by taking his hand. He sat on the bed and let Jesse wrap him in his arms; it felt natural to do anything else but that, to feel the young man's warmth enclose him for a change. Being as big as he was, Orson had always played the hugger. But not that night, he let Jesse take control, and there was nothing that could persuade Orson to endure otherwise for the next wee hours of the morning.

TWELVE

FROM THE BED, Orson noticed how the room had turned to blue. The street lights that had tinted the room a pale orange had shut off suddenly to reveal the first rays of the sun blazing through the large window. Both men had been laying sleepless for a while without saying a word to one another. Orson had been spooning Jesse for quite a while, pondering on how natural it felt. Both their right arms rested above the bed sheets while their hands held gently. The man enjoyed looking at the contrast of their skins, one next to the other. Earlier, during lovemaking, Orson would catch a glimpse of their reflection in the large mirror next to the armoire door and recalled getting exceptionally aroused by the sight of black over white. He tried not to let that thought linger too much on his mind; he was appreciating that moment of quiet, so he let it be for a little longer.

It lasted until he called out "Red!" out of the blue. "Is it OK if I call you Red?"

"Red?" Jesse asked, lifting his head slightly, taking him two seconds to figure out why Orson had come up with that one. "Sure, but never tell anyone why you call me that. I don't need anyone trying to picture me naked, please!"

"OK!"

"Plus, I get to call you Mr. Nipples."

"Deal!"

Jesse turned his head around and kissed Orson on the lips and rested back to his place.

"Red, I still can't get over my kissing you like this."

"Why, don't you like it?" Jesse asked, already knowing the answer.

"Are you kidding? I am loving it. I'm just saying—and don't get me wrong—we've been buddies all this time without it remotely crossing my mind that we would ever hook up. I told you before, I'm not into white dudes, but you, my friend, you've done something to me that no one of any color ever has."

"Wow, that's awesome, Orson. Beautiful." Jesse said as he moved his hand to Orson's forearm and squeezed it hard.

Orson kissed the back of Jesse's neck repeatedly.

"Jesse, do you remember yesterday at the Pig Pickin'," Orson said after a long silence, "I mentioned in passing that the story you're writing resembles my life more than you think?"

"I do. Listen, I am sorry." Jesse raised his head to face Orson. "I had no idea, and in front of your friends . . ."

"Don't worry about it; you had no way of knowing. I was so stunned when you mentioned this to me a few weeks ago. It was uncanny. At first, I thought maybe Ambar said something . . ."

"Said what?"

"What I'm about to tell you. Something I'm not proud of. I don't like talking about it, really. Probably the worst . . . not probably, for certain, the worst day of my life."

"Orson, you don't have to tell—"

"I want to, Jesse, I want you to hear everything there is to know about me, but—"

"Hey," Jesse turned over and lay on his other side to face Orson. "One thing at a time will do. Whenever, no rush."

"Do you remember me telling you about L.C.?"

"Of course."

"How our thing went on for years, before, during, and after being married to Genna? Every time L.C. would come down to Memphis with his band, we saw each other. He would call, and I would drop everything I was doing and respond to him like a loyal dog. On this particular day, he called the shop."

"The car shop?"

"Yes, he wanted to meet up at lunchtime, but we couldn't go to his hotel, I forget why. So, I suggested my house. Genna was at work. I don't know what I was thinking."

"Dude, your house?"

"Please, Jesse." Orson was getting impatient, "Oh! I remember now, one of the boys in his band was sick, and he and L.C. were sharing the room, so we couldn't meet there."

"Man, but where you lived with your wife?"

"Please, this is difficult as it is. May I go on?"

"When was this again?"

"About twenty-five years ago. My daughter was fourteen, so, twenty-seven years ago."

"What was her name again?"

"Man, what else do you wanna know?"

"Sorry I need details."

"Damn it, boy!" Orson raised his voice slightly, "I'm baring my soul here, and you keep cutting me off."

"You're right, I'm so sorry, Orson." Jesse got a hold of Orson's hand and kissed it. "I won't say another word."

"L.C. got there late, as usual. Anyway, after we finished our business, we both fell asleep. L.C. woke up at some point and lit up a cigarette. I remember the smell when he woke me up with his elbow because he heard a noise downstairs. As I was about to react, that's when I saw Genna standing by the bedroom door."

"Oh shit!" Jesse squeezed Orson's hand.

"Jesse, that look on her face . . . I'll never forget her eyes staring back at me. Man, that look of heartbreak, disappointment, betrayal . . ." He paused. "She ran downstairs, I put on my work overalls the best I could, with the top hanging behind my waist and went after her barefoot. When I made it downstairs, she was already out of the house. I kept yelling out her name: 'Genna! Genna!' I went outside, and I saw her trying to get her key to open the car. I almost made it to her, but still, she wanted nothing to do with me and ran off again." Orson went silent. Jesse reached for his other hand and moved both close to his lips and kissed them. "I watched her cross the street like a mad cat, and that's when a speeding pickup truck hit her." Orson paused again, then continued, having trouble speaking. "I saw her fly a few feet in the air . . . it all seemed like a bad a dream, everything moving in slow motion. It was all too fucked up to be happening to me. I've never been able to get the horrible sound out of my head ever since; the way she hit the pavement. Jesse, right in front of my eyes."

Jesse, hardly blinked as he listened.

"I ran to her, half naked as I was, she was already dead when I got to her. I fell on my knees and held her lifeless body, crying out for her not to leave. I don't remember how long I was on the floor like that, but at some point, I remember looking towards our house, and there was L.C. getting quickly into his car and taking off. I couldn't believe it, Jesse! I was numb from that point on. It was too much for me to grasp. Shortly after, an ambulance came, and I went with them to the hospital, not that I remember getting in it. Ambar showed up at the hospital, and she said L.C. told her what had happened. She was furious at him for running out on me, so she felt compelled to go to the hospital right then. She and L.C. used to be good friends up until that day. She never really forgave him. She and I were just acquaintances then. L.C. had introduced us at The Grasshopper, but we weren't really friends then.

"She basically took charge, and I was in some state of shock because when they confirmed that my Genna had passed, I was lost, not really knowing what to do. She stood by me when the police came to question me about what happened. She helped me with the hospital paperwork. She even drove me to pick up my little girl from school.

"Ambar was just great. Well, you know her. She's beyond a friend now." Orson stopped; trying to find words while struggling hard not to cry. "Man, it was rough having to tell your daughter that her mother had just died. I wasn't able to do it alone. Ambar sat through it with me." Orson finally gave in to his tears, a bit embarrassed to be crying in front of Jesse, who didn't say a word and just slid closer to Orson and hugged him. The man was tempted not to talk anymore and was willing to be cuddled to sleep, but instead, he continued: "My own kid seemed to hold me responsible. Even though she never learned the details of her mother's death, she treated me like it was all my fault. Well, she was right. It was my fault."

"Wait a minute, Orson . . ."

"I know. Let me finish, please, Red." The man reached out for Jesse's face and caressed it. He didn't want to lose his train of thought because he was on a roll. He hadn't talked about this in years, and it felt a bit redeeming.

"After the accident, all I did was drink beer and smoke weed all day, for who knows how many weeks. My own flesh and blood didn't want to stay with me, nor did I want her, or anyone, to be around me. She ended up moving in with Ambar for a while. I stopped going to work. I lost a few clients and a lot of weight.

"Ambar eventually convinced me to seek therapy, which I did, and that was good. Not only did I deal with my wife's death, but I also came to terms with my sexuality. I'm pretty much over the whole guilt thing, even though at times I feel it's still pretty much my fault. After all, I had no business taking that nigger to the house that my wife and I shared to have barely fifteen minutes of sex on our marital bed."

"Man, you're too hard on yourself."

"The only upside was that I got my self-esteem back even though I never knew I'd ever lost it, but that was months later. I didn't think very much of myself before all that happened, and I haven't told you the half of it yet."

Orson stopped talking to study Jesse's face, concentrating mainly on his eyes. He began to look deep into them, feeling drawn to what he suspected was the young man's essence. It took him a few seconds to notice Jesse was weeping in silence with a soft, yet shy smile. He realized he had never glanced at anyone's eyes that way before, feeling a true connection. Orson was certain that the man in front of him felt the same he did. He tried to remember if he'd ever looked at Genna that way, realizing right then and there that she had felt more like a sister and certainly not a lover. Orson thought of L.C., and it was so obvious that this occasional bedmate never felt the same for him. As if love could be measured and compared, Orson now acknowledged to himself.

"Halfway through therapy," the man continued. "I did get better and sober. My daughter moved back in with me, and I got my shit together. But for the longest time, I'd lost interest in music altogether, and that's why I'm telling you all of this. This was my traumatic experience, as you very well put it. Playing the piano only made me think of L.C., and all that happened, and I hated it. Besides, I always felt that I was only mediocre; music deserved a better player."

"So, since the accident, you haven't played?"

"Zilch, not a single note, nada. But I still write. I eventually started doing that again. I carry this notebook around . . ."

"Really? You write music? Cool." Jesse lifted himself, resting on his left elbow. "So that's that little notebook you carry around? That night I ran into you at the storage place, I saw a little red notebook laying about, was that it?"

"Probably."

"Oh! At what time do you need to be at work tonight?" Jesse asked as he leaned back as he was before.

"Shit, I almost forgot! Ten o'clock."

"I haven't . . . Where was I? Oh yes . . . when do you usually write? I've never seen you do it."

"You've been keeping me busy, son. Not a minute's peace since I met you!" Orson teased Jesse. "Whenever I'm bored, or I have to wait for something or someone; also, when I can't sleep. I play these notes in my head and then put them on paper before I forget. It drives me crazy when I don't have my notebook on me. Many times, when I'm in the car, and I get inspired, I'll pull over to write. You don't know how many times I've forgotten a tune that I thought I would remember to write down later." Orson paused for about half a minute. "I must have about fifty of those little notebooks and many napkins, receipts, and pieces of papers with notes on them. I figure one day I'll compile them all into a complete blues symphony."

"I'd love to hear at least one song. In fact, I'd love to hear you play the piano, period."

"For you, Red, anything."

"Hmmm, then I think I'll marry you."

Orson didn't know how to reply to that, he just smiled with his eyes, touching Jesse's face again and then moving up his fingers to caress his hair.

"Would you really play again, or you're just teasing me?"

"No, I mean it. I've been giving it some thought lately. The other day, the boys actually gave me shit again, at the cookout, for not playing. And I'd kind of like for you to hear me play, you know?"

"But haven't you missed it all these years?"

"Kind of, but I have my notebooks, and that kind of keeps me in touch with music. Plus going to The Grasshopper and the records I listen to at home and on the radio."

"Man, I'd love to hear you play," Jesse said, raising his head again and looking Orson in the eyes. "But whenever you're ready, no pressure from me. In fact, I will never mention it again."

"I will, Red, like I said, for you…"

Jesse moved closer to reach Orson's lips and kissed them softly. "You know? Now that you opened your heart to me this way, I feel it is my turn to tell you about Steve's OD and how I ended up in Memphis, and we can close the exes chapter once and for all. Well, you know a little bit of it already, but I feel like I owe you the whole story."

"You owe me nothing, Red."

"You're right, and I don't want to spoil our first day as . . ." Jesse didn't know how to finish.

"Our first day as a what?"

"I don't know . . . I'm a writer. I should come up with something good without sounding corny."

"Yes, Jesse, think hard, and don't disappoint me, please."

"Got it! Our first day as unforeseen lovers."

Orson laughed out loud.

"I stand my ground," Jesse continued waving his index finger back and forth between them. "Us, like this, is the last thing I expected to happen this weekend—so there: unforeseen lovers, that's who we are."

"I hear you, Red, come close and kiss me." So, Jesse did.

"It feels good getting to know you. All those tidbits I keep getting about you, little by little. Like you play the piano, you can write music, you're into guys, not white guys, but you'll do me anyhow. And most importantly, you're the best kisser I've ever tasted. Why did you ever keep that from me so long, about liking men?"

"Honestly, I almost did tell you, when you first said you were married to Steven, I figured I would never see you again, but I did. And then I didn't want any tension between us, like you thinking I was being friendly with you because I wanted to get you in the sack. You yourself, once said or complained to me that sometimes you get too much attention for being handsome. I love that you're so humble about your looks and about your talent. Also, and to be honest, I never even considered this, us, in bed like now. But now, that you got me, it's hard to pull away. You are something else, Jesse. I've been having the time of my life since day one."

"Man," Jesse caressed his lover's face once more, "who are you, Mr. Davis?

"Just any other man, but unlike any other man you'll ever meet."

"Well said, Mr. Nipples." Jesse raised his hand, and Orson did the same, giving each other a high five.

Orson kissed Jesse again passionately enough to make the guy nearly melt in bed. Jesse had to pull away at some point to try and catch his breath. They rested back and looked into each other's eyes for a little while longer.

"Listen, Jesse, I've been thinking; I want to take you someplace today. A short detour from our trip home that I think you'll like."

"Another surprise? I'm game, but not before we take another shower together. I feel we have unfinished business under that waterfall showerhead you like so much."

"Hey, it's not my fault that you couldn't stand on your two feet last night. You shouldn't drink and shower, it could be lethal."

"You are lethal, man, how the hell did you learn to kiss that way?" Jesse said, shaking his head in disbelief. "So, it is very much your fault; no drug or alcohol has ever had such an effect on me."

Orson took Jesse by the head and kissed him again, and like a few hours earlier, he breathed his passion into him. Sometime before noon, they eventually made it to the shower, a memorable one for Orson. Jesse got on his knees and pleasured him under the water stream. The man had to cover his own face with his forearm to muffle the loud profanities that kept coming out of his mouth until he finally climaxed.

Downstairs in the dining room, there was a small table for two in front of the window. On top of it sat a small vase with fresh flowers, silverware, and two upside down coffee cups on their saucers. A cold pot of coffee stood at the other end of the room, waiting for the only two guests of the Bald Cypress B&B who never came down for breakfast.

THIRTEEN

THE RENTAL CAR WAS HEADING to Mississippi under a bright and cloudless sky, quite a contrast from the previous days, Orson admired from behind the wheel. He suddenly laughed, which caught Jesse's attention.

"What?" asked Jesse.

"I was remembering your little shower joke from this morning."

"Oh . . . welcome to Fellatio Falls?"

"The very one."

"Y'all come back now, you hear?" Jesse joked again with the best southern accent he could pull off. Orson went on smiling as he shook his head from side to side. Jesse just stared at him for a few more seconds. "You know, now that I know you more intimately, I'm beginning to see you in a whole new light."

"Oh, yeah? And what do you see?"

"Oh! I don't know . . . you look different to me now. It's like sometime between the hot tub yesterday and now, you became yummier."

"Yummier? No one's ever referred to me in gastronomical terms."

"Well, this morning, you proved to be quite the delicacy."

"Damn it, boy." Orson swung his head again to his side, but this time he pulled out his collar as if to release a breath of air. "You shouldn't talk to me that way while I'm driving."

They stopped at the town of Port Gibson, Mississippi, where they had a bite to eat at a small diner where Jesse had catfish for the first time. After lunch, Orson insisted on fueling before heading back to Memphis. What he really wanted to do was to ask someone for the best way to get to their destination. He had purposely avoided using the GPS to keep their journey's end a surprise. He took advantage of their expense agreement and asked Jesse to take care of the bill inside the minimart. Orson spotted a local hefty tow truck driver who had just pulled up beside them with hopes the rugged man could give him directions. This driver, who was as tall as Orson, was the right person to ask because he knew exactly how to get to Port Gibson.

Orson quickly memorized the instructions for driving to his surprise destination. It turned out the place was easy to get to and only six miles away from the gas station. He wondered why Jesse wasn't out yet. He approached the store glass door and looked inside. He spotted his friend in the last aisle in front of the coolers. His guy was talking with two young men, both the bodybuilder type. One of them had a short-trimmed beard. They seemed pretty friendly with Jesse like they knew him. Orson realized he was being nosy, so he decided to wait in the car.

From the driver's seat, he saw Jesse going to the register to pay for his purchases while the two young men walked out of the store. As they passed in front of him, Orson opened his window to see if he could pick up what they were saying as they got into their car. They were raving about Jesse and how hot he was. This made the veteran feel tall and proud of being Jesse's lover. Jesse finally returned to the car and handed Orson one of the two small bottles of water he just bought. As the man started the car, he immediately asked about the two young men. Jesse said that he met them at the gay bar he went to on his first night out in New Orleans. He added that the one with the beard came on to him and even bought him a drink, but Jesse played it low. He assured Orson that going to some stranger's apartment for a fleeting encounter wasn't his thing.

Orson got on State Road 522 to find the landmark he had asked about. As the truck driver had told him, 522 detoured onto Rodney Road, and he immediately found a small metal sign that read "Windsor Ruins." Jesse was intrigued because the name suggested mystery. Orson turned right onto an unpaved driveway that was sided by tall and narrow trees with brown and yellow leaves. The Spanish moss hanging from the branches seemed more intrusive in this landscape than on the woods surrounding the main road. The forest disappeared on the left side, revealing an open field with fewer trees while the right-side scenery remained the same.

They rode for several more yards until they came to a clearing where the driveway ended in a sort of cul-de-sac.

Orson, who was very glad no one else was there, parked at the end of it. For the last several yards, Jesse had been staring in silence out of his window at twenty-three magnificent brick columns that stood alone in the middle of the field. The solitary structure was all that was left of the old Windsor plantation that burned down in 1890. Orson explained to Jesse that he had come here on a school trip when he was a small boy and always wanted to come back. Who better to go with than Jesse! They got out of the car. Orson walked around the vehicle and met up with his friend, who was admiring the pillars. Jesse looked at him quickly and smiled and then looked back at the enigmatic monument. They walked a few steps to stand in front of the two main columns where there was once a grand metal staircase that led to the mansion. Orson felt Jesse's hand rest gently on his back, their eyes met briefly, and then both went up to examine the perfectly crafted cast-iron capitals that crowned each pillar. Jesse pulled out his cell phone to take a few photos starting with a selfie of the two of them using the columns as a backdrop. He was already thinking about what part of a story would be most suitable for using this scenery.

At first, they strolled side by side, but eventually, they drifted apart to explore on their own. They both appreciated the time alone though it didn't take long to tour the site. The ruins of the mansion were all that remained; the gardens, the stables, the slave quarters, and the cotton fields were merely ghosts in the once colossal estate.

Orson was coming back from his short excursion to the outdoors pit stop in the woods when he heard music and voices in the distance. He spotted another car that was somewhat familiar; a red car parked near theirs. Watching from behind the columns, he realized Jesse was standing by the vehicle, talking to someone who just came out of the passenger door. It was the young man with a beard who Jesse had been chatting up at the gas station. "What the hell?!" Orson thought out loud to himself. He felt as if a lightning bolt had struck him on the head. He felt vulnerable. He realized his old insecurities flourished, reviving emotions he hadn't felt in years. He turned around and walked towards what looked like an old abandoned road, perfect for a quick getaway. Inevitably, L.C. came to mind, as well as all his stories, and sorry ass excuses pulled out of a hat every time he was late or never showed up for whatever occasion. Flashes of all those men and women Orson saw L.C. flirting with right before his eyes at some bar or stage the musician happened to be performing on. Lost in his thoughts, Orson disappeared down the old deserted path.

Jesse had been sitting in the passenger seat, waiting for more than half an hour, regretting that he let Orson drive. The man had the car keys, so Jesse could neither beep the horn to call him nor start the car to keep warm. He tried phoning Orson a few times only to have his calls picked up by voicemail. He even yelled Orson's name a few times. Every five minutes, he would give himself five more before going out to find his buddy, but then he finally saw him walking from a few yards away towards the car. Orson moved at a slow but steady pace. As he got closer, Jesse saw the serious look on his friend's face, one he did not recognize.

"Dude, where in the hell have you been?" Jesse asked as Orson approached.

"I went into the woods and lost track of time." He stopped by his door and reached for the keys.

"I was worried about you."

"Well, I'm here now." He opened his door. "Let's go." He said as he got inside the car. Jesse did the same.

"You would never guess who followed us here." Said Jesse as he was putting on his seatbelt. "A little creepy, now that I think about it."

"Don't you mean who followed you here? I saw you talking to those guys earlier before I . . ." Orson started the car and drove off slowly, "got lost."

As Orson reached the end of the driveway, ready to get on the main road, Jesse, who sensed the hostility in his friend's voice, extended his arm to get a hold of his hand to ask him what was wrong but was not able to. The man stopped the car, put it in park, and switched off the engine. Orson turned to face Jesse.

"Jesse, what are we doing here?"

"I don't know. You brought me here."

"No, Jesse, I mean us."

"What do you mean? Wait! You don't think I told those guys to come all the way here, do you?"

"You said they followed you here. I believe you, that's not it."

"Well, what then?"

"C'mon Jesse, I mean you and me and whatever it is that we're doing."

"I think we're great, to be honest."

"You're not feeling me, Jesse. Where do you want to take this?"

"I don't know, I like what's happening now, and it's fun. You said it yourself last night; you're having the time of—"

"Yes, it is fun now," Orson cut him off, "but what about later, when you pack your stuff and disappear back to LA, and I stay here. I'm telling you, I ain't flying 2,000 miles back and forth to see you."

"Dude, we're getting to know each other. We don't even know if . . ."

"Jesse," Orson interrupted. "Do you know how old I am? I'm sixty-three years old. Sixty-three," he repeated, emphasizing it, "and what are you, thirty-five?"

"Thirty-four."

"What's that, a thirty-two-year difference?"

"Twenty-eight."

"Damn it, boy! That's not the point. The fact is there is a huge age gap between us. And that's not all: I'm a simple blue-collar man, and you are some rich kid out of UCLA who has it all. I've got nothing to give you."

"That is such bullshit, Orson!" Jesse's voice began to break. "I don't want anything. Look, a year ago, I thought I had it all, and I lost it."

"Not all."

"I lost all that was important to me, and what was left was a joke, a big farce."

"I doubt that. Sure, we're having fun now, but what will happen when we run out of things to say? You and I have nothing in common, son."

"Stop calling me that!"

105

Orson ignored Jesse and continued, "And another thing, what will happen when I turn 80 or if I make it to 90? Have you thought about that? I'm not getting any younger, you know?"

"Well, neither am I."

"I don't think we're thinking this through. Jesse, only yesterday, you were visiting your husband's grave. I'm concerned that I might be your rebound."

"Orson, that is not fair," Jesse was on the edge of crying. "Why are you doing this? Just a few hours ago we were saying how . . . Dude, don't to this, it's us . . . we're good together!"

"Think about it, man. You are still grieving Steven's death. You're not ready . . . I'm not ready."

Jesse couldn't think of anything else to say, he turned his face and looked out the window instead. He thought for a brief moment that Orson was starting to make sense. Then he remembered the first time he slept in his arms and thought what a shame it would be to let all that go; to watch it fade in the sky like a red helium balloon, Jesse's mind wandered. He turned back to look Orson in the eye, but he couldn't hold it for long.

"So, this is it?" Jesse asked with tears running down his face.

It took Orson a few seconds to reply. "I think we shouldn't hang out as much for a while. Let our hearts heal a bit."

"C'mon Orson; we barely started this a few hours ago. My heart is not broken, and neither is yours. There is nothing to heal, unless . . ."

"Jesse, I don't wanna do this." He went on. "I don't want to get involved, not anymore. I'm too old for this. You're young. You have your whole life ahead of you."

"Is that the way you want it?"

"That's the way I want it." Orson took Jesse's hand. "Hey, let's give each other some time. Enjoy being alone for a while. Let's meet in a few weeks and see how we feel about each other then."

"Forget it, Orson, you've already made up your mind." Jesse gently pulled away his hand. "I don't need time. And what? Meet with you again and find out that I've already lost you? Pass." Jesse was going from sad to angry. "It's clear to me; you are afraid of whatever the outcome will be.

You want to play it safe, but I must tell you, I'm disappointed. I thought it was going great. And I wouldn't have minded flying back and forth to get to know you, because I think you're worth it. If it's an age thing, or class, or race, or whatever, that's bullshit. We've proven to be good together, dude, and you're chickening out because it's getting too big for you."

Orson knew Jesse was right. But the man had decided. He was certain he wanted no heartaches nor disillusions, and he wasn't taking any chances. He felt safer pulling away from Jesse.

"I've had a wonderful time these past few weeks. I loved every second of it. But my past experience tells me not to go on. I am much better off alone. I don't want you to wake up one day and realize you got into this for the wrong reasons. Think about it, Jesse. Heal your heart first, be alone for a while. Man, I'm repeating myself. I'm doing this now before we get in too deep; before it gets painful. I know what I'm doing, Jesse." He looked down at the steering wheel. He waited nearly a minute before turning the key to start the car and put it in gear to go back.

Not a single word. Not a single note of the blues from the radio. Not a single stop. It was a straight drive from Port Gibson to Memphis. The longest cross-country trip ever traveled between neighboring states for both of the men. The first stop was the T&R Storage. Orson's shift was about to start. He just sat at the wheel, wanting to say something before he handed the car over to Jesse.

"How are you getting home?" Jesse asked.

"I'll call Ambar and ask her to pick me up."

"If she can't, I can come and get you. One last thing . . ." Jesse opened his side of the door to put the light on. "I want to see your face again."

Orson couldn't deny this to Jesse. They stared into each other's eyes, longer than Orson could take. He was neither ashamed nor sorry for his decision. He just couldn't bear to keep looking into Jesse's sad eyes, he turned the other way, and without saying a word, he slowly stepped out of the car. He opened the trunk and got his bag and hesitated for two seconds to make a decision. He chose the yellow umbrella and closed the trunk, then walked straight to the gates, fighting hard to turn his head and at least wave at Jesse. He heard the guy get out of his side of the car to go into the driver's seat. He knew Jesse was watching him. As Orson opened the entrance and walked inside the gates, he heard the second door slam, and the car finally drove away, the cue that he needed to put Jesse behind him, glad that it was all over and done with. 'Sure, I will regret it,' Orson thought, 'and sure I will miss that boy of mine, Jesse, my sweet Red. But I'll be sparing myself the future pain, and that's what's important.' Whatever his heart had felt the last few hours, days, and weeks, he was then immune to it, or so he thought.

FOURTEEN

A FOURTEEN-YEAR-OLD black girl with dark straight hair down to her shoulders was showing Jesse the way down the hallway at Frayser High. She was nearly dragging her feet, or so it seemed to Jesse, at the pace she was going. She was wearing white pants and a green sleeveless shirt with a big F in the heart area, part of the school's softball team uniform. She was leading him to the amphitheater to meet Mr. Emerson, one of the English teachers, also in charge of the drama club. Jesse was amused by his guide, who seemed to know her way around blindly, as she only stared at her cell phone screen for the whole walk. Usually, he would be annoyed by this antisocial behavior, but he was feeling good about the meeting he'd just had with Mrs. Young, the school's principal. They had been exchanging messages in previous weeks regarding her interesting proposition, and after several emails and more than a few phone calls, they were able to finally meet again.

Jesse had intentionally set *Amazing Graceland* aside for the moment being. Every time he worked on the story, it made him think of Orson, which hurt him to the core. He did manage to put together an outline to pitch the show for his friends at HBO. They loved the idea of a series based on the blues and wanted to see a finished script for the pilot by the following summer. The time frame was a little over eight months, which gave him enough time to do both: write the script for HBO and lead the seminars he had just discussed with Principal Young.

Even three weeks after he and Orson parted ways, he would still get angry at the big guy for giving up on them so quickly. When the nights seemed too long to bear, Jesse drove back to some of the spots his friend had taken him to, trying to convince himself it was part of his research, when in reality, he was hoping to run into Orson. But being the only white man in some of those joints did not always make him feel welcome, so there were only two places where he felt at ease. Conveniently, one of them was The Grasshopper, but he only went early and on nights when he knew Orson would be working late at the storage place. If he drank a bit too much, he'd stay longer those nights. He often wondered if Ambar tipped Orson off that he was there because the man never showed up any of the nights he visited her bar. Nonetheless, going to watch live music certainly got him in a better mood, and dancing did more than that. Diving into the blues seemed to release whatever anxiety was clouding his spirit.

It was on one of those late nights at Ambar's place that 45-year-old Mrs. Young approached him and asked if he was, in fact, the screenwriter/producer Jesse Santos, whom she recognized from an entertainment magazine. They got to talking, and somehow, after a few drinks, she ended up convincing him to give creative writing seminars at her high school.

The teenage girl stopped by the side of a brown metal double door, and without saying a single word, she pointed at it with an aloof grin on her face. Jesse thanked her and watched her leave at the same slow pace. Jesse thought, 'If I ever include this encounter in a story, I'll have her chewing gum.' He opened one of the doors to step into what at first seemed like a dark room. His eyes quickly adjusted to see the well-lit stage at the bottom of large space. There were eight students performing the middle of a scene from *Rope* by Patrick Hamilton. The young actors were casually dressed, obviously to him rehearsing the final scene. Offstage, there was a black silhouette of a stocky man with thick dreadlocks down his back standing in front of the first row with his arms crossed facing the actors. The darkness covering the seating area was perfect for Jesse to sneak in without being noticed. He sat down in the last row, right next to one of the two long aisles. He was spying innocently on the English teacher; studying how he engaged with his pupils. Watching him work excited Jesse about his plan to teach creative writing classes in that school. In fact, teaching could not have come at a better moment, for he was not in any particular rush to get back to the west coast. He had been purposely taking his time getting rid of stuff from his inherited home. He wanted to stay through the rest of fall and probably part of winter. He was still not ready to let go of the house, nor was he willing to return to LA just yet. And the reality was that Jesse had too much time on his hands.

After sitting in the dark for 15 minutes, Jesse was finally spotted by one of the actors on stage. She pointed him out, and everyone below turned to look at him; he simply waved at all of them. Mr. Emerson looked at his watch and then dismissed the actors. After giving his final input to his kids, he started up the stairs to meet the man sitting in the shadows. Jesse met him halfway.

"Mr. Santos?" said the teacher extending his hand.

"Please, call me Jesse." As he shook Emerson's hand, he realized the teacher was about the same age as him. He was surprised to see a younger man with a fair complexion. The backlighting from the stage that created an effect that made Emerson seem older and much darker. "What should I call you?"

"Professor." He said with a straight face. "That's quite a handshake you got going there."

"Oh, I'm sorry, professor, I've been told about that. Something I picked up from my father."

"Hank. I was kidding. Please, call me Hank."

"Principal Young apologizes for not introducing us personally. She had an unexpected visitor."

"I know she texted me, that's how I know it was you up here."

"By the way, that was really good. Your students were great. Congratulations!"

"Thank you. That's nice, coming from you. We'll perform this Friday and Saturday. It'd be great if you'd come." Hank then pointed the way upstairs to go out, "Shall we get out of here?"

"I wanted to meet you quickly since we're going to be working together next week. Mrs. Young assured me you wouldn't mind I'd showed up here."

"No problem. I have a lot to ask you." He stopped briefly, "Wait, what are you doing now? Do you need to be anywhere?"

"No, I have time."

"Shit! Never mind, I have to pick up Suki—" he seemed to say to himself, "that's my daughter—and take her to yoga class."

"Don't worry about it. I'll see you next week, then." They started walking again.

"Then, I'll walk you out to your car." Hank stopped again, "Unless . . . listen, while my daughter is in class, I have to sit and wait for an hour in a tiny hall with a bunch of moms, no offense."

"Yikes!" Jesse joked back, "none taken."

"They have a coffee place right next door. We can talk there."

Jesse agreed and walked with Hank to the school's parking lot. They rode together in Hank's car to pick up his daughter from her grade school.

When Suki got in the car, she stared at the stranger, eyeing him with suspicion for taking her front seat. Her father introduced them, adding that Jesse came from Hollywood. This caused her face to soften with a friendlier look. She turned out to be an outspoken 8-year-old with the same light skin tone as her father. Her hair was tied up in a top-knot, a mature look for an 8-year-old. Again, Jesse was expecting someone much older, for some reason. It must have been the yoga lesson that set him off. Not the usual activity for a small child, though he remembered some young kids in LA taking yoga and decided maybe it's not that unusual. Just then, Suki started on a questioning spree asking Jesse things about Hollywood; some he could answer, most he could not. Her questions were mainly about shows and very young actors he had vaguely heard about. Lucky for him, the yoga place was around the corner from her school. Hank accompanied his little girl to the center while Jesse waited in the coffee shop at a table for four near the window. To kill time, he browsed through his laptop, which he had brought for the meeting with the principal, just in case. He scanned through some old files he hadn't seen in months, even years: his first drafts for series that materialized and others that stayed in limbo. He heard the door opening and looked up to see Hank walking in. It was at that very moment that his notion of writing seminars for Frayser High shifted into a more ambitious concept. He almost jumped up with excitement about his new idea, but instead, he urged the teacher to take a seat and then waved at the waiter to come and take their order. Jesse ordered two coffees and outlined his new idea.

What Hank thought would be a timid talk on a mere extracurricular activity gradually developed into a passionate discussion about creating a web series. He was thrilled about Jesse's new concept; both men agreed about the bigger picture. They were shooting ideas left and right, shaping all possibilities. It reminded Jesse slightly of the brainstorming sessions he'd had with Steven. Jesse suggested gathering forces from some of the after-school clubs to create a production team. The English club would cover creative writing; the drama club could handle acting and directing; the jazz band could produce a soundtrack; the audio-visual club could take care of the technical aspects like lighting, filming, and editing. The production team would work under Jesse and Hank's supervision as the executive producers—as they named themselves.

Hank's cell phone rang, interrupting the enthusiastic brainstorming session. It was the yoga instructor asking why Suki hadn't been picked up yet. Jesse told Hank to go ahead and get her; he would settle the bill and meet them by the car. When Hank left, Jesse walked to the register to pay. For a brief second, he wished he could tell Orson about this meeting. He pulled out his phone, and while the check was being tallied by the same waiter who served them, Jesse felt compelled to text his friend. He was feeling happy about his new project and wanted to share it with his big guy, whom he missed so much. The cashier called out the total amount and snapped him out of making what was probably a mistake; the phone went back in his pocket. He met Hank and Suki outside, and the teacher drove him back to Frayser's parking lot.

Jesse got in his car and stayed there without starting it. He was contemplating the following options for the long night ahead:

Go home and work on *Amazing Graceland*—not likely.

Sit at home and work some more on the project he talked about with Hank—maybe.

Have dinner out alone—definitely.

Go to another local gay bar to meet some stranger and talk him to death with no intention of getting laid—not tonight.

Drive out to The Grasshopper and dance and hope Orson might show up—yes!

FIFTEEN

THE STEAM WAS TOO THICK to make out anything beyond you. There I was, with my arms spread up high with each hand against the corner walls while the hot water was splashing on my back. And there you were looking up at me, trapped inside, between me and nothing else. I lowered my left hand to take yours, slowly raised it to where mine used to be just few seconds before, then held your arm gently by the wrist against the wall. I whispered a dare in your ear, and you immediately responded. You moved your free hand and got a hold of my dick, stroking it slowly, just as I dared you. Your grip was soft but firm, and I began to grow the very moment you touched me. I lowered my right hand and placed it on the side of your head and tenderly tilted it to the side. My lips moved close to your neck, I opened my mouth and sank my teeth into your smooth skin but without biting you. You moaned with pleasure, and I knew you wanted more. I softened a bit and moved your head closer to me to assure you that you were safe with me. Without leaving your flesh, my mouth slid over to your scalp, which made you gripe even more. I sensed your legs trembling, but at the same time, I felt your hand stop pleasuring me. I commanded you to continue, and you did as you were told. My teeth danced smoothly around your head. You could hardly stay put; my passion kicked in momentarily. I released your arm, moved you close to me, and held you tightly between both of mine. You embraced me back. We stood there under the shower with hot water streaming down our bodies for who knows how long.

I stopped hugging you and placed my hands to the sides of your face. I pulled you away to take a good look at your lovely face to lose myself in your eyes, those intense green eyes with deep, dark pupils that dragged my soul into yours. You stared back at me and nodded softly as if as reading my thoughts. Consent. Allowing me to give you all of me. I kissed you hard, trying to pull you in as you surrendered to me. I slid my hands down your arms and made you turn around and face the corner, where I held you captive. Without me telling you, you raised your arms and placed your hands against the wall, you spread your legs and offered me yourself. I held you by the waist, pulling you against me, and with one thrust, I made you scream, begging me to stop. I couldn't; I wouldn't. I wanted to explore you, get to the center of you. You stopped resisting, whimpering with desire, which made me all the more feverish. I let go of your waist and wrapped you in my arms without releasing you. You pulled your arms back and placed them by the sides of my neck, placing your hands behind my head, holding on to me. I kept pulsing into you. In one constant tempo neither of us wanted to end. But then I began to have that sensation again, as if I was climbing a mountain, almost reaching its peak, not exactly wanting to make it, yet longing to be at the top. Then, there was no turning back, I reached the sky and floated in the air, melting into you. I felt the universe surround me and rush into my head. I opened my eyes, and you were gone.

There I was, in my bed and all alone thinking of you; another morning without you, jerking off myself to death since I let you go. I couldn't take it any more. I never had it so bad for anyone, not Genna, not L.C., just you. I remember getting angry at myself. And what the fuck was that? My bullshit fantasy of having you surrendering to me; when you're everything but submissive. But hey! It was my vision. I could do you as I pleased.

These kinds of thoughts had been going on for three weeks, the more I fought them, the more you popped into my head, and I was fed up with it; I wanted nothing to do with you. I put on a robe and went around the house looking for my cell phone. There it was, on the kitchen table, I sat down and went through the phonebook and found your name: Jesse, not Santos, not Red, just Jesse. I hit the erase button, and out you went. No more temptations to call you. Sure, I could have driven to your house, but that would have taken some heavy thinking on the way there, and I would not have made it past my seat belt. Boy! You don't know how much willpower I have, nor how stubborn I am. It was harder for me to erase all your photos, the ones at the Pig Pickin', hanging out in New Orleans, and our last selfie at the Windsor Ruins.

I basically threw the cell phone on the table and sat back with my arms crossed. I stared at the table, looking at nothing in particular until my eye was caught by that little bright yellow notebook. The one you must have bought somewhere on our trip to New Orleans and sneaked in my bag at some point when I wasn't looking. Even though I got rid of everything else, I wasn't about to get rid of that. It was my only memento of you. I put on my glasses, the ones I look so cute in according to you, picked up the notebook and read the note you left for me again.

Although I am not good at poetry,
I thought I would give it a shot for you.
There's magic between us we both agree,
Came unexpected and out of the blue.

I got you this pad for you to compose
Beautiful music straight your heart;
For all of those moments with highs and lows,
Here is my token to master your art

I sat there for a long time, reading your poem countless times, wondering if there was any purpose to our being together. I didn't want us to be pointless. Besides the great times we had together, I wanted it to have some meaning. I thought about all our talks and how bewildered I felt about some of the things you said. I admired how you would have an idea and immediately figure out how to make it happen. I loved that about you, I envied the drive that got you going.

I stood up and went to the kitchen counter and opened the top drawer, the one next to the silverware, and pulled out three small notebooks, of similar size to the one you'd given me. I left them on the table, and went to the living room, opened the drawer underneath the stereo and found at the bottom of it eight more notebooks and grabbed them. I went to the foyer, to the drawer in the narrow chest where I usually leave whatever comes in the mail to read later, there were five more. I then found fourteen more in different parts of my bedroom, one in the bathroom, and six more inside my desk in my little office, purposely leaving behind a handful of napkins and little pieces of paper scribbled with notes from the middle drawer. I had gathered a total of thirty-seven, including your gift. I gathered all of them on the kitchen table. I sat down and looked through all of them, one by one, trying to put them in sequence. Imagine placing in order dateless bits and pieces of unfinished music dating back from the 1990s up till now?

I felt the urge to call in sick to work, which I did. I was anxious and melancholic at the same time. Sure, I was still missing you madly—hell, the same way I had every day since we broke it off. But this day was different. There was a plus to it, an upside. I was on a roll.

I numbered the cover of each notebook in red marker, to the best of my memory. I fixed myself some lunch and looked at them some more, making sure I got them in the right sequence. I finished eating and cleaned up. I grabbed all the notebooks and opened the door to the basement, where I only go for laundry and to put away stuff I no longer need, but won't dare to throw out or give away. I went down the stairs and found myself in front of lots of boxes. Some with books, others with LPs, cassettes, videotapes, some army stuff, and things from the old house. The great majority of this stuff belongs to Angela. It's stuff she just doesn't want to throw away, and I have been keeping for her for years, all labeled and dated. My only tangible way to feel like I'm a good dad, I guess.

I battled my reluctance—not knowing exactly if or where to start— thought about it momentarily, and then went for it. I set my notebooks on one of the steps of the stairs and started moving boxes, finding my way to what I had deliberately buried in the back of the basement years ago. My old piano, the one Papa Joe left me. The old abandoned upright wooden friend that I could depend on taking me back to a different time. When I moved to my little house, I was so close to giving it away. I feel grateful that I didn't.

I picked up more boxes, moving and piling them against the wall to make room to breathe and let the sunlight in from the only small window in that basement—on the opposite wall to the piano and close to the ceiling. It was a beautiful day out, but I had made up my mind to stay in to continue doing what I set my heart to do: dust away years of neglect and remove bad memories once and for all. I grabbed an old rag from the shelf on the top of the dryer and did just that; I cleaned the hell out of that piano, and I did the same to the window.

I sat down on my stool, and it felt strange. At first, I thought my butt had grown, which is more likely, or that I got taller because I had the impression of being further from the piano. I looked at the lacquered black of the surface for a bit, not daring to lift the lid. But when I finally did . . . oh, my dear Jesse, I swear to you, I got goosebumps. I placed my fingers on the keyboard, barely touching them, almost caressing them with my fingertips. I finally hit one single note, and I was back, back from wherever I'd gotten lost. Back from all the time I had been hiding from pain and betrayal—maybe. It had been so long that it no longer made sense why I left in the first place—all those years of putting off that very moment. You know?

I got the notebooks from the stairs and looked for a pencil in my toolbox; then, I got back to the piano. I put them all on top of the baby grand, but kept your notebook handy, and sat down again. I opened the first page and read your dedication again. To be honest, I couldn't have enough of it. Every time I did, I'd smile. No one had ever written me a poem before. I turned to the next blank page. I played a note and then another. I took the pencil that was tucked behind my ear to write what was coming out of my head. Red, you can't imagine what it was like to dive back into the blues. My emotions were funneling through my fingers to the keyboard, playing notes I didn't think I had in me, an overwhelming feeling went through me as I composed.

I had an epiphany. I wasn't meant to play the day before, nor the day after. It was as if all my experiences since I stopped playing led me to that moment. Like there was nothing wrong with me not playing for so long. It simply was what it was. And then I felt peace in my heart.

I kept playing and writing. That afternoon and all through the night, I went through every single notebook I've ever written in since Genna's passing. I can't recall if I ate that night, or if I ever went to the bathroom. The fact was, I was back. I was back to my groove, back to my friend— the good the ol' blues. Thank you, Red, for pointing me in that direction.

SIXTEEN

JESSE WAS WAITING in his car, still a bit anxious after his first meeting with the students. Even though Hank had been prepping them for a week, Jesse did not know what to expect. The gathering had taken longer than anyone had anticipated, which for Jesse was a good sign. It was nearly 7:00 p.m., and he thought it was a good idea for he and Hank to go for a bite and get some feedback from him. Jesse jumped in his seat as Hank suddenly opened the passenger door.

"Sorry, man, I didn't mean to startle you," said Hank as he sat down and immediately fastened his seatbelt.

"Believe it or not, I'm still nervous."

"Really? You? I figured you have meetings with big producers and famous people every day. That would scare me."

"Sure, I know how to handle them; it's high school kids who intimidate me." Jesse chuckled as he started the car. "So, how did you like the presentation?"

"Man, why are you asking me this? You saw it yourself—the kids were all excited."

"Where are we going?" Asked Jesse with his index finger on the GPS screen.

"To Southern Hands, on Winchester Road, it's about twenty minutes," Hank said while placing his backpack on the car floor, between his legs. "You made it look easy. Are you sure we can pull this off before Thanksgiving?"

Jesse finished typing in the location. "A fifteen-minute pilot? Piece of cake. I can tell already, the kids in the audio-visual club know their shit, so I wouldn't be too concerned." Jesse pulled out of the parking lot onto the road. "When my husband and I did our first web series, we started from scratch, did it all ourselves at home."

"*Dames from the Dammed?*"

"Yes"

Hank paused for a few seconds wondering, and then he asked, "Do you always mention your husband like that, so casually?"

"What do you mean?"

"We're in Memphis, Tennessee; it's Baptist country here."

"Oh, that. Not really, only because I knew you Googled me. You saw it; the students didn't seem to mind, at least most of them. Mrs. Young was the same; everyone who Googles me also finds Steven."

"I hear you."

"So, I don't worry about it."

"I wanted to ask you. You told me the other day you were on sabbatical. Why Memphis, of all places?

"I needed a break from LA, so I came down to sell Steven's grandparents' house. The truth is I'm liking it here."

"Really?" Asked Hank, surprised at Jesse's response.

"Actually, it's the music scene, but I don't mean the one downtown. I'm talking about the real blues scene. I met this cool dude about a month ago who took me to the meanest blues dives in and around town."

"Awesome."

"To that point, I even got an idea for a new show in the process."

"Like, a series about the blues?"

"Well, not really about the blues, but that music plays an important part in the story. I was inspired by the man who showed me around. Actually, he's the first person I met in Memphis. The story is loosely based on some aspects of his life." Jesse paused for a few seconds, "Anyway, I used to wait until he got off work, and we hit those off-the-beaten-path dives at one or two in the morning. Man, the places this guy took me to. I don't think I ever danced so much. I loved every second. Afterward, we would go out for dinner or breakfast. Whichever we decided on in the wee hours of whatever morning, we would be out till sunrise."

Hank waited, not sure if he was stepping over the line with Jesse, but they had spent a few days working together, and he felt no reason to be shy at this point, and staying quiet was not in him. "I take it you two had a thing."

"Why do you say that?" Jesse asked, loving the remark and looking forward to how Hank would answer.

"Just the way you're talking about him."

"That obvious?"

"Your tone changes a bit as you mention him. I notice these things, I'm the drama teacher . . . Sounds like you two had a blast."

"We sure did." Jesse reminisced.

Hank turned to Jesse, who seemed to be someplace in his head. "You really like this guy, don't you?"

"Man, I really do . . . But it's weird too, because I've never been attracted to older guys. Never."

"My wife is older than I am."

"Thirty years?"

"No, man. That's a lot of fucking years."

"I know, dude. I am used to guys close to my age, you know? But this guy; this guy caught me off guard. He took my heart and put it in his pocket close to his."

"Man, you're a true poet."

"I wrote that for a pilot that never took off."

"He must be quite a guy."

"Well, he is. But you see, we hung out for weeks and weeks, and there was not the slightest hint of flirtation. But one weekend in New Orleans changed everything."

"That's New Orleans for you. The Big Easy will do that." Hank lifted his hand and pointed to the left, "It's better if you turn here."

"And an interesting weekend too. Little did we know we would end up hooking up, and man did we ever."

"This is the same man who is thirty years older than you?"

"Well, technically twenty-eight years, but, yes, the only one I'm talking about, Hank." Jesse made a left turn where Hank had suggested to. "I'm telling you, I never had it so bad for anyone, not even my husband, who hopefully rests in peace."

"Wow, now I really want to meet this guy. Call him up, tell him to join us."

"I wish. He broke it off on the way back from New Orleans."

"I'm sorry to hear that."

"I know, he was concerned about us being too different and the fact that I would go back to LA at some point. Maybe he was right, but I miss the hell out of him."

"When do you think you'll be heading back to California?"

"I don't really know; maybe January. Definitely after all the holidays are over. Steven was a real holiday buff, so going back home now is out of the question for me." Jesse spotted the sign that read "Southern Hands" in big, bold lettering on the side of the road. "Is this the place?"

He didn't have trouble finding a parking spot, probably because it was a weeknight. Once inside, Jesse realized the place was nothing like he had imagined. The name suggested something homier and rustic. Instead, it was like other places he had been to in the south, where the decor has nothing to do with the name, always with surprising results. As he looked around, he noticed the beige resin dishware that seemed more appropriate for a school cafeteria, but he wasn't discouraged or deterred. He was confident Hank had chosen the right place.

They were seated, and after reviewing the plastic-covered menu, Jesse let himself be guided by Hank for what to order. This was not something he normally did, but since he moved to the south, his new go-with-the-flow behavior proved to work to his advantage. Hank ordered his all-time favorites items from the menu: catfish filets and Kam's pork chops, both with the same side order of mac and cheese and black-eyed peas. The waiter brought their beers first.

"I was asking you if your wife is a teacher also."

"No, a lawyer."

"How long have you guys been together?"

"If Suki is eight, we've been married for eight years now."

"Oh yeah! Let me see those pictures she wanted you to show me with her new yoga outfit, please."

Hank reached over his brown leather briefcase, where he always kept his phone. He searched for it in the two front pockets, found it on the left one, and took it out. He hit the photo archive icon and showed it to

Jesse. As he passed through the photos, Jesse could read the look on Hank's face. He was proud and very much in love with his daughter. Suddenly the phone screen went black and "Dad calling" was displayed on it. Hank picked up.

Jesse could not help but hear, so he turned his head so as not to seem so obvious. Thankfully, it was a quick and good-humored conversation.

"Your dad?" asked Jesse.

"No, my father-in-law. I call him Dad. My father died before I was born. Anyway, he's been helping me out by picking up Suki after school since you and I started working on the series. He's just great."

"Is he the one who's also a big blues lover?"

"The same. You guys oughta meet." Hank picked up his beer mug and had a drink. "Too bad we don't see each other that much."

"How come?"

"Angie and her dad don't get along that well. We only see him on important dates. And to be honest, if it wasn't for me, he would miss out on most of Suki's events. It just doesn't occur to Angie to call her own dad and invite him."

Jesse realized Hank wanted to open up. This usually happened to him, but not so much since he moved to Memphis. He would meet people randomly, and for some reason, they would confide in him very personal information. He liked Hank, and if the teacher needed an ear, Jesse had no problem listening. The food had just arrived, and Jesse was eager to dig in. He also figured that once Hank put some food in his stomach, he would open up. And he did.

Over dinner, Hank basically told Jesse his married life story; how he and Angie had met in graduate school while they were both living in DC, his home town. Shortly after they started dating, she got pregnant. They were very much in love then, so they married without blinking an eye. After they moved in together, they slowly discovered how different they were from one another. She complained to him about not being mature enough; he hated how she became way too serious from one day to the next. He admitted that he was not around much while she was pregnant. When she was sick, she was no fun to be around; so he would be out with his friends. But soon after Suki was born, his attitude changed overnight,

125

and he became a devoted father. Things between Angie and him got slightly better for a while. This lasted until they both finished their master's degrees, and she started hinting about going back to live in her hometown. Hank hated the thought of moving south; to Memphis of all places. Washington, DC had so much more to offer the three of them, but Angie never saw it that way. She saw a city high in crime and a terrible place to raise children, and there was no way to make her see it any other way. Angie threatened to leave without him, and he could not bear the thought of waking up without seeing his daughter each morning, so he eventually caved in, and the three of them relocated to Memphis.

By then, Hank was much more in love with his daughter; and completely out of love with his wife. That was Jesse's takeaway from Hank's storytelling. He felt bad for Hank for living in a loveless marriage. Though he could definitely relate to Hank's feelings, he didn't know Hank well enough to offer his opinion or advice. That opportunity might come once he got to know Hank better and felt more like a friend.

At the end of dinner, both men were very much full and tipsy. Their plans to go out for a drink afterward were wisely decided against. Hank insisted on getting the bill, but Jesse wouldn't have it, thinking about what a teacher's salary in the south would be. Hank finally had to trick Jesse by pretending to go to the bathroom; instead, he went to the cashier.

Jesse dropped Hank at home and was glad to find out he knew the neighborhood. About five blocks later, the guy was sitting alone in his rental car, parked at the corner facing Orson's house across the street. He didn't know if it was all the talking earlier about his man or the extra beer he had during dinner. Probably both, he thought. The truth was he missed the old guy. He had a perfect view of the house, and he could see the dimmed lights through the closed venetian blinds. 'Is Orson there at all?' Jesse asked himself. If the man didn't love that Lincoln Continental more than his own life, his car would be parked outside the garage like everyone else's. Jesse grabbed his phone and browsed for Orson's number. Look at you, Jesse, he said to himself, you are basically stalking the man, what the fuck?!

Suddenly, his phone rang, which gave him the second scare of the night. It was Hank, making him jump in his seat again.

126

"Hey Jesse, what are you doing?"

"Don't ask."

"OK, OK, sorry. I'll be quick. Listen, I've been talking to Angie here. If you're not doing anything on Thanksgiving, we'd . . ."

"I'd love to!" Jesse hardly let Hank finish his invitation. "What should I bring?"

"Cool!" Hank nearly laughed at such a quick reply. "Nothing, you don't have to bring anything."

"I know; I could bring some great Spanish wine. Do you guys drink wine?"

"Sure, wine sounds great, but you don't really have to bring anything."

"Of course, I will. For how many people?"

"It'll be us three—my mom, my aunt, Dad, and his girlfriend . . ." said Hank, then a female voice in the background seemed to correct him. "OK, she's not his girlfriend. And you. Eight in total. Perfect; an even number."

They worked out a few more details and finally hung up. Jesse put his phone back in the compartment below the radio. He looked at Orson's house again, but this time all the lights were out. 'What I wouldn't give to be laying on that bed with Orson,' he wished. But he found himself in a better mood. Hank's phone call had come in the nick of time, saving him from doing something stupid. It would be fun to spend Thanksgiving with a bunch of strangers and his brand-new friend. He then thought, 'Christmas will be a whole different story, but I won't think about that now. I'd better go.'

SEVENTEEN

IT WAS CLOSE TO 3:00 P.M., and there was some tension in the Emerson kitchen. Angela seemed a bit more stressed than usual because there would be complete stranger joining them for Thanksgiving dinner; all Hank's idea. In any case, she wore a rather elegant, slightly tight pastel blue dress that accentuated her slim figure and her dark skin tone. Every time there was a newcomer in the house, she unpurposely wore her hair up with curls hanging beside her cheeks.

It irritated her how calm Hank always seemed to be during what she'd consider a crisis. All the guests had arrived, except for Jesse, but they were all family, so there was no need to pamper anyone. They could all take care of themselves. Basically, the crisis was all in Angie's mind.

"Does your friend have a habit of being late?" asked Angie as she closed the oven door and lowered its temperature slightly.

"Not really," lied Hank, not knowing if Jesse had the habit of being tardy. He looked at the clock on top of the fridge, while wiping clean the last wine glass of the set with a white cloth. "It's only eight minutes past three." He put the wine glass on the counter with the others and then called out, "Dad!" hoping to be heard beyond the kitchen door.

"Remember what happened the last time we had one of your guests over for Thanksgiving?" Angie asked, trying hopelessly to wind up Hank for a possible argument.

"That was five years ago, let it go!"

Angela's father entered the kitchen.

"How can I help?" The man asked as he clapped his hands once and rubbed them against one another.

"Dad, could you please help me with these wine glasses? Set them on the table." Hank was holding five of the glasses. The doorbell rang. "Never mind, could you get the door instead? That's Jesse."

"Wait! What?! Who?!" The man asked.

Jesse was standing in front of the Emersons' red door, holding a brown cardboard gift box by its handle in one hand and a bouquet of white tulips in the other. He looked up to the sky as it started drizzling at that very moment. He wondered why in hell he made the last decision to leave his orange umbrella at home before getting in the taxi cab. 'And hold it with what, my teeth?' he reasoned. He scanned himself again to make sure his shoes were clean and that his pants and black leather coat were looking the same as they did when he saw them last in his bathroom mirror. But no, he was now damp, and the longer it took for someone to open the door, the worse it got. Finally, he heard the door unlocking, so he poised with a smile.

"So, guess who's coming to Thanksgiving dinner?" Orson joked as he opened the door, knowing Jesse would appreciate movie humor. He then laughed at his reaction. "Red! My boy. I wish you could see the look on your face."

"What da…" Jesse whispered as he looked all confused at the number on the house by the side of the door.

"Yeah! You're in the right house, son." The man laughed, "I'm Hank's father-in-law."

"Nooo! Fuck me!" Jesse said slowly, close to whispering and in complete shock, not concerned anymore about getting rained on.

"C'mere!" Orson stepped out and hugged Jesse. "How you've been, son?"

"I've been OK." He hugged back as hard as he could with both hands full. He was surprised to sense that Orson was trembling, probably as much as he was. "Did you know I was coming?"

"No, I found out two seconds ago when Hank said a certain Jesse was at the door." Orson tried to pull away, but Jesse held on a few extra seconds. "Your hair is a bit darker." Orson got a hold of the box Jesse has holding, "Let me help you with that."

"There are two bottles of wine in there, be careful."

"Please, come in." Orson let him go in first. "Please, tell me you brought that great Spanish wine."

Orson showed Jesse into the living room and started the proper introductions. There was Hank's mother, Gladys, a plump woman with a contagious smile and thick eyeglasses, with a handshake as firm as Jesse's to go with it. Her sister, Evelyn, seemed just as lovely and friendly; she had given up on flirting with Orson years ago, about the time Ambar started being invited to these occasions. Jesse took off his coat at Orson's request and walked straight to Ambar, who was very much surprised to see him walk in. She welcomed Jesse with a warm hug. Suki was sitting on the sofa watching as her new favorite beau was embraced by her Auntie Ambar. The little girl made a clear point of wanting a much bigger hug for herself to everyone's amusement. Jesse had no problem complying with her wish and picked her up and held her until her grandfather came to the rescue and took her off his hands.

"C'mon Gennie," said Orson setting the girl on the floor, "Jesse still has to say hello to your mom and dad in the kitchen."

"We'll have plenty of time to play later, OK, Suki?" said Jesse.

"Oh no, you too?" Orson complained, "Is it so hard to call her Gennie?"

"Orson, give it up already," Ambar added.

"Never!"

Jesse recalled just then how his friend referred to his granddaughter by her diminutive name instead of her nickname, which Orson disliked so much.

Orson picked up the box with the Spanish wines and let Jesse get the flowers they left on the table by the sofa. They headed to the kitchen, going straight through the dining room. The table was already set, and most of the food was on it, except for the warm dishes.

"Please, tell me you made the mac and cheese you always brag about," Jesse begged his friend, who assured him it was part of the menu. Orson pushed the door open to the kitchen, placing his other still shaky hand on Jesse's back. They walked into the kitchen to find Angela and Hank disagreeing on what to take first to the table. Orson put a stop to that by gently pushing Jesse holding the bouquet towards his daughter.

"Hello Angie," said Jesse, finally getting rid of the flowers, "we meet at last."

"Thank you so much!" Her face brightened up with a smile that reminded Jesse of Orson's, making their resemblance more evident. Her reaction gave him the impression that it had been a long time since she received flowers. Jesse made a mental note to remind either husband or father later to repeat the gesture; it was worth that smile. He watched as she opened one of the top kitchen cabinets to look for a vase.

"You guys would never guess," started Orson, all excited, "Angela, do you remember last month when I told you I drove to New Orleans with a friend to see my army buddies? I went with Jesse. I know this guy!"

"You're shitting me." said Hank with a smile of disbelief. "Get out of here! You know each other already, really?"

"Yeah," the man replied. "We met at the Piggly Wiggly, and then we started getting acquainted."

"Oh, yes! Your friend who wanted to write about the blues. I thought it was an older guy, for some reason," said Angie, finally finding a plain cylindrical vase for her flowers, she went to the sink and filled it with water.

"So did I," added Hank. "Man, what are the odds?"

"Dad, please get the turkey out of the oven, I'm taking these and calling everyone to the table," said Angie before walking out of the kitchen with the flowers, "Hank, please bring out the coleslaw."

Hank went straight to the fridge; the moment he opened the door, he froze. He realized he knew more about that weekend in New Orleans than he should care to. He didn't know what to say or what to think. He grabbed the dish with the coleslaw, nearly knocking down a carton of milk and a bottle of juice in the process. He quickly and clumsily closed the fridge door and followed his wife to the dining room in a hurry.

"Jesse, fetch me those mittens, will you?" Asked Orson as he opened the oven door. "So, how've you been?"

"Keeping busy," said Jesse handing him the oven mitts. "Orson, I still can't get over this, you, Hank's father-in-law?" he shook his head slightly.

"I think I'm doing a pretty good job not showing you how nervous and freaked out I am that you are here."

"No, dude. A terrible job," Jesse said. "Your forehead is sweating like crazy."

"That's because I'm standing in front of an open oven." Orson quickly changed the subject. "Hank told me he was working on a series in school, but I thought it was him and another teacher. It never occurred to me it could be you. I figured you'd be back in LA by now."

"Orson, do you think I would leave town without saying goodbye?"

Before Orson had a chance to answer, Hank walked into the kitchen.

"Dad," Hank walked straight to his father-in-law with a serious look and checking for the door in the meantime. "Is there anything you need to tell me?"

Orson grabbed the hot tray with the turkey by both ends, pulled it out of the oven, and then set it on the counter. He looked at his son-in-law with a confused look on his face. Jesse then volunteered to explain.

"Orson, Hank knows about us . . . our weekend in New Orleans."

"What the fuck, Jess?" Orson nearly yelled, he took off his mittens and threw them on the counter.

"Hey Dad, it's cool," Hank said, placing his hand on Orson's shoulder. "It actually answers a few questions, but you need to talk to Angie."

"Jesse, why the hell did you have to say anything? This is a personal matter."

Jesse didn't appreciate Orson's tone of voice. "Hank, can I take this to the table?" He got a hold of a kitchen towel and grabbed the dish with the macaroni and cheese and headed for the door.

"Don't you walk out on me, son," Orson said, trying hard not to raise his voice. Jesse stopped cold by the door.

"Easy, Dad. Jesse didn't tell me. You did, just now. You said the two of you went . . . he didn't know you were my father-in-law." Hank opened a drawer and pulled out a few more kitchen towels and placed them on the counter, next to the turkey. "You have got to talk to your daughter. I don't keep secrets from her, and I'm not about to start."

"There's nothing to tell. Jesse and I are no longer involved. Everything is back the way it's always been."

"No, it is not," said Jesse, with tears on the edge of his lower eyelids,

"Go to hell, Orson!" and walked out of the kitchen.

"What the hell, Dad!" Hank snapped at his father-in-law, "Jesse still cares a great deal for you." He kept watching the door for Angela to come. "You should have heard the way he talked about this great man he went to New Orleans with, meaning you! He's pretty cool, you know?"

"Who's cool?" asked Angie, who had just walked into the kitchen.

"Jesse is," Orson replied while getting a hold of the baster for the turkey.

"That's what Hank keeps saying." Angie picked up a basket with biscuits, "Those are lovely flowers he brought," and another with cornbread. "Guys, you need to bring out the turkey, everyone's at the table already."

Hank was holding a hot plate with string beans and would not take his eyes off of Orson. "Yeah, Dad, the turkey needs to come out." He then followed Angie out of the kitchen again. Ambar and Jesse entered right after.

"What can we bring out?" Ambar asked.

"Take the baked ham. Ambar, I need ten seconds with Jesse. Do you think you can keep everyone at the table? The turkey is the only thing left to bring out."

"Sure, no problem." Ambar took two hot pads from the counter, grabbed the tray with the ham, and left.

"Red, hand me that big dish behind you," said Orson putting on a pair of green silicone gloves. Jesse did as he was told, curious about what Orson had to say. He watched him transfer the turkey from the pan to the dish the guy had just given him. "Hey, do you think you and I can talk after dinner? I realize I must have sounded awful. I'm very sorry, Red."

"Please, don't call me Red, it saddens me." There was a silence that lasted an eternal 15 seconds while the two just looked at each other. "You could give me a ride home. We can talk then if you'd like."

"Good idea," Orson said while opening a drawer and pulling out a carving knife and a serving fork. "Oh! I started playing again."

"With yourself?"

"Well, that too. But no, the piano." Orson smiled right after, getting Jesse's smart-ass remark.

"No, shit! Really?" Jesse smiled right back. "That's fantastic, Orson, I'd love to hear you play one day."

"Sure." Another weird silence. He handed the knife and fork to Jesse, and then Ambar opened the door.

"Everyone's ready and hungry. C'mon." She said.

Orson picked up the platter with the turkey and led the way while Jesse followed with the utensils to carve the bird. They entered the dining room, and everyone in it stopped talking. They turned to watch Orson, who centered the Thanksgiving turkey on the table.

As the Emerson tradition called for, if there were a guest of honor, that person would sit at one of the ends of the table. So Jesse became the center of attraction during the feast, not only because of where he was seated but also for his charms and the information he was all too happy to share. Orson had the best view of them all, sitting opposite his friend and once again watched him being interviewed again by people he loved. This time by the older ladies who wanted to know all about life in Hollywood. Jesse told stories of movie stars he had met and worked with, almost all done by request. As he did a few weeks ago with Orson's friends, he volunteered anecdotes and gossip from Tinseltown, some of them, rumors, and others from the horse's mouth. Hank and Orson tried desperately to sway the conversation to give their guest a chance to catch his breath, but it was hopeless. Folks always came back to Jesse and show business. This went on throughout dinner and dessert. Orson would look at his son-in-law, and they would both laugh out loud every time that happened.

During coffee, Hank and Jesse made a promise to hold a private screening of the pilot of their web series right after supper. *Better Daze Ahead* was the proposed title suggested by the students. Everyone at the table loved the title. They thought it was inspiring for a series dealing with high school pregnancy. Something they took seriously at Frayser High, for that represented 11 percent of the students. Jesse and Hank thought it was brave and mature of them to choose that topic for their show.

After clearing the table and cleaning up a bit, the two younger men retired to Hank's studio upstairs for some rough editing. The women waited in front of the TV set, not really watching anything in particular.

Little Gennie kidnapped Orson to her bedroom. She amused herself by showing off her latest artwork because she thought her granddad was a much better critic of her work than anyone else in the household. She sat him on her bed as if he were part of her stuffed toy animal collection. The first thing Orson noticed as he looked around the room was the absence of the grey fox terrier dog pictures little Gennie always included in her drawings. He also realized she had taken down the few photos of dogs of the same breed he had seen posted on the walls the last time he visited— on her 8th birthday.

"Gennie, what happened to all the pictures of Knookie?"

Her enthusiasm for displaying her artwork dimmed a bit: "I don't want a puppy anymore."

"What?" asked her concerned grandfather. "Knookie was in all your drawings, and you were so looking forward to adoption day. What happened?"

She would not answer.

"Did your mother talk you out of it?" Orson regretted what he just said. "Or was it your dad?" That didn't make it any better, he thought.

"I talked me out of it."

"But why? You wanted him forever."

"I had my personality reasons."

Orson bit his lip so he wouldn't laugh at her statement. He insisted and persisted until he finally got her talking.

"Allie, my friend from school. Last month, her dog Mocha got sick, and then she died."

"Do you mean Mocha died?" He said as he caressed her hair gently. She nodded. He was relieved to know that it was the dog and not her friend. "I am sorry to hear that, Gennie. Your mom and dad forgot to tell me."

"Allie was so sad for weeks and weeks."

"You do know dogs and cats don't live as long as people," said Orson, not sure that bit of information would help. "I'll bet Allie's parents will take her to get another puppy."

"No! She was so sad she never came back to school."

"What?"

"Yes, and she left school without saying goodbye, too, and I don't want to leave my friends either."

"I don't understand why she left. Did she get sick or something?"

"Daddy said her father joined the army, and they moved to Boulder."

"Oh! I see now. But that won't happen to you. Your dad is never going to join the army. Believe me."

"Really?" Gennie finally looked up as if to reassure herself this adult could be trusted.

"Knookie will only bring you joy."

"Yes, but then one day she will die, and I will be sad beyond consolation."

Orson could not stop himself from laughing. Oh! How he loved this little drama queen. Which movie did she pick up that from? He wondered. He did some fast thinking before saying anything. One faulty word could mark her for life. He realized just then where she got her drama from.

"When you finally meet Knookie, it will be a day to remember. You two will start a new friendship that will last for a long time. You can't begin to imagine how fun it will be to come back from school to find your favorite puppy ready to play with you. You can take her to the park and the lake and watch the little fellow get bigger and bigger."

"Yes! But one day, she will die and go the heaven."

"Right! I mean, no!" He scratched his head and quickly said, "Gennie, do you mean to tell me that you are going to miss out on all the good times because you're worried about Knookie dying? All those hours, and days, and months, and years of fun. All the love that little creature can give you . . ." Orson stopped. He found the most obvious epiphany slapping him in the face with Jesse's name written all over it.

"I guess you are right, Grandpa. I change my mind then."

"You know little Gennie, why don't I help you write a letter to Santa and ask him to bring you Knookie? If your mom and dad say it's OK, she'll be here in three weeks tops. Three weeks! That's just around the corner."

"I'd like that."

Orson swooped closer to her and put his big arm around her. "And then, you make us a new drawing of Knookie for us to show to your mom and dad. You can even send it to Santa tonight, so he'll know what Knookie looks like."

The suddenly excited Gennie slid over the edge of the bed and landed on the floor. She walked to her small white and pink plastic desk for her crayons and her large drawing pad that's half her size. She sat on the floor by the side of the bed, and Orson climbed down to be by her side and watched as she drew and colored for Santa.

EIGHTEEN

ORSON FOUND IT PECULIAR that Jesse had just told him that he loved driving in the rain. 'It must be an LA thing,' he thought, 'because it's always sunny over there.' The guy said the sound of the water hitting the roof of the car was almost like poetry in motion to him, especially right then, when drops were falling hard with brief gaps of silence between them. To relish the sounds, Orson suggested they'd stop to listen, but in reality, he wanted to park to talk to Jesse, even though they had barely left the Emerson's home. They sat quietly, listening to the rain. Orson had certainly heard that sound many times, but he never found it as romantic as Jesse did, certainly not while inside a car.

Jesse noticed that Orson's left knee started bouncing up and down softly but at a steady pace. He secretly loved it when the man did that. He found it endearing and knew that eventually, Orson would soon say whatever he had locked up in his mind. To make Orson loosen up, he started:

"How did you like the pilot for our web series?"

"I loved it. Honestly, I thought it would be more trivial, and I don't know why. But no, it was raw and direct; I was surprised. Pregnant high school girls? Wow!"

"You have to give credit to the English teacher. Your son-in-law is very passionate about his students, and it was actually the kids' idea. They did great, don't you think? Writing and acting . . ."

"I'm sure you had your hand in there somewhere." Orson added, "By the way, I borrowed your show, *Random Highways* from the library."

"The whole series?"

"Well, season one, but never got around to watching it. I ended up returning it. Sorry."

"That's OK; it was incomplete. Steven and I always felt frustrated about that show. It got canned after the second season; it was too expensive to make."

"Shall we continue? Getting you home, I mean."

"Sure, let's go."

Orson started the car and drove. They continued talking about Jesse's series and television in general, something they never did before. It was one of Jesse's favorite subjects and certainly his area of expertise, but it felt like small talk with Orson. Their conversations together had never felt this dull, the guy thought. For the first time in their brief history together, neither was saying what was really on their minds. But Orson had had enough and meant to put a stop to it, so he pulled over and parked again.

"Jesse, let's cut the bullshit." He turned to Jesse. "We're both behaving like complete assholes."

"Thank you!" Jesse couldn't agree more.

"First of all," said Orson while taking off his seatbelt, turning and facing his friend. "I want to apologize for sounding like a jerk earlier in the kitchen. Hank caught me completely off guard while I was holding the ready-to-serve Thanksgiving turkey in my hands. I keep thinking about how cruel I must have sounded, and I'm very sorry."

"Orson, no need." Jesse noticed Orson's knees shaking again. "You apologized already. Is that what you wanted to talk to me about?"

"Well, no. I wanted to find out how you were doing since we . . . you know, parted, but . . ." He stayed quiet for a few seconds, but his right knee wouldn't stop moving.

Jesse took off his seatbelt and turned to Orson, he reached out and put his left hand on his friend's knee and pressed down gently to stop it. "Hey, what are you trying to say?"

Orson placed his hand on top of Jesse's and squeezed it. "When I broke it off with you, I kept thanking myself, congratulating myself even, for being wise enough to cut it clean before getting more attached to you. You see Jesse; I kept thinking; you, so good-looking, blonde, rich, young . . . what the hell were you doing with an old fellow like me? At times I thought of you having daddy issues and just wanted to know what it was like to be with an older black dude, or because you were on the rebound, or simply for kicks. That's what I kept saying to myself, really. Let me finish, please." He stopped Jesse from interrupting. "When the truth is, I was afraid of being hurt. I am so tired of feeling hurt. That motherfucker L.C. drained the trust out of me for any man. I've never really given anyone the time of day since. Not that I met that many guys, but certainly not anyone like you, I'll tell you that." He stopped talking. He just looked at Jesse. "Earlier in the kitchen, when I asked you to have a chat later, an apology is what I had in mind. And like I said before, I wanted to know how you were doing, curious about how you were getting by without me. But seeing you tonight across the table, telling your stories, making me and everyone feel so close to you. I started realizing . . . you have this way of . . ."

"Orson, stop it!" Jesse said as tears began to slide down, "Please, tell me what I think you really want to say. I can't take it any longer."

"Jesse! I want to be with you. I want to spend more time with you, get you to know much better than I already do. I don't care if you go away in a few days, weeks; I will deal with it. I'm a big boy; you know that." Orson smiled and got a hold of Jesse's hand. "I love being with you so much, and I don't want to miss out on the fun with you. Thank God I get a second chance."

"Orson, you know? That day, during that long drive back to Memphis, man, I was beating my brains, thinking that maybe you had something there. That I was not really over Steven yet, that it was too soon. But that evening, after I dropped you off, it hit me like a ton of bricks. The void you left when you drove away, man; I was so sure about us, I don't know why . . . Wait! I take that back; I know exactly why." Jesse pulled his hand away from Orson's and slid over closer to him, raising and folding his left knee on the seat and placing his left hand on Orson's shoulder. 'That's what's so great about this old Lincoln Continental,' he thought, 'you can just easily slide over that large seat.' "Just the way it all evolved, our long talks in the car, dancing to the blues 'til who knows when, the late dinners at those greasy spoons, the sex— Oh God! The sex!—New Orleans, and man, the coincidence of this evening. Dude! Wow! When you opened that door this evening, I thought

I was high or something!" Jesse watched Orson laugh silently, he moved his hand and placed it on top of his thigh. "I learned a long time ago not to take coincidences for granted." He then took Orson's hand and placed it between both of his. "And now this. You and I here, the sound of the rain. I could not have written anything better."

They looked at each other in silence for a few seconds until Orson laughed quietly through his nose.

"What?" Jesse wondered.

"Now I get what you mean about the raindrops hitting the roof of the car. I like it too."

"Good."

"Red," Orson gently squeezed one of Jesse's hands, "may I call you Red again?"

"God, yes! please call me Red."

"Red, there is nothing more I would like to do right now than to take you to my bed and stay there all weekend long." With his head, Orson pointed to his house, right across from where he had parked the car.

"Hey, that wasn't there before, who put your house there?"

Orson threw his head back and chuckled. "So what do you say? Do you want to spend the weekend here with me or what?

"Is there enough food in the house?"

"Thanksgiving leftovers."

"Sold!"

Orson started the car again, pulled it into the driveway. He hit the remote control to the garage door and drove to the back end of the path and into his usual parking spot. It had started raining harder, and he figured they would get very wet for he wanted to go through the front door instead of the kitchen's, which was closer. The reason being, Orson really wanted to show off his home and what better way than to begin at the foyer. They got out of the car and ran while the garage door closed behind them. Each one carrying one plastic bag filled with the leftovers, they made it to the little porch while. They went inside the house, Orson switched on the lights and did not give Jesse a chance to take off his coat, and he dropped his bag on the floor and grabbed his guy by the coat lapels and pulled him close to him. He then placed his hands on the back of Jesse's head and

142

moved close, bending down slightly and kissed him.

Feeling those dark lips pressed against his again, brought Jesse nearly to tears. He let go of the bag from his hand, and his knees started to shake, he realized Orson quickly picked up on it. The man wrapped him with his arms to hold him, just as he fantasized so many times before. If someone had told either one they would end up together by the end of Thanksgiving Day, neither would have believed it. They finished kissing, and Orson finally took off Jesse's coat and his own and hung them on the wall rack. The man proceeded to give Jesse a tour of the house. He thought if his young friend was spending the weekend, he might as well know his way around the place.

Jesse was very surprised by the décor. Scandinavian mid-century modern was the last thing he expected; he considered it was too LA even for Orson, who seemed more conventional to him. The man explained that he bought the house with the furniture in the late 1990s from an older couple who was moving to a retirement home. He loved how the clean-edged look blended perfectly with his new little 1920s bungalow. Back then, he did some research on the internet at the local library, and that's when he discovered what it was actually called and learned that Scandinavian originals were the best pieces of its kind. This was way before eBay or Google, he clarified, so he found some great deals to furnish the rest of the house. Orson had the kitchen completely redone; it needed to be contemporary and functional because he loved cooking, and a vintage flair would be impractical. He was particularly proud of the bathrooms. He did nothing to the main one; everything was original. It had survived the test of time, except for the plumbing, which he had completely redone. He eliminated a small bedroom between his bedroom and the additional bathroom to make both spaces larger. Creating direct access to that bathroom and adding a spacious walk-in shower, all in beautiful dark furnishings.

Jesse complimented Orson on his taste as the tour went on, commenting on the creative vein hidden in the man. Opportunely, they found themselves in Orson's bedroom, a medium-size space decorated slightly more traditionally. He explained that for a man his size, he needed to go for more sturdiness than design. Nevertheless, Jesse thought it was a beautiful room to spend the rest of the weekend. He still could not get over the fact that he was in Orson's house and was about to spend the night with him. Throughout the impromptu tour, all Jesse could think of was why we weren't in bed already. He desired more than anything to feel Orson's naked body next to his. He wanted to indulge him with tenderness, something he suspected the man had never received from any other man, based on bits and pieces he'd gathered from Orson himself.

The house tour officially ended when Orson moved over to Jesse and held him by the arms with his large hands. They stared at one another in silence, thinking what was next. Jesse took the lead, held Orson by the hand, led him to his bed, and sat him gently there. He proceeded to remove every piece of the man's clothing, starting with his shoes. Jesse got down on his knees and untied Orson's left sneaker and then the right. Orson just sat there quietly, following with his eyes every single move his young lover made. He breathed deeply, overwhelmed by the pampering he was receiving, living second by second in the now. Jesse took off Orson's pants and his underwear and finished by unbuttoning his shirt slowly. He held the man's hands, kissed them, and then gently nudged Orson to lean back and lay in bed, arranging a pillow between the headboard and his head. Not taking his eyes off the man, Jesse undressed. Not too fast, not too slowly. He then picked up every item of clothing and placed it on the chair next to the window that Jesse figured had that purpose. Then he rushed to hop in bed to be with Orson. They both lifted the blankets and playfully got under them. They looked at each other while their heads were resting on their respective pillows; neither could hide their joy and much less their smiles. They had wished for this moment for so long, convinced it would never happen. But there they were, together again, back in each other's arms . . . 'Home at last,' Jesse thought.

NINETEEN

ORSON WOKE UP and found himself alone in bed. He turned to look at his clock on the night table and read that it was a quarter to six in the morning. He got up and walked to the window as he does every morning. He looked out and saw that it was drizzling still. It seemed like it hadn't stopped since the night before. He made a short trip to the bathroom and put on a pair of boxers and pulled out a long-sleeve gray t-shirt from a drawer. As he stepped in the hallway, he put on the shirt and headed for the living room where he thought Jesse would be. Sure enough, he found him there, sitting in the middle of the sofa, naked with one knee bent next to his chest and the other leg folded below it. Orson watched him from the hallway, not wanting to disturb him. For a second there, he could not believe his luck, having that beautiful young man in his home. A gentle soul, who seemed to love him, bathed by the soft blue morning light from the window.

It didn't take long for Jesse to notice Orson. "Hey, Babe!" Jesse said softly, "How long have you been there?"

"I was going to ask you the same thing." Orson notice Jesse had been crying but didn't want to say anything yet. "Let me get you a blanket." he opened a narrow door in the hallway, pulled out a quilt, walked over to the sofa, sat next to Jesse, put his arm around him, and lifted the blanket open and covered themselves.

"Did you just call me Babe? I like it."

"You don't let me call you anything else."

"Have you forgotten about Mr. Nipples? You only called me that once."

"You're right! I'll make a note of that." Jesse squeezed himself next to Orson's body, while the man hugged him hard. "What time is it?"

"A little before six." Orson waited to ask: "Are you alright, Red?"

"I had a bad dream, and then I couldn't sleep."

"The same one? The one with Steven and the party?"

"Yeah, but it was different this time." Jesse paused to gather his thoughts, "this time the party was not at exactly my house, it was at the Windsor Ruins. It was weird because it was our house in LA, but there were no walls, and I was still going room by room looking for Steven. The place was still crowded like in the other dreams, and it was hard to get by." Jesse turned his head to Orson, "Do you remember you told me that the Windsor Ruins had a cast-iron stairway that was now in some college?"

"Yes, I do."

"Well, I got to the back entrance of my house. In real life, it takes you out to a patio with a swimming pool. But in the dream, when I opened the door there was Steven going down those cast-iron stairs. I remember feeling relieved because it seemed like I made it on time to save him. I was out of breath again because I'd been frantically looking for him. I wanted to go after him to catch him, but the stairs were gone. By now, the party was gone, and I found myself in my empty house with no walls. I turned to look at Steven, who was walking away. He turned his head to look at me; he smiled and then kept walking. I could not get to the ground because I was too high above it, but also it was getting dark. So I stayed there watching him going down a path, the path I saw you coming from behind the ruins that day. I was so frustrated and angry because I couldn't go after him that I woke up."

"Is that why I found you here crying."

"Well, I started crying sitting out here, thinking about the dream. It was strange because it was more of a dream than a nightmare this time, there was a comforting feeling to it."

"I don't know much about interpreting dreams, but I think you are done with this nightmare."

"That's exactly what I was thinking, and that's why I was crying. It feels like a farewell from Steven. Lauren would probably see it that way. By the way, I texted her about the dream, so she might call me back. She usually does when I text her. Even though I don't believe in her mumbo jumbo, I always find what she has to say about dreams amusing."

"Mumbo jumbo?" Said Orson, raising his left eyebrow. "That ain't nice. You're talking about what Lauren does for a living. You should be a bit more respectful of your mother's beliefs."

"But it's all speculation and theories about things that cannot be proved."

"It doesn't matter. Can you prove they are only speculations? It is important to her; it's what guides her world."

"Wow! Orson thanks. I never saw it that way."

"Well . . ."

"Who are you, Orson Davis?"

Suspicious, Orson looked Jesse in the eye and realized the guy was teasing him this time. "Get out of here." The man pulled away from his lover's hand and laughed, then moved over to kiss him on the lips.

"Jesse, I don't know if I've told you already, but once I Googled you and Steven. I saw a lot of photos of you two, and you both looked really happy. I remember feeling a bit envious."

"Well, it wasn't all fun, as I once told you, especially in the last couple of years."

"Oh, I'm sorry to hear that. I don't know why I assumed . . ."

"There were definitely some good times, but when it got bad, it was rotten."

"I'm sorry, Red; I didn't mean to be stirring up bad feelings. We can talk about something else." Orson began to get up. "I'm gonna make some coffee."

"Babe, please stay." Jesse grabbed him by the arm and stopped him. He then turned to the man, keeping his leg on the sofa and putting his other foot on the floor. He wanted to face Orson, who also postured himself to do the same. "Everyone thought we were the perfect couple. That's why they were all so shocked when the shit hit the fan."

Orson didn't want to interrupt; he rested his arm on top of the back pillow of the sofa, placing his hand on Jesse's shoulder.

"When HBO discovered our web series, and we started working with them, the money started coming in. We were ecstatic. Man, those were

147

the days. We started meeting a lot of people in the business; we were somewhat swallowed by Hollywood life. HBO produced our next show *Crescent Hill,* and it was also a hit. Right after that, we wrote *The Sketch Artist* for George Clooney, and with that money we bought our house in Laurel Canyon. Big place with a fantastic view of LA."

"Like those mansions in the movies, where you see the flat city with the little lights?"

"Just like it. When we first moved there, I would wake up every morning and actually pinch myself; I couldn't believe it. It was weird to be living the life most people moved to Hollywood for. We had it. It all seemed perfect. Steven was loving every minute of it. He came from old money, so he was used to the lifestyle. But it was all new to me, and at the beginning, it was weird to spend money so freely."

"I can't begin to imagine what that feels like."

"Well, it's fun, believe me . . . Anyway, we started throwing parties at home, and I guess that's when the dream life got distorted. Those parties got wilder every time. Of course, there were drugs; a lot of drugs. We started with a little bit at first. Then we were doing more. We even began using them to be creative with our work. We did psychedelics, and that led us to sex parties with trios and orgies with young aspiring models and actors—you name it, we did it."

Orson's eyebrows could not go any higher. He could not believe what he was hearing from Jesse's mouth; he even decided against joking about whether any of those actors were now famous. "Wow, really Red? You?"

"Yes, not just me, both Steven and me."

"But wasn't he bipolar? Taking drugs and all . . ."

"He had been lying to me about his medication for a while by then. But then he would get a bit scary sometimes."

"How?"

"Things he would sometimes say, sudden reactions he would have; things he wrote even. I convinced him that we should both go into rehab. Which we did and got out with flying colors. And it worked for a while . . ."

"Damn, you're blowing my mind. You? Rehab?"

"I hope I'm not freaking you out."

"Are you kidding?" Orson took both of Jesse's hands and squeezed them as he kissed his boy. "You just revelead a whole new dimension of you to me." He couldn't help thinking, 'I can't believe this badass boy is truly mine.'

"After rehab, we started writing *Desperate Hearts*. That script saved us for a while. It was kind of like in the beginning, taking our work seriously again. Well, as you know, the movie was huge." Jesse felt comfortable telling Orson details about his past, the details that very few knew about, not sensing the least trace of judgment from him. "We still had parties, though not as wild . . . at first. The sex with others did continue, and little by little, I started wanting to have less sex with Steven, unless there was a third or fourth person in the room with us."

Orson kept shaking his head.

"The drugs found their way back to us, and we ended up in rehab again, before it got out of hand, like the first time." Jesse continued, "That time I quit for good."

"But you drink and smoke pot with me."

"Yeah, but I can quit any time I want to. The difference this time is that I don't miss the drugs. I enjoy a good joint here and then, but I never think of is as a means of escape. But Steven struggled this time; it was hard to watch. He began having writer's block. He kept writing scripts with me, and he still had his way with words, but he had trouble coming up with creative ideas. He confessed this to me, but I could see it as well. Then he started micro-dosing to be creative and hid it from me. Orson, I was so pissed when I found out, I almost kicked him out of the house. We were working on *Random Highways* then. That was crazy, we were writing and producing, and on top of that, I had this crazy idea that I could direct most of the episodes. I guess that's when I lost perspective of what was really going on with Steven. I didn't notice Steven falling off the wagon again, and that's when everything went down to hell."

"The OD?"

"What a fucking nightmare that was. When I arrived at the house and found . . ."

Jesse's cell phone rang. It was Lauren inquiring more about the dream her son shared with her by text. Jesse took a big breath and decided to answer. He set his cell phone on speaker mode for Orson to hear.

Lauren was overjoyed to find out where and with whom her son was spending the weekend. But she was blown away by the sheer coincidence of the two men meeting again. She immediately announced it was destiny that caused their chance encounter; she was convinced of it. As usual, the son disregarded her observation, while Orson was fascinated and considered the possibility. She began to flirt a bit with Orson again to tease Jesse. The man went along with it; he could not wait to meet her. Jesse was glad they got along so well. When mother and son got talking about the nightmare, Orson left the room to give them some privacy. He finally went to the kitchen to make coffee. The phone call didn't last long, but she interpreted the dream just as Jesse had suspected she would.

Nonetheless, it was comforting to get reassurance from an expert—even if he claimed not to believe in her "mumbo jumbo." When he hung up he got off the sofa, went straight to the kitchen, barefoot, and wrapped himself in a blanket. He walked straight to Orson and put his arms around his big man. Orson took advantage of the situation and got a hold of the guy's lips and kissed them, the way that made Jesse shiver. After what appeared to be one or two minutes, Jesse was able to cut himself loose from Orson's power.

"Do you want to kill me? I haven't had my coffee yet!"

"You're right," Orson clapped his hand and rubbed against each other, "So, are we hungry on this glorious drizzling Friday morning?" He poured a cup. "Here, Red, have some coffee."

"I'm starved."

"Let me think . . ." He moved closer to Jesse and gave him another but short kiss, "Since this is your first morning at my house, how about my famous banana chocolate pancakes."

"I don't think I ever had those."

"Well, are you in for a treat, but I need to go to the store real quick to get some butter and bananas and eggs."

"Basically, everything. You work at a supermarket. You should have everything, always."

"Mr. Hucklebuns, we have a situation!" Orson joked, putting his arms around Jesse. "Let me hop in the shower, and I'll be on my way. You can stay here if you'd like, it's shitty out."

"Oh good, I can snoop around!"

"I got nothing to hide, snoop all you want," he got serious suddenly, "but don't go into my night table."

"I was just kidding, but . . ."

"So am I." Orson smiled again.

"Do you mind if I hop in the shower with you?"

"Oh, no! I'll never get out of here."

"Please, Babe, I promise I'll be good." Jesse smiled like a little boy. "I'll wash you."

That was enough for Orson to agree upon. Getting Jesse in his shower again was something he'd longed for. He had invested many hours on how, when, and what he would do to his boy, Jesse, under a water stream.

It was nearly eight o'clock when they made it out of the shower. Orson offered Jesse a large-size robe Hank and Angie had given him two Christmases before and a pair of slippers just as big the robe. Instead, Jesse declined to put on his own clothes but accepted the slippers because they were at least dryer than his own shoes. Orson got ready to go to the store, but could not find his keys or cell phone. He grabbed the spare car key from a kitchen drawer, and since Jesse was staying at home, there was no need for the house keys. Before Orson left, he took Jesse to the kitchen and walked him to the door to the backyard and taught him the Davis family password knock to let him when he got back; the old-time "Shave and a Haircut, Two Bits."

'That's it?' Jesse kept to himself.

Before Orson walked out the door, he gave Jesse what began like one of his long kisses, but purposely cut it short to tease the guy. The man opened the door and ran to the garage so he wouldn't get wet. Jesse watched from the door with shaky knees and a smile until Orson drove off. He closed the door behind him.

Not ten minutes had passed when Jesse heard a car pulling in the front driveway, and sure enough, it was followed by the Davis knocking code on the door.

"What did you forget?" He asked as he swung the door open,

"Angie!"

She was holding Orson's keys hanging from her index finger and was as surprised as the guy. "Jesse! What are you doing here?"

"Please, come in," he held the door while she entered. "Or you'll catch a cold."

"These were hanging from the lock, probably all night." She set the keys on the table in the foyer, and Jesse followed her into the living room.

"Your father was just looking for them all over the house."

"That's not the only thing he forgot," she opened her purse and pulled out Orson's cell phone and kept it in her hand.

"Did you spend the night here?" She asked with an incredulous look on her face.

"Yes," He pointed at the convenient quilt on the sofa. "Last night, your dad and I got to talking in the car, and we ended up here interviewing him about Graceland, then it got late, so he let me spend the night." He regretted saying anything at all. He was very sorry for not taking the advice from many to study acting when he first moved to LA. If there was one thing Jesse knew about himself, he was a terrible liar.

"Is my dad around?" She kept a skeptical look on her face. She then scanned down on the sly and noticed Jesse was wearing her father's slippers, then raised one of her eyebrows.

"He went to the store to get bananas."

"Don't tell me he's making those awful banana pancakes of his."

"Yes, why don't you stay for breakfast? He said he'd be right back."

"No way, thanks," She handed Orson's phone to Jesse. "Just give him this and ask him to call me." She turned and headed for the door.

"I will." Jesse followed her and tried to somehow fix the awkwardness he had created. "By the way, dinner was great last night."

"Mm-hmm." That's all she murmured as she walked out the door. Jesse stood on the porch until she left, expecting her to look back so that he could wave goodbye.

She just backed up her car and drove away.

When Orson got back a few minutes later, Jesse told him about Angie's visit. The man was not amused, but realized his guy might have broken the ice by starting "the talk" with his daughter, which was a good thing. Besides, he was feeling too great for having Jesse over and back in his life, so he happily began making his breakfast for two.

TWENTY

"ORSON, PLEASE, can we take a break?" Jesse was panting, "I don't think I can come again today, or ever again."

"But you sounded so close." Said Orson sneaking out from underneath the blanket to face his lover. "I can go on longer."

"I know you can." Jesse said between breaths, "Did you say you were 60 or 16?"

Orson laughed and moved over next to Jesse, laid sideways, resting his elbow on the pillow and his head on his hand.

"I'm sorry about earlier," the guy continued, "it hurt too much. It's been years since anyone tried to fuck me. But I'll get there, don't worry."

"Oh! I'm not worried." Orson said, half-joking, half not. "I'm getting you, boy! Sooner or later."

Jesse pretended to swallow saliva, "Yikes!"

"Maybe you're too high. I told you to go easy on the weed."

"That's not it. Could it be . . . maybe . . . just maybe, that I've come four times already in less than . . ." Jesse raised his head to look at the clock on the night table, "thirteen hours."

"Five."

"Thirteen, it's three o'clock in the afternoon."

"No, five times, you forget I blew you in the shower. That's five for you and four for me."

"For a man with so little experience, you sure are a master at it."

"Who told you I have little experience? I had my occasional quick and anonymous in the woods and rest areas off the interstate, but I was much younger. I've lost interest; cruising was never really my thing."

"Gee and I thought I was dating a . . ."

"Whoa! what? Who said that?" Orson interrupted and raised his head, and with funny, quick gestures, he swung it as if looking around the room. "Are we dating?"

"Well, we haven't had what you would call a date. Official or formal, but I'm totally into you. Dude, am I ever!"

"Well, you know, I'm nuts about you, Red! And I want you to be my boy. Are you my boy?"

"Anything I say back at you will not do justice to how I feel about you, Orson." Jesse paused briefly and then added, "And yes, I'll be your boy."

"I'm telling you, man, this is so new to me. You caught me so off guard that I never . . . at 63 . . . who would've thought? I confess I'm a little scared; I will hate it when you go."

"I'm not going anywhere, not for a while, at least. Hell, I'll be damned if I let you get away again. You mean too much to me, Orson."

"Be careful with what you say. Anything that comes out of your mouth I believe."

"I mean it, dude. You are it! There's no question about it." Jesse lifted his arm and caressed Orson's face. "Don't worry about it, Babe, we're creative people, we'll figure out something to make this work."

"Damn, Red," said Orson swinging his head from side to side slowly, "you are something else."

"Well, remember these words if you are ever unsure of us: You are stuck with me, Mr. Nipples." Jesse stopped caressing and went for Orson's right nipple and pinched it with his thumb and index finger. Orson dropped himself on top of Jesse and began tickling him with one hand aiming for Jesse's slim belly and the other hand for the armpit, and finding out how ticklish his guy was in process. The laughter led to kissing and eventually to cuddling. Orson rested his head on Jesse's chest for the first time. He tried to remember if he had ever done that before. Naturally, L.C. came to mind. He wanted that bastard to stay off his mind and keep him out of that almost sacred moment. Then he remembered that Ambar had mentioned on Thanksgiving that L.C. was trying to get a hold of him. Orson was glad he hadn't talked to L.C. in years. Therefore, he never had to worry about his ex showing up at his doorstep because he didn't know his bungalow. Ambar would never tell L.C where Orson lived. Now the bastard was trying to creep back into his life, he reckoned, and he would have none of it. He wasn't too worried about Angela running into Uncle L.C. The chances for that were slim. Besides, they hadn't seen each other in over 20 years and probably would not recognize one another. Orson still regretted meeting with L.C. a few times after Genna died, even though he swore to L.C. and himself that he never would.

But L.C. was a charmer, Orson thought, full of shit. To this day, he couldn't figure out why he had it so bad for L.C. for so long. It definitely wasn't his looks. Maybe because L.C. was his first time or maybe it was simply the sex. No, that wasn't it either. The son of a bitch would just lie there, expecting to be pleasured. The truth was that every time he saw L.C., Orson had less patience with him, until the day came when he had none. That was about the time he found his 1920s bungalow. In it, he saw the opportunity to dispose of L.C. from his life for good, and that's the way it had been ever since.

Orson loved this new side of the unknown, not certain if Jesse would go to LA or when. One thing the man was sure of, Jesse loved him, even though the word had never been mentioned, but the man was happy with just that. At that precise moment, Orson felt Jesse's arm reaching for his back; he loved the sensation of the guy's fingertips dancing softly behind him. The man held tight to his lover, finally understanding what Jesse had meant about that very first night they slept together in New Orleans, of having found home in his arms.

A few minutes had passed, maybe an hour, in silence, just the soft sound of rain outside the window, and then Orson opened his eyes.

"Red, are you hungry?"

"Not really, we had a big brunch . . . You were right about those pancakes . . ., and the sausages . . ., and the eggs . . ., and the hash-browns. Ten times better than the ones we get at the Waffle House."

"I told you!" Orson rolled over his side of the bed after quickly kissing Jesse, "I'm going to the kitchen to find myself some cereal or something." He got up, "Do you want anything?"

"Yes, please, some of that apple juice." He lifted his torso and rested it on his elbows. With his eyes, he followed Orson naked, going around the bed and couldn't help biting his lower lip. "Man, am I lucky or what? Hmm! Please, hurry back."

Orson laughed while he reached for his robe from behind the bathroom door and put it on before stepping out to go to the kitchen.

Jesse woke up when he heard his name being softly called; he opened his eyes to find Orson sitting down gently right next to him on the bed. His first thought, after seeing his smile, was I could get used to this, so he smiled right back at him. Blues music had been playing somewhere as part of his dream state, but it was just then that he noticed it had been coming from the living room all along.

"Red, dinner is almost ready," Orson said in a soft voice. "I didn't know if you wanted to take a shower before or . . ."

"Dinner? What time is it?"

"It's almost eight."

"Have you been up long?"

"For about three hours. I came back with your apple juice, and you were sleeping like a baby, smiling and all, and I didn't have the nerve to wake you."

"Have you been cooking for me all this time?"

"If heating up Thanksgiving leftovers is cooking, then yes."

"Did you say Thanksgiving leftovers?" Jesse reached out for Orson's hand and pulled it to his face and kissed it before getting up. "That's the main reason I stayed over for the weekend."

"Please, remind me later, after dinner . . . to kick your ass!"

Jesse smiled and lifted the blankets and got out of bed. He kissed the man on the cheek before going to the bathroom. Orson stayed and roughly made the bed. Jesse came back to the bedroom, and the man was by the door holding his robe, offering it to Jesse, who quickly accepted the gesture. Orson swung his arm with palm pointing up, showing out the way for the guy to go first. Jesse walked down the hallway and felt Orson's heavy hands on each shoulder from behind. He loved the sensation; there was safety in those arms.

As he approached the end of the hallway, Jesse was surprised by the orange flickering coming from the living room. By then, the music grew more intense; he was glad to recognize the tune that was playing, it was

"That Evening Train" by T-Bone Walker, the one they sang out loud on their third night in the streets of the French Quarter. When he entered the living room, the fireplace was the main source of light; the flickering glare combined with the mellow blues created a cozy, yet romantic atmosphere. Across from the fireplace, Orson had the coffee table set up as the dinning one, with silverware in carefully folded cloth napkins, and wine glasses. Jesse turned to Orson, who was smiling softly right behind him, he raised his arms and wrapped the man's neck with them, and he pulled and kissed him. Orson then excused himself and went into the kitchen. Jesse walked to the coffee table and got a good look at the setting Orson had put together. The whole ambiance reminded him of a movie set, ready to be shot. Symmetrical table placement set up, logs on the fire, a record player spinning, perfectly folded blankets and cushions on the sofa, low-dimmed lamps on each side. On the table closer to the fire, a small brass and black enamel tray with a couple of rolled joints, a book of matches and a pair of condoms. It seemed that Orson had it all planned out: dining, smoking, and lovemaking all designed and prepped for an all-nighter. He loved how neither of them seemed concerned with time, no restrictions, no rush, no need to get anywhere nor do anything. Jesse sat in front of the fire on one of the cushions he grabbed from the sofa, stared at the flames, and enjoying the heat brushing his face. For an instant, he remembered his married life in LA and how every time they had a similar romantic moment, it would always be his idea and not Steven's. He realized that was the first time anyone had done something like this for him, similar to scenes he had written in his stories. Now it was happening to him.

Jesse heard Orson moving plates around in the kitchen and humming the song playing on the record and felt his body overwhelmed by goosebumps and watery eyes followed.

He heard Orson again, "Red, are you ready?" pushing the door open. "Here the moment we've all been waiting for."

Jesse knew for certain, just then, he was very much in love with Orson.

TWENTY-ONE

JESSE WAS COMING OUT of a deep sleep. Once again, the music that had pulled him back to reality was blended again in his dream. Muffled sexy piano notes playing softly seemed to come from a few rooms away. 'That's Orson playing his music.' That thought rushed to his head as he opened his eyes; he stared at the ceiling while he listened. This is close to heaven, he mused; sensuous music while laying on soft pillows on the floor and covered by a thick blanket next to a fireplace that was almost out but still warm. By the mood of the music that was playing, 'Orson must be feeling good,' Jesse joked to himself, 'celebrating having got his way with me.' A little pot and a lot of patience were all it took to welcome the man inside him. Jesse reminisced about being more aroused by Orson's desire than the penetration itself. The animal look in his eyes, followed by his groaning excited Jesse beyond any expectation. As he laid on his back, he watched the whole of Orson thrusting away; making Jesse surrender in a manner he didn't know it was possible. Who would have thought that a casual encounter in a supermarket would scale up to what they have now.

Enthralled by the music, Jesse wandered away, imagining Orson living in California. Hell, the man's house was already so LA. Would he get used to the traffic? To one season? Or the lifestyle? Jesse had thought about the possibility of moving to Memphis. I could write from here, then fly back for shootings. Or could they live half a year on the east coast and the rest on the west? Was Orson even ready to talk about it?

Too much thinking for the wee hours of the morning, Jesse concluded, so he got up and wrapped the blanket around his nakedness. He followed the music and almost went into the hallway when he realized it was coming from the kitchen. He entered through the swinging door, and it still wasn't there, even though the melody sounded clearer. He opened what seemed to him to be the door to the basement; there were stairs, a light on, and blues playing at the end of them. He descended slowly, so as not to disturb the player. As he made it to the last three steps, he sat down quietly and listened. For the very first time, he watched Orson playing his blues. The man looked very focused, reading music from a small bright yellow notebook. Jesse recognized it as the one he had hidden in the man's suitcase while he waited for him at the Windsor Ruins many weeks before. He also noticed the eyeglasses; he loved it when Orson wore them. 'They make him look so cute and so distinguished,' he thought, 'I must ask him to wear them more often.' Jesse watched him stop and pick a pencil from behind his ear to fix a note on paper, the perfect moment to interrupt him. Jesse cleared his throat.

"Damn it, boy!" Orson jumped on his seat, then turned around to face Jesse. He picked up his phone, which had been sitting on the piano, and switched off the recorder. "Are you trying to kill me?"

"Sorry, Babe." Jesse got up, walked to Orson, embraced him from behind, then leaned over and kissed him.

"How long have you been sitting there, watching me?"

"Less than a minute, but I heard most of it from upstairs. It sounded great. What was it?"

"Please, Red." He had eased down, moving the glasses to the top of his head. "Don't sneak up on me like that, I don't like it. I think it's a reaction that I brought back from Vietnam, so bear with me."

"I won't do it again." Jesse moved over by the piano to face Orson.

"What was that piece? Was it one of yours?"

"Yes, it's mine, but it is not finished."

"Finished or not, it sounded great."

"You're not just saying that, are you Red?"

"No, it was really cool. I liked the sexy flair you got going there."

"You're just saying that because it's me."

"No dude, I'm no musician, but I've got good intuition for music. And that was good. Short, but good."

"Damn! That's good to hear." Orson smiled at Jesse while lowering his head, not to see him through his eyeglasses. "That's what my buddies tell me."

"What else do you have?" Jesse pointed at the notebook Orson had been writing on. "I see you kept the notebook I left for you. I figured you would have burned it or something."

"No! Of course I kept it. You got me with the dedication you wrote in it. I had to keep it."

"You told me one time that you have a few of those notebooks. How many do you have so far?"

"Funny you should ask." Orson got up and lifted the lid from the piano stool and revealed the rest of them. Upright and proud, he said, "I've got thirty-seven."

"Wow!" Jesse leaned over and took one of the notebooks, one with a blue and green stripes cover, and flipped through the pages. "And you haven't played anything from them."

"Hardly. I make up the music in my head and put it on paper, but I never played them until recently."

"So, do you know them all by heart?"

"Of course not, are you kidding? But most of them, if not all of them are just melodies, no intro, no bridge or end."

"What? Really?"

"I get bored easily. I stay with the essence."

"I hope you don't get bored with me one day and toss me under your piano stool."

"You? Naah!" Orson reached out with his hand, pulled Jesse closer, and kissed his cheek. "Like I said, I keep the essence." He watched Jesse go through the notebook some more.

"Have you ever written complete pieces?"

"Yes, I have complete music sheets and everything."

"I'd love to hear them."

"I'd love to hear them too. But I have to find them first. I lost them a long time ago in one of my moves."

"Can you remember any of them?"

"Not really, if it wasn't for all the years passed and all those jays I smoked, my memory of them wouldn't be so distorted. Seriously, they date back to my army years. I can recall only a few notes, that's all."

"Oh! For a minute there, I thought you were some kind of genius."

"Thanks, pal." Answered Orson with playful irony.

"No! I mean, you are a genius . . ."

"Forget it, Red," Orson interrupted with a smile, "too late to fix it, buddy."

"Mr. Hucklebuns, we have a situation."

Orson laughed out loud, and without a sign or warning, he uttered, "I love you, Jesse." He suddenly turned as pale as a person of his shade of black could get, while his eyes opened wide.

"Don't look so spooked, man." Jesse smiled, "I love you too, silly. C'mere." He opened his arms and moved towards Orson, the man met him halfway, and they embraced. "There, we said it. Doesn't it feel good?"

"It sure does." He squeezed Jesse hard before releasing. "Hmmm!"

"Now that that is out of the way, I would love to hear some more of your music."

Jesse leaned over the open stool and started browsing through the notebooks, "Would you indulge me?"

"Now?"

"Sure, why not. We don't have to be anywhere this weekend."

"You do remember I'm working tomorrow night, right?"

"I know, I wanna get some work done in the meantime, plus I wanna go running, too."

Jesse chose a small red notebook that looked like it had a few years on it, "but now is now, and I would love to hear you play for me, please."

"Do you know what time it is?" Orson picked up his phone from the piano to look at the time.

"Please don't tell me, I don't care to know." He watched the man putting it back without looking at the screen. "I think we have some kind of jet lag."

"Don't you mean sex lag?"

Jesse laughed. "Good one! Do you mind if I borrow it for a script?"

"Be my guest." Orson looked at Jesse's notebook selection and began flipping through the pages. "Number sixteen, that's one of my oldies, but horrid." He gave the notebook back to Jesse. "So, which one do you wanna hear?"

He flipped through the middle pages again. "I like that they at least have titles." He stopped at a fold. "How about this one? 'Broken Blues.'"

Orson moved his glasses from his head and slowly swooped them back to his nose. "Let's see . . ." He read the first four notes as he sat back on his stool. "You should sit down for this one. It may depress you." He told Jesse, then placed the open notebook leaning against the music rack, turned on the recorder on his phone, and started rehearsing out the first few notes.

Jesse scanned around the room to find a place to sit down. Orson swung his head, pointing to the back of the room. The guy looked over some boxes and then went to where the man suggested and brought back a vintage butterfly chair with brown leather seating, then placed it next to the piano.

Orson tried to stay focused while Jesse sat; he was doing good until the guy revealed himself from his quilted garment and sat naked on the chair. The man stopped playing and watched Jesse repositioning himself on the butterfly chair unconventionally, placing his legs on each side of the right corner and then resting his head on the opposite larger one. It was obvious to Orson that Jesse was familiar to this cool, but rather uncomfortable at times, classic piece of furniture. Finally, Jesse spread the quilt over himself and settled in.

Jesse watched as Orson played away, concentrating on the piece. It was obvious the man was trying to make a good impression since it was the very first time he played for him. Jesse was mesmerized by the notes, how one followed the next in a flawless tempo, creating a melancholic atmosphere. He could almost feel the room turning gloomy, breathing its sadness, even. 'Changing the mood of the space, the same way a score does to a film,' Jesse thought as his eyes closed. He was glad to be sitting down, for he sensed he was growing more blue by the minute, intoxicated by Orson's melody.

By the fourth piece in a row from notebook 16, Orson looked at his one-man audience and saw that he had fallen into a deep sleep. He understood. Such a passionate weekend could drain anyone causing them to look the way Jesse did again, smiling like a child. He switched off the recording, then turned sideways on his seat, and leaned over to face his boy Red, resting his elbows on his lap and joining his hands. He studied his face for a couple of minutes. He recalled that during their break up, he had a hard time remembering the details of Jesse's face after deleting the photos from his cell phone. Orson admired the lack of flaws in his lover's face. Perfect nose, faded blonde curls, stunning green eyes hidden under those eyelids with precious golden lashes. He had to stop at the lips, those sensuous reds he fantasized kissing so many times during their hiatus. 'Why would anyone so fucking gorgeous give me the time of day?' Orson wondered. 'Jesse could have anyone, and he chose me; fortunate bastard.'

Orson looked over behind him, to the opposite side of his piano, at the small cellar window next to the ceiling and realized daytime was showing signs of coming. He stood up quietly and walked to the light switch next to the stairs and turned it off, all the time watching Jesse, making sure not to disturb his sleep. Then he walked towards the window and stood right in front of it, grateful again he was tall enough to have a perfect view of his backyard. He folded his arms on the sill and rested his chin on them. He truly loved the soft morning light, showing his favorite shade of blue; and to top it off, it had just started raining again. Orson felt hypnotized by sight and sound, not even blinking at the sublime, yet timid setting. Jesse's voice snapped him out of his trance. The words that came out of Orson's own mouth right after left him baffled. "What, love?" he had said while he turned to look at Jesse, who was very much asleep and had mumbled a few nothings. He turned to his window again, thinking about those two words he had just spoken. The mixture of melancholy and pure joy produced shivers all over his skin. Then it hit him: insight, notes, impulse, and rhythm, all into one. He took one last look outside, wanting to permeate the sensation. Gently, but quickly, Orson walked over to his piano and sat back on his stool. What he had in mind was perfect and wouldn't bother Jesse. He switched the recording app back on and started playing two soft notes repetitively, something sweet that emulated rain. He looked over at Jesse a second time, and his boy looked the same way as he had left him, with his eyes closed and a soft, yet sweet grin on his lips. Orson continued playing, adding notes to what he had begun creating, and birthing the blues texture he needed. He then stopped and wrote in his small notebook. He looked at Jesse one more time and briefly paid attention to the rain, then he played again some more and wrote some more.

TWENTY-TWO

RED, DO YOU RECALL that day when we rode to the lake in my brand-new Imperial?

Remember? You were in the shower at my house when I decided to surprise you with a short country road trip. I had left you a note on top of your clothes to meet me in the garage out back. The look on your face when you found me all leathered up and ready to go . . . I was so surprised you were familiar with the bike; little did I know it was featured in one of your shows, *Random Highways*, I think you said. By the way, we haven't named the bike yet. When you wake up, that's the first thing we'll do: name it and go for a spin.

It was nice to be outdoors for a change. Thanksgiving weekend was still not over yet. It had been raining for days, and finally, the sun had come out, and I thought we needed a bit of fresh air. The perfect excuse to take my new bike for a spin and hopefully score a few more points with you. The sun was beaming and warm on us among the autumn winds. Once we left the highway behind and drove on the back, lonely roads, you timidly put your hands on each side of my belly. And yes, I noticed when you caressed me discreetly, not knowing if I'd mind. Well, I didn't; I loved it.

Anyway, once we got to the lake, I didn't dare to tell you that it was actually my secret place. I couldn't put those words together. I thought it would sound so corny, so I held back. I remember putting my arm around your shoulder while we walked. I was amazed at myself by this display of affection out in broad daylight. But with you, Red, I did many things for the first time.

Well, the trees along the edge of the lake seemed to be showing off for us, all golden, bright orange, and brown. Their reflection on the water made them all seem bigger than life. The sound of stepping on dry leaves has always been music to my ears, in the fall especially. Each season has its own particular sound, and I regret not having shared that thought with you then, the same goes for not telling you that that was my secret place. Well, I'm doing it now.

At some point during our walk, you mentioned your concern about Angela's unexpected visit two days before. Like Hank, you wondered when I would have "the talk" with her. You felt that since we had taken our story to the next level, it would be good to get that out of the way. I still had my doubts as I do now.

"I actually never had to tell anyone."

"What about L.C. and Ambar?" You asked. "You told them."

"No, I didn't," I added, "with L.C., we never talked about it. Ambar just knew because she was friends with him. But the word gay never came up. There was never a need to do so. I didn't have to tell anyone I was straight, either. Everyone just assumed I was, for my size, I guess, and the way I act."

"Yeah, you had me fooled for the longest time."

"I never felt like what people refer to as gay. I simply happen to like men. Besides, I hated having to put another label on myself. You know how I feel about labels. Being black is enough of a label for me. You white folks never have to label yourselves as such, but you do when you're other than straight, Christian, and white; in this country, anyway."

"Wow, I never saw it that way; you are right. It's like, I am half Hispanic, but because of the way I look, no one ever questioned me about it. Sometimes, when I say my last name . . ."

"That's not what I mean at all, but I hear you. I dig what you're saying."

"So, Babe, have you thought about what are you going to tell her?"

"I don't really know. I guess I'll start with Uncle L.C. and take it from there." I remember pausing for a second. "I can already see the look on her face when I do."

"I think I know the look, the same she had when she saw I had your slippers on."

170

"I'm going over to their house next weekend. Hank wants me to take a look at his car, and I will probably stay for lunch. So I guess after lunch, it will be as good a time as any."

"Don't you think Hank may have told Angie already?"

"If I know Hank, he's waiting for me to tell her. He would never say anything."

"Hank's great." You added. "I could see the two of us becoming best friends until you came back into the picture . . ."

"Hey!" My reaction was to stop and turn to face you.

"Mr. Hucklebuns . . ." You then raised your heels with a smile and kissed me on the lips, and we continued on our walk. "Hank's all excited about us, you know? He texted me about it yesterday, or the day before, I forgot to tell you."

"He sure is the best," I reaffirmed. "Between you and me, Red, sometimes I think Angela takes him for granted. In fact, I've come to think she doesn't even love him."

"Dude, I don't wanna talk about this, Hank's my friend."

"I'm not really sure. It's what I sense when I go see them."

"Hank has told me a few things for me to suspect that that's the case, but I prefer if you and I didn't discuss this, I don't think Hank would like it."

"I just hope they're OK for Gennie's sake."

"Hey, do you want me to go with you next weekend?"

"No!" I stopped, removing my arm from around your shoulder. "Is hard enough for me to tell her I liked men all my life, but to show up with the young white boy I am shacking up with, I think not."

"You're right, Babe. I realized it wasn't a good idea halfway through my question."

"It will be better if you're not there." I put my arm on your shoulders again, and we both continued walking. "I will probably tell Hank to take Gennie out for ice cream or something. Angela's tough. We don't see eye to eye on many things. It's always been like that, even before Genna died."

"Always? Really?"

"Well, for as long as I can remember, Angela and I never liked each other. I love her; don't get me wrong; she's my only child. We got along well when she was little, but she was always more loving and responsive to her mother. When she turned ten or eleven, we just didn't enjoy spending time alone with one another. I would tell Genna about this, but she wouldn't hear of it, she thought it was nonsense. She said I had to work harder to gain Angela's love. And then when Genna was killed, it got worse. Angela became reclusive and hostile towards me."

"Did she ever blame you for Genna's death? I know you told me she doesn't know the whole story."

"If she would have known, believe me, she would have brought it up in many of our fights. Jesse, when I think about those fights that she and I used to have, man, am I glad those teenage years are done with."

"I'm sorry to hear that. I didn't know it was that bad between you two."

"It's really not that bad anymore. Nowadays, we respect each other's boundaries. But we do love each other, we do, but in our own particular way. Hank has played a big role in the way things are now between Angela and me."

"What do you mean?"

"When Angela first met Hank, she became a whole different person. I went to see them in DC one time, and she was happier than I'd ever seen her before. When she introduced Hank to me, it was love at first sight for me. He felt like the son I never had. Then she became a bit jealous of us. Hank and I hung out in the city, you know, to show me around DC, and she would get all upset.

"In any case, thanks to him, she and I talked on the phone more to each other, well, the three of us, actually. Then I know Angela and Hank started having serious ups and downs until she got pregnant with Gennie. They thought getting married would be the best for them with a baby on the way and all . . . After the baby was born, she seemed a much happier and loving person. I thought for a while that the old Angela was gone for good. That was about the time they first moved to Memphis. But I guess the routine of everyday life took its toll on her, and she started returning to her old self. Well, maybe not as bad as before, but she became all serious again." I stopped in front of a bush and pulled my arm from you again. "Listen, Red, that's not why I brought you here; definitely not to

172

talk about Angela, so do you mind if we change the subject?"

"Not at all. I'm sorry I brought it up."

"Don't be," I then took you by the hand, "just follow me."

I turned my back to you and bent over a little to get through an opening in the bushes that had a path underneath. I pulled you inside, and we walked a few feet with shrunken shoulders before I led you to a large and massive rock. A large limestone formation of about 15 feet high and probably about 20 feet wide. Why am I telling you this? You were there. As you saw, it's totally irregularly shaped, but it was easy to climb. I went up first, and you followed. I remember being too concerned about your safety, but you seemed to know your way around the rock. I was a bit disappointed that you didn't need my helping hand. I wanted so bad to show off my gentlemanly ways. You must have noticed it because you took my hand at the last step up. We walked over the basically flat top. You wouldn't let go of my hand, and I loved it. I took you to the opposite edge to admire the lake from above.

"Wow!" You said, then turned to look up at me. "This is absolutely gorgeous. How come there's no one here?"

"It's private property, and it belongs to a friend of mine, an old client from when I had the shop. He lets me come whenever I want."

"Orson, I wish I had friends like yours."

"Well, the truth is I don't have that many friends. You've basically met them all." I unzipped my jacket and using your hand as aid, I sat down on the hard ground facing the lake. I stretched my legs and leaned back with my elbows on the rock. "I know lots of people, but true friends, I can count them with a hand and a half. Anyway, I call this place 'My Meditation Rock.'"

"You named it that?"

"Yes, I've come quite a few times. When I am feeling down or lonely, I bring my music player, a couple of beers, and maybe a doobie. This is the first time I didn't come alone."

"Really, Orson?" You asked as you sat down next to me but preferred crossing your legs with your stretched arms behind you with your hands on the ground. I liked that you sat so close to me, with your arm touching my knee.

Not thirty seconds had passed when I caught you smiling. When I asked you about it, you pointed out that I was swinging my foot left and right like a windshield wiper at top speed. According to you, that was a dead giveaway that I had something on my mind that sooner or later would come out. I recall feeling flattered that you knew me so well, and at the same time, I wanted to come clean. I announced I had something for you. From inside my jacket, I nervously pulled out a set of earphones and let them hang from my hand.

"Gee, thanks," You extended your hand open. "I always wanted an old secondhand set of these."

"You're spoiling the moment, Love."

"We're having a moment?"

"Jesse, do me a favor and shut up, will you?" I opened the other flap from my jacket and took out my phone and started searching through it. "Early this morning, I came up with a little piece of music I think you'd like."

"You mean when I slept right through your performance this morning? Babe, I can't apologize enough."

"I'm glad you fell asleep; otherwise, there would be no surprise for you."

"Cool!" You said as I was still looking for the damn song I couldn't find on my phone. Then you snapped: "So?!"

"Patience."

"No! What else do wanna say? Your foot is shaking again."

"Damn," I finally found the song. "Stop that. It freaks me out that you know me this well."

"So, what is it?"

"Actually," I reached out for the headset you were holding and plugged the end jack to my phone. "I wrote it thinking about our last couple of days and how we have been able to . . ." I paused for a few seconds until I finally got the courage to tell you, "Hell! I wrote it for you." Today, I still don't know what I was so nervous about, but Red, I wish you could have seen the look on your face at my words. It was beautiful. Your face glowed, and your eyes instantly watered. Your reaction moved me; it made my heart beat stronger. I asked you if you were ready for the song. You could hardly nod, much less speak. I hit play, and you immediately turned your head to look at the lake. You either wanted to concentrate on the song or didn't want me to see you get emotional. And boy, did you get emotional! You moved your hand over to me and took mine while you listened; you squeezed it from time to time. I enjoyed watching you, swinging your head from side to side; I assumed in disbelief, all of that while trying to restrain your tears. No such luck, that's what I love about you: it's all out there with you.

When the song was over, you pulled out one bud from one ear and then the other; then turned your head softly to look at me. I read the whole world in your eyes. No one had ever looked at me that way. If I wasn't sure before that you were in love with me, I was convinced right then and there. And I fell right back in love with you too, all over again. I had never felt such goosebumps before, on my feet, my legs, my arms, my spine, my head, and on up to the tips of my hair.

"Wow!" You moved your open right hand towards your heart. "That was beautiful, Orson. Look at me; I'm a mess." Then you started to wipe the tears with your fingers.

I reached into one of the side pockets of my jacket, pulled a small pack of tissues, opened it, and offered it to you.

"What else do you have in those pockets?" You picked a tissue and then blew your nose.

"Funny, you should ask." I reached into my other outer pocket and pulled out a hand-rolled joint and a mini lighter. I placed it on your lips and lit up. You took a long puff and held it for a brief few seconds before letting go.

"What a gift, Orson. I love the song."

"Do you really, Red?"

"Yes, I could almost hear the words to it. What's it called?"

" 'Gentle Rain.' "

"Perfect. Just perfect." With the help of your hands, you got on your knees and moved closer to me and kissed me. I'd never been kissed at my lake, at my secret place, on Meditation Rock. I wrapped you in my arms, and you let your body fall gently on me, and at that moment, I felt I had it all. I needed nothing else.

One minute later—or an hour later, who knows—I released you and took a long drag off the jay.

"So why don't you?"

"Why don't I what?"

"Put words to the song."

"I could try."

"It will be your gift to me." I said, "I'd love to hear what you'd do to it."

"Send it to my phone; let me see what I can do. I don't guarantee anything, but . . ." You moved over back to where you were seated before, but rested your body on your elbows with your legs stretched out, just like I was. "And, please send me any other songs you think I would like. I don't care if they are not finished. Hell, send me all you got. I'd love to hear them all." You turned to look at me again, "Thank you, Orson. Thanks for the song. The best present, no kidding. It's the ultimate love offering."

You then rolled to your side, resting your head on your hand and your elbow on the rock. I turned the same way to face you. We stared into each other's eyes and didn't say a word. It didn't take long for me to start kissing you again. I just couldn't help it. Not sure whether it was your soft young lips that I loved tasting or your trembling response to what I was doing to them. In either case, I was heaven bound.

I remember that you stretched your arm over to reach in my pants. By the time you undid the third button, I was already hard. You grabbed my cock and stroked it a few times. Although I was extremely turned on, I stopped you by pulling your hand out of my pants. Without giving any kind of explanation, I got up, holding my pants by its opening with one hand. Your surprised eyes just stared at me. I offered you my other hand to pull you up. I started walking to the opposite edge of the rock from where we came. Puzzled, you had no choice but to follow me in silence. I went first, and this time you let me hold your hand all the way as we climbed down the rock. Once we reached level ground, I stopped, and I turned around. Just when you were about to ask what the hell was going on, I looked at you, and I could tell you had read my mind. Sensing that I was telling you to trust me, I felt the surrendered grip of your hand.

I turned back to the path that continued around the lake. You followed me again. I wonder if you remember all of this as vividly as I do. We walked a few feet down the trail, and when you least expected it, I took a sudden turn into the woods. I knew exactly where to go; you just tagged along, trusting my every move. The sounds of nature seemed more enhanced as we ambled our way into the forest. Maybe it was the weed; it didn't matter. I just wanted to get to the spot I had in mind. A few more feet and I finally found it—a clearing in the woods, a space of almost 10 yards in diameter. I led you to the trunk of a tree that had fallen many years before. I sat down on it, finally letting go of my pants. There was no need for words, you had started something, and we saw to it that you would finish. You got on your knees between my legs, not caring to take off your pants and getting the dirt on them. I just sat there feeling like the king of the forest staring at the beautiful view. The sun, the sky, the trees, my beautiful lover looking up at me with those deep green eyes. All of it belonged to me.

TWENTY-THREE

IT WAS PAST TWO in the morning when Orson pulled into Jesse's driveway for the second time that night. He saw Red coming out of the house before he stopped the car. The first thing he noticed was Jesse's wet hair and change of clothes. When Orson had dropped him off six hours earlier to go to work, he left him with muddy jeans and the same clothes he had been wearing since Thanksgiving. 'If I know my Red,' the man thought, 'he must have been busy and left the shower for the very last thing.' He watched Jesse turn the lights off, close the door behind him, and getting quickly inside the car with a big smile on his face.

"What happened to the bike?" Jesse asked right after kissing Orson.

"It was too cold to ride at night, so I went home to get Abe after work, that's why I'm late." Orson started the car and drove off. "You look happy."

"Happy to see you, Babe." He grabbed Orson's hand and squeezed it. "Also, I got a lot done. I even went out for a run. I feel vitalized. By the way, I talked to Lauren again."

"How's she doing?"

"She's good. She's back in San Diego." Jesse moved over to kiss Orson on the cheek and got back to his spot and put on his seatbelt. "That's from her. She sends her love."

"Red, are you high?"

"No! Why?"

"You're acting all juiced up."

"Well, I wanted to talk to you, but I want to wait till we get back to your house."

"What is it, is Lauren OK?"

179

"Yes, she's fine," Jesse said, confused about why Orson brought up Lauren again. "No! It's about your music."

"What about it?"

"I've listened to all the tracks you sent me. A few times, as a matter of fact. And I love them, every one of them. Your music is great, dude."

"You think?" Orson turned his head to look at Jesse.

"Why are you still so surprised?" Jesse asked. "Hey, I'm no blues expert, I'm merely learning about the genre. Your music, my friend, blew me away. Hell, I'm even thinking about you doing the score for this thing I'm working on."

As he kept driving, Orson turned his head a few times to try and catch a glimpse of Jesse's eyes, to be certain his boy wasn't kidding.

"Dude," said Jesse raising his eyebrows and opening both palms facing one another. "I'm dead serious! I know music. Who do you think picks the music for our shows? Orson, I don't mean to brag, but the soundtrack for *Random Highways* did really well, and the score for *The Sketch Artist* was nominated for a Grammy, so I think I have enough authority to say what's good, even if it's blues."

"My music is very basic."

"Wait, why do you think that?"

"I don't know. I always thought it was average."

"Bull! Not only do you play well, but what you write is great. I'm curious," he paused "who put that idea into your head, that your music was just OK? Even your friends say you're great."

"Well, L.C., probably," Orson paused. "He used to say that I should make a career in anything else but music."

"You're kidding, right?" Jesse was annoyed. "Who made L.C. such an expert?"

"Well . . ."

"Orson," Jesse interrupted with an irritated tone. "whatever he said to you is such bullshit. He was probably envious of you."

"I haven't thought about it in years, but he used to say my songs, my playing, and even my singing was average. But I just kept doing it as a hobby because I loved it."

"But aren't you upset that L.C. would say such a thing about your favorite thing to do? You could have had a great music career."

"I don't care about that. I had a great career as a mechanic, and I loved every minute of it." Orson turned his head briefly to Jesse. "You're obviously upset enough for the two of us. Are you OK?"

"I'm fine. But I'm telling you, every time L.C. comes up in conversation; it becomes clearer to me what an asshole he really is. And yes, I'm pissed off, because you're not only good, you are fantastic!"

"I know I haven't said anything nice about him, but in Nam, he was very insistent that I learn music theory. If it wasn't for him, I wouldn't have written all these songs that you think are so great."

"Listen to yourself. Your songs are great. Now I have to convince you that they are. C'mon, that guy obviously distorted your self-esteem…"

"Jesse, take it easy." Orson saw Jesse's face changing. "My self-esteem is just fine."

"Your musical self-esteem, then." Jesse realized he might have been overreacting a bit. "I'll bet you're a good singer, too."

"No one ever complained."

"I heard you hum a bit, even sing a few notes at home, and you sing just fine. In fact…" Jesse stopped talking, sorry he had started the sentence.

"What?"

"Well, I've been thinking. Maybe tomorrow night, we could go to The Grasshopper for open mic night. You could play a little. You don't have to sing, just play."

"Fuck me . . ." Orson nearly whispered.

"What is it?"

"Just an hour ago, I was considering the same idea. It's like you read my mind, son . . . I mean, Red!"

"So, that's settled, you're doing The Grasshopper tomorrow night."

"Sure, why not. But just the piano! I ain't singing in public. Only you get to hear that." Orson took his right hand off the wheel momentarily and got hold of Jesse's left cheek and caressed it. "Ambar is going to get a big kick out of it. She's been trying to convince me to take part in the Sunday Night Jam Session for years, and you've done it in less than five seconds."

"Well, you've been thinking about doing it too."

"You know what this means, don't you?" Keeping his eyes on the road, Orson leaned a little bit towards Jesse while pulling his hand; he then kissed it. "We have to stay in tomorrow, I would have to practice all day, and I don't wanna make a fool of myself."

"You mean in a few hours? That's cool. I'll have a rehearsal concert all to myself. I also could get some work done; I brought my laptop with me," said Jesse patting the backpack he'd put on the floor between his legs. "It will be fun. We could work a bit in the morning, make a little love, work some more, order pizza, make more love, take a nap; does that sound to you?"

Orson just laughed as he listened. He realized he had been the subject of conversation throughout the drive home. He wanted to know all the things that Jesse had claimed had kept him busy. When he asked, Jesse seemed evasive at first, but when they finally arrived home a few minutes later, he responded.

Besides going for a run, he explained, he did a bit of laundry, talked to Lauren and consequently to his parents, and caught up on his emails. Most importantly, he had been working on *Amazing Graceland*. Orson got excited about it. He wanted to hear more about it; during their falling out, he had wondered every now and then whether that story was still in the works, but he had forgotten to ask.

While they were getting ready to go to bed, Orson kept bugging Jesse to tell him all about the work in progress. The guy told him to be patient; he would make the tale a bedtime story; those were magic words for Orson. Jesse finished brushing his teeth and walked into the bedroom, finding Orson sitting shirtless under the blankets with his back against the headboard, all poised like a good schoolboy. A golden halo on his head and a small bell will ring at any second now, Jesse imagined as he smiled back at his man. He couldn't help it. He literally ran to Orson and jumped on the bed to join him.

"Picture this," Jesse started, "Hurricane Katrina hits the south, Memphis is flooded, and Graceland closes to the public for repairs of damage caused by the rains. During renovations, two reel-to-reel tapes surface labeled 'Otis and Elvis' in The King's handwriting. They turn out to be a series of blues tracks sung by Elvis accompanied by a single piano, all unknown songs. No one knows who the hell Otis is. The Graceland staff contact a local newspaper to get the story out. Enter James Sanders, a freelance writer for *Rolling Stone* magazine."

"So you're in the story too."

"Of course I'm in it, do you think I'm going to leave you all alone on this? Anyway, James is thirsty for new work and starts his own search for this Otis person in the hopes of getting good money for the story. Through the studio label on the reel-to-reel tapes, James finds out the recordings were made in Graceland, concurring with the time RCA set up a temporary recording studio in the Jungle Room."

"Did you make this up?"

"No, this is actually a fact. Elvis's contract called for RCA to release two albums a year. By 1976 he was touring a lot and insisted on spending as much time as possible at home, so basically the Colonel and RCA brought the studio to him, and the Jungle Room was the best place for it."

"You've been doing your homework."

"Of course, this is how I make the big bucks." He air-drew the dollar sign with his right index finger.

"Please, go on, this is great."

"Well, James discovers that an Otis Danson worked briefly as a security guard in Graceland between 1975 and 1976. After many phone calls and countless dead-ends, he eventually tracks down Otis, retired and living in Chicago with his son. He flies there to interview him. Otis tells him that at the time he worked in Graceland, he was going through rough times. His wife had kicked him out of the house, and he was basically living in his car, so whenever he had the chance, he would spend time inside Graceland. One night after a recording session, Otis thought everyone had left the mansion to go out drinking or something. I'm still not sure, but anyway, he went into the Jungle Room and found the piano there. The sight was irresistible to him, and thinking he was all alone, he sat at the piano and started playing. About twenty minutes after Otis began playing, who walks in in his silken robe with a big golden monogram?"

"Liberace?"

Jesse could not believe Orson's funny reply. He laughed out loud and leaned over his shoulder and pressed his head against it briefly.

"Anyway, Otis freaked out, convinced he would be fired on the spot. But, no. Elvis knew Otis and liked him. One of the reasons The King hired him in the first place was the fact that he, as Elvis had, had also served in the army and at the same camp in Friedberg, West Germany, though at different times. Elvis wanted Otis to play some more, intrigued by all the unknown material. Otis told him they were his own compositions and that it would be an honor to play them for him. Elvis loved the sound. It had been years since The King had wanted to go back to basics, and he saw in Otis' music a vehicle to do so. That night Elvis and Otis had bonded through music. What do you think so far?"

"Wow, Red! I love it."

"I haven't figured out yet how and when Elvis learns the songs, whether or not they make the recordings that very night or how these tracks get lost."

"I have no doubt you'll figure out something great."

Orson was blown away by his boy's imagination. How a writer could come up with various characters and give them fully developed personalities was always amazing to him. A sudden pang of guilt hit him for not having watched Jesse's work on any type of screen. He almost did, during their break up, but he thought it would be too painful to see, hear, or feel any trace of Jesse during that period. In any case, he loved his talent and was happy to learn the guy felt the same about his. Jesse always had great respect for composers; he admired the gift of fusing notes to create a melody, the guy had grown very fond of Orson, not only as a lover but as a music maker.

Like on the previous nights, they talked, played, and giggled till they fell asleep, not knowing exactly who had dozed off first. Eventually, one of them would wake up to find the lights on. He would switch them off and would turn himself sideways and hug his way to sleep. If it were Orson, he would spoon; if it were Jesse, he would find his spot within his man's arms. "Sweet dreams," one would whisper softly to the other as their eyes closed.

TWENTY-FOUR

JESSE STILL COULDN'T BELIEVE he was driving Orson's precious Abe. He had begged Orson to let him drive it a few times, knowing he would get 'no' for an answer. Little did he know that all that teasing would finally pay off. But now that he was behind the wheel, Jesse was paranoid, fearing that something would happen to his boyfriend's most sacred possession.

The truth of the matter was that Orson was extremely nervous, having second thoughts about performing that very night, and regretting what he'd gotten himself into. The Grasshopper's Sunday Night Jam Session was well known among blues lovers and definitely not amateur night. It was too late to back out now; Jesse was all excited about it, and Orson had just texted Ambar that he would take part in the open mic night at her bar. And it was likely that she had already spread the word around the joint.

From the corner of his eye, Jesse could see Orson moving about in his seat, switching on the light and flicking his visor to look at himself in the mirror again. For the fourth time, he had watched the man opening and closing the glove compartment looking for nothing in particular. But then Orson started asking weird questions, like if he should have worn a bowtie or if his sideburns were even. They were driving on Millington Road, off the North of Westside, Memphis, and were just a couple of miles away from The Grasshopper. It was an empty stretch of a two-way lane surrounded by trees, and Jesse had seen the perfect spot to pull over. He slowly drove onto the side of the road on the grass. He switched off the car but leaving the lights on. He then turned to Orson with a gentle smile.

"What's up, Babe?"

"Nothing, why?"

"Hey, I know you." Jesse reached over with his arm and caressed the back of Orson's neck with his fingertips. "You're nervous about tonight, aren't you?"

"Me? Nervous? Nah!" Orson remarked. "I'm scared shitless. Jesse, I haven't performed in public since the nineties."

"Fuck, I didn't know it's been that long. But hey! What's the worst that can happen?"

"That I'll make a fool of myself?"

"Orson, you've been rehearsing all day, and you sounded great."

"You're probably right, but your words don't help, I'm grateful, tho—"

"How about a blow job?" Jesse blurted out. "Would that help?"

"Say what?" said the surprised Orson.

"You heard me. Would that help?"

"Damn, Red." He looked at Jesse in the eye, half-smiling, thinking his guy was joking. "You are serious."

"Of course, I'm serious. I'll do whatever it takes to help you relax, and I'll have a little fun of my own in the process."

Jesse watched Orson as he quickly started unzipping his jeans. The man looked back at him with a naughty look in his eyes.

"Fuck!" Yelled Orson jumping in his seat as his playful face had morphed into fear.

Jesse quickly turned to see what got his lover so spooked. An old dark orange Camaro was halted right beside them, evidently on the wrong lane. The driver's face was just a few inches away, staring at them, and he wasn't alone. There were two men, both in their early twenties, it oddly occurred to Jesse that the one in the passenger seat had something under his nose you could barely call a mustache, the driver had a similar thing going on under his chin. 'Are these two brothers?' Jesse thought completely out of context, 'they look so alike, but who the fuck cares?' They both wore black t-shirts and had the same hostile look on their face. Jesse felt his heart beat faster than he ever recalled. Orson's felt the same as it did in Vietnam when under fire.

186

The four men were motionless as if all had frozen in time until the man with the so-called mustache yelled something Jesse could not make out. The windows in both cars were not rolled down, so it was hard to hear what was being said. The driver just laughed at whatever the passenger said, and he drove off slowly. Just when Jesse felt at ease enough to take a breath, he heard Orson's door open. He turned and saw him stepping out of the car in a hurry. He watched the man walk quickly around the back of his car on to the asphalt chasing the Camaro. Jesse's neck couldn't turn right anymore, so he rolled his automatic window down and stuck his head out to find Orson in the middle of that dark and lonely road. He was standing 30 yards away, yelling at the disappearing car. The guy could not believe Orson's cursing. He had never heard him yell like that, nor had he ever seen him do something so idiotic. The Camaro suddenly hit the brakes, and it seemed as if the screeching had drowned out any other sound around, including Orson's tirade. The night seemed to be on pause again.

Jesse just stared at the man's silhouette framed by the red lights from both cars. Jesse broke the night silence by pleading out loud to Orson to get back in the car. But no one moved, not Orson, not Jesse, nor the orange Camaro or its occupants. For eleven seconds, their lives were on hold, but then Jesse saw how the two red eyes from the back of the Camaro dimmed down as the car finally roared away out of sight. Jesse saw Orson turning around and walking towards his Lincoln Continental. Jesse settled back in his seat, not realizing his right hand hurt from gripping the steering wheel so hard. He released, then opened and closed his hand a few times until Orson stood right by the door.

"Love, are you alright?" asked Orson leaning over the window. "You were yelling something at me."

"What fuck, dude?!" Jesse had lost it. "Are you out of your fucking mind?"

"Calm down, Red. They're just a couple of jerks."

"It's redneck country out here, man, you don't know if they were armed. Look at me!" The guy stuck his trembling hands out. "And please, zip-up, will you?"

"Jesse, you watch too many movies." The man said as he pulled up his zipper.

"Orson, don't you ever pull a stunt like that in front of me again. Steven used to do stuff like that, it drove . . ."

"Whoa, whoa, whoa! Hold on a sec there!" Orson didn't let him finish. "Don't you ever . . . and comparing me with your late husband in one sentence? I don't think so!"

"Orson, if we're gonna fight here, you better get—"

"Jess, let me in." Orson opened Jesse's door. He was obviously angry. "Slide over, will you?" He got in the driver's seat and put his fingers on the ignition key.

"What are you doing?" Jesse asked. "I thought you didn't wanna drive?"

"I'm seriously thinking of going back home after I drop you off at your house."

"You're just plain scared about playing tonight, and you are trying to…"

"I'm not trying anything. Stop that! I just don't appreciate having some white dude telling me what I can and cannot do. I'm way too old for that shit."

"Wow!" Jesse shook his head slightly. "I can't believe you'd do that."

"Do what?"

"Pull the racial card on me. What does my color have to do with anything? Why? You wouldn't be insulted if I was black and had said the same thing."

"Maybe, but you aren't black."

"Fine! But you had no business chasing after those guys. That was so stupid . . ."

"Don't you call me stupid, son."

"Babe, I haven't called you stupid, I simply said . . ."

"Don't you Babe me now!" Orson interrupted. "You're the one who wanted to stop and blow me in the first place."

"I was just trying to calm you down."

"Let's just stop talking. I don't wanna fight with you, and on our first night out in months. And you're right, I had no business chasing after those boys, but I just couldn't bear it. That kid was calling you that."

"What did he call me? I heard nothing."

"Never mind . . ." Orson was pensive for a few seconds. "Maybe we're spending too much time together."

"Hey, don't blame this on our last three days. I think they've been the best."

"They have been great, haven't they?"

"I'm sorry about . . ."

"Hush! No need." Orson put on his seatbelt and turned the key halfway. He leaned over to kiss Jesse. "Let's not ever fight again."

"Man, I hope all our fights are this short." Jesse slid closer to the man and put his arms around him, but immediately released him. To amuse Orson, he turned his head around, looking out of each window in any possible direction. He stopped at Orson and smiled, "All clear," and finally kissed him.

"Hey!" Orson cut the kiss short. "I've never had make-up sex. I've heard it can be explosive."

"Easy, lover!" said Jesse smiling as he slid back to his spot. "Let's just stick to tonight's plan." He then buckled up. "We've had enough excitement for now, and the night is still sort of young."

"Party pooper," said Orson throwing a mischievous smile at Jesse. "But you do owe me a blow job!"

"We have plenty of time to abuse our bodies anyway I want, I mean, you want. Are you sure you don't want me to drive?"

"No, I'm cool, I guess it's all the adrenaline pumping through me." He started the car and got back on the road.

Orson's cool didn't last very long. The moment he and Jesse walked into The Grasshopper, reality took a bite out of him. The place was packed with people, and the music jammed so hard that Orson could almost sink his teeth into the party mood everyone seemed to be in. This tensed him very close to his limit. He needed a drink, and he needed it bad.

Jesse, from his vantage point, was in awe. He got a good look at the dance floor and felt the energy that pulsed to the point he actually saw steam coming out of it. He then realized it was cigarette smoke. 'For a second there, I thought the smoke was coming out of people,' he took a mental note of that. He figured the smoking laws in Memphis were quite

189

different from LA's. He started to regret having suggested Orson perform that night, not knowing the bar would fit such a huge crowd. He considered apologizing to him for insisting, but that would have made things worse. Instead, he smiled and patted Orson's back as a sign of encouragement.

Orson wasn't feeling encouraged, though he knew Jesse had good intentions. He scanned the place looking for Ambar, who had just spotted him from the bar. He had a brief jolt of pleasure watching her and Bad Ass Jimbo serving drinks and taking orders from customers and waitresses. They looked so smooth that their motions seemed rehearsed, like a dance in near-perfect synchronicity. He saw Ambar waving them over, she was wearing red for the occasion, and Orson was flattered by her vote of confidence. He took Jesse briefly by the arm and guided him to the bar. They made it through the multitudes; Orson greeting more than a few on the way. Jesse loved that he knew so many people. Ambar saw them coming and asked the usual barflies to make room for her friends. The two men sat down on still-warm stools and ordered two beers.

"What's going on tonight?" Orson asked Ambar, pointing at the crowd with a quick swing of his head.

"Crazy, eh?" She replied. "Some big shot player is showing up tonight."

"Who?"

"Who the hell knows?" she handed him two glasses of draft beers. "It's all over Twitter. It could actually be anyone or no one at all. First, people were posting that it would be Watermelon Slim, and then Eden Brent's name started trending."

"Fuck!" Orson turned to Jesse and toasted with a wink and a lift of his glass.

"You're not backing out, right?" Ambar asked. "I've waited so long to hear you play. That's why I'm wearing this!" She pinched her dress softly.

Jesse leaned over the big man to get to his ear. "You'll be fine, Babe." He said as he caressed Orson's back.

"And I guess we have to thank you for tonight." Ambar said directly to Jesse.

"I know exactly how to get through this guy," joked Jesse, as he rubbed Orson's bicep up and down. "A little tenderness goes a long way with this one."

Orson just cringed, not believing what he was hearing, but then he surrendered to laughter.

"Hey, Orson!" Yelled Jimbo from the other end of the bar. "When are you getting on stage?"

The man turned to Jesse and asked, "You are driving tonight, right?" He saw Jesse replying with a couple of quick nods and then turned back to Jimbo. "Come over here and bring Jack with you, will you?"

The bartender got a hold of a bottle of Jack Daniels and walked towards the trio. Ambar was already setting up the shot glasses in front of her four friends. Jimbo poured the drinks quickly and picked up his glass.

"To Orson's big night." Jimbo said.

"The pressure is on." Orson whispered to himself while they all raised their shots.

"To Orson." Ambar repeated, Jesse followed, and they all tossed their shots back.

Orson took the bottle from Bad Ass Jimbo and served himself another shot and swallowed fast. "I need to go and sign up, right?" he asked, looking at Ambar.

"Yes," she replied, "go by the stage and find Ernie, he'll put you on the list."

Orson put his glass back on the counter and gestured to the dance floor for Jesse, "Shall we?" Each got off their stool and went in that direction. On their way to the stage, Orson said hello to a few more people, occasionally introducing his boy, Jesse. They made it to the stage's side stairs. As the man went to put his name on the list, Jesse went straight to the dance floor, magnetized by the thermic passion generated by the mob. Orson eventually joined him.

It was time for the first set break, and Orson learned from Ernie that he was the next in line. The musicians would start in 10 minutes. His buzz from the whiskey wore off at that very instant. 'I literally have to face the music,' he thought, and worse yet, play in front of one euphoric crowd. He started feeling sorry for himself thinking about those poor amateur musicians facing nasty judges on those talent shows he ran into on YouTube. 'Why would anyone go through the painstaking task of playing in front of anyone if you have much more fun doing it alone at home?' He was about to do the same thing; face about a hundred people, some of whom he knew by name, who were going to do just that, judge him for what he likes best. 'Stop it, Orson,' he said to himself, 'don't go there. You'll be just fine. You got this! Jesse told you so. You trust him, don't you? So snap out of it and man up!' He tried hard to feel at ease. Being on the dance floor with Jesse a few minutes earlier had helped him release some steam. He didn't need to share his insecurities with him.

Jesse watched as the next round of players got on stage, they all seemed to know their way around except Orson, even though the piano was the instrument that was easiest to find. Not that the man couldn't see it, it's just that he went straight to it without looking anywhere else as if he had the fear of getting lost along the way. Jesse saw him sitting on the stool and pulling out his reading glasses from his shirt pocket, again, only looking at the piano. He looked like a big nerd, Jesse thought as he loved this new shy side of Orson. Jesse felt proud of Orson, admiring him for finally daring to play in public after thirty-something years. The guy looked around for a place to watch his man without distracting him. He found a spot next to a wall that had a long ledge for drinks. From there, he had a perfect view of Orson, who finally noticed the other musicians getting ready to give each other the go.

The band took off with "Black Snake Moan," a song Jesse liked. He first heard the song in the movie of the same title. He was tempted to go back to the floor and dance, but he wanted to give Orson his full attention while on a stage for the first time. There would be plenty of times to dance to his piano playing, he thought, in private or in public. He only had eyes for Orson, who was trying not to miss a beat. By the end of the first song, he seemed a bit more relaxed; the more he played, the more confident he seemed to be.

At some point during the third song, Jesse was out of beer but didn't want to leave his perfect spot. Lucky for him, Ambar came over with two beers, one for him and one for herself. She was finally able to leave the bar to check out her best friend up close. Ambar raised her beer and toasted with Jesse before screaming for her best friend, who now was more concentrated on his music than on anything else around him. During his piano solos, Orson seemed really lost in his music; absorbed by the notes; he played as if they were waves he was surfing on. The man seemed to touch the hearts of everyone in the crowd. The applause grew louder and more frenzied with each solo. Orson's confidence on stage was soaring by the sixth song. It was during this number that Jesse heard Ambar say: "Oh shit!"

TWENTY-FIVE

ORSON'S ROUND WAS UP; another piano player was on the list to go on stage. He was ready to take a break, satisfied with his performance, but mainly amazed by the response from the audience. As he stepped down from the stage, he heard Ernie the MC announce his full name followed by raging applause and cheers. As he tried to get around the dance floor to find Jesse, people came up to him and congratulated him as he walked through. He tried to conceal his excitement by scanning the room, looking for his lover. His eyes hit the bar, and an involuntary "fuck me" came out of his mouth, but then he heard Jesse call out his name. Orson spotted him and Ambar closer to the stage than he thought. He walked to them and was greeted enthusiastically. Jesse lifted his heels in an attempt to kiss him. Orson found himself automatically responding by bending over a few inches, neither of them realizing it was the first time they had kissed in public. Not a big deal, at The Grasshopper, anything went, and no one cared.

Jesse immediately offered Orson a drink, but none of the waitresses were nearby. He spotted one near the bathrooms, so he squeezed through the crowd to reach her just as the next set began.

"L.C. is here" was the first thing Orson said to Ambar when Jesse was out of sight and earshot.

"I know; I saw him."

"Does Jesse know?"

"He does." She picked up her glass and drank the little beer she had left in it. "He said he and L.C. better not cross paths, otherwise . . ."

"Otherwise, what?"

"That's all he said." She set her empty glass on the narrow counter.

"I like Jesse. I'm glad someone is looking out for your best interests for a change."

Orson totally dismissed what Ambar had just said, "Out of all the nights that nigger had to pick tonight to be here. You didn't tell him I was playing tonight, did you?"

"I should take that as an insult, but I'll let it slide 'cause you're nervous tonight. But I told you, he's been in town for a while now."

"He looks old."

"I know; he doesn't look too good. When was the last time you saw him?"

"Saw him? About a year ago. I haven't spoken to him in about 12 years."

"He really wants to talk to you. He's been here about eight times, always asking about you. He's going back to Atlanta soon."

"Are you kidding me, Ambar? After our history together? You're the one who bitched at me all those times for going back to him. I really can't believe you're telling me this. Honestly, I really don't feel like having him near, so I'm glad he's going back to Atlanta. Our story is so fucking old. Anything that needed to be said has already been said."

On the other side of The Grasshopper, Jesse missed the waitress he was chasing after, so he went to the bar to order. As he got close, he saw Jimbo talking to a small group of people at the end of the counter. When Jimbo saw Jesse at the other end of the bar, he went to him, revealing the person behind him. It was L.C., who noticed Jesse had seen him. Jesse got a better look at L.C. this time. He wasn't impressed, he saw a very skinny, tall, black dude with large buggy eyes and sunken in cheeks, wearing a white Panama hat with a white blazer over a black t-shirt and white jeans on an Autumn night. 'I'm surprised he's not wearing sunglasses,' he thought. The guy went ahead and ordered three draft beers, and as he pulled his wallet out, Jimbo told him to put it away. The bartender explained that the golden rule at The Grasshopper was that anyone drinking with Ambar was treated by her. He hesitated before putting away his wallet, as he and L.C. kept exchanging looks. Jesse decided on the spot to conduct a little experiment. He ordered two whiskey shots from Jimbo, telling him they were for himself. He laid his money on the counter. While he waited for his change, he saw L.C. leave his entourage and approach him with a smile. Jesse's experiment worked. He made it seem that he was treating L.C. for a drink. He then drank one shot after the other before the presumptuous man reached him.

"Hey!" L.C. greeted Jesse. "You're Davis's boy, aren't you?"

"I beg your pardon?"

"I said if . . ."

"I heard you just fine L.C. I was fucking with you."

"So you know me then."

"I know who you are and plenty about you."

"What did my buddy Davis say about me?"

"You really don't wanna know."

"Oh yeah? C'mon, I'm curious."

"Curious? No, he didn't say that about you."

L.C. laughed out loud. "You're pretty cool, and the more I hear you, the more I like you. Davis always had good taste."

"Wait! Are we talking about the same Orson Davis?" Jesse could not believe what was coming out of his mouth; he was on a roll.

"Ouch! Good one!" Said L.C. as he signaled Jimbo, who stood nearby, to serve them another round of shots. "Please, let me buy you a drink."

"My beers are getting warm; I gotta go, dude." Jesse was having second thoughts about speaking his mind. "My friends are waiting."

"Here, have another shot." L.C. handed one of the shots to Jesse; he kept the other one. "Cheers."

"Cheers." Jesse decided to stick around a few more seconds.

"C'mon, I really want to know what Davis told you about me. Seriously"

"He said you were unreliable, arrogant, and a lousy lay."

"Really? He said that?"

"Actually, only the first one. The second one, it's just been proven; consequently, the last one is a given."

"Well, you should come to my hotel later, and I'll show you what I got between my legs. You'll definitely change your mind."

"Please, don't go there. I'm not the least interested. Besides, I already

197

caught a glimpse of what your dick is like."

"How so?"

"By looking at you, man." Jesse was feeling the buzz from the shots and was getting some looks from the people near him. "You are such a prick."

"How about another shot, boys." Jimbo interrupted, trying to make peace, "On the house." But he was ignored.

"Listen, kid," L.C. went on. "I've come to you in good spirits; there's no need to . . ."

"Bullshit!" Jesse said loud enough to get a few more heads turned their way. "How so? By wanting to show me your dick? When you very well know, I'm with the one you call your friend." He finally put his empty shot glass down. "Why do you do that? Orson was more than a friend to you, dude. That is not cool." Jesse then closed with, "You're such a loser."

"Jesse, buddy. C'mon." Jimbo was very uncomfortable and tried to calm him down.

"Listen, kid; you obviously don't know who I am." L.C. was angry but did not lose his cool. "No one talks to Leroy 'Lazy' Cooper like that."

"Wait, you're Lazy, Cooper?" Jesse's face became pale. He looked around and saw everything but friendly faces staring back at him. "Oh, fuck! Orson never told me you're The Lazy Cooper."

Jesse looked at L.C. in the eyes, but measured his words for a few seconds, then spoke as soft as he could to be heard only by the musician, given the loud music in the background. "I suppose you want an apology, but I'll give you something better."

"And what is that?" said L.C. putting his shot glass down.

"A thank you. If it weren't for you and the way you treated Orson, he would have had a completely different path, and he and I would have probably never met. So I want to thank you for that, Mr. Cooper."

"No apology then?" said L.C. with a straight face.

Jesse didn't really want to reply, but: "That's right. So long, stranger." He picked up his three beers with both his hands, turned around, and walked away, sensing plenty of eyes from L.C.'s fans on him from about a 20-foot circumference. Then he heard Jimbo say, "OK, the show's over. Who needs a beer? L.C., what can I get you? Whatever you want . . ."

Jesse was glad to find Orson and Ambar standing in the same spot he had left them. His heart was pumping fast and could not contain his excitement.

"Red, why are you smiling like that?" Orson asked him as he was arriving. "Wait a minute; you met L.C."

"Yep!" Jesse responded with a grin as he placed the three beer glasses on the ledge.

"I know that look. You said something to him, didn't you? What the fuck, Jess?!"

"I couldn't help it; he practically laid it out there for me."

"And you're drunk too. C'mon Jess; you said you would drive us home."

"Just a couple of shots, I'm fine."

"You're not driving my car; I'll tell you that."

"Hey, boys!" Ambar grabbed her new beer. "Keep it cool; otherwise, take it outside. I'm gonna check on Jimbo." She let them be and walked straight towards the bar.

"Good idea." Orson took a long drink of his beer, leaving the glass nearly half empty. "I need some air, c'mon." He pointed the way out with his open hand to let Jesse go first."

'He's still a gentleman, even when angry.' Jesse thought, which made him smile briefly.

"This isn't funny, Jess," Orson said as he followed the guy.

"Is that your new thing? Calling me Jess when you're upset?"

"Not here!" Orson wanted to play it cool, trying hard not to show his anger in public. "Out!"

"Fine!"

The music had stopped on their way through the crowd. Orson was congratulated a few times for his performance, which briefly delayed their exit. He smiled politely but did not reply to anyone. He then heard Ernie on the microphone announcing the mystery guest. Sure enough, Leroy "Lazy" Cooper was welcomed to the stage with a roaring applause, whistles, and screams of pure joy. 'It is just as well,' thought Orson, 'that we're almost at the door.'

Jesse and Orson exited the bar passing by Mick, the bouncer, outside.

A large black man, as tall as Orson, but not as wide or as dark, was sitting on a stool smoking a cigar, pretending not to care who came in or out. The two walked away from the door to the corner of the building for some needed privacy.

"Jesse, what did you do back there? What did you say to L.C.?"

"What's the big fucking deal?"

"You had no business talking to him."

"Why on earth not?"

Orson realized he had made a dumb remark and didn't reply to Jesse.

"Hey! I did thank him for the way things turned out between you two; otherwise, you and I would have never met. After, I told him he was a loser."

"Really? Orson tried successfully to conceal a smile. "You said that?"

At that very moment from inside the bar, it sounded like L.C. had found his way to the microphone after the big applause. He greeted his audience and then did the unexpected: he mentioned Orson Davis and invited him to the stage to accompany him and the rest of the band on the piano. Neither man outside could believe their ears, but Jesse saw an undeniable look in Orson's face.

"Please, tell me you not even considering going on stage and play with that asshole."

"Why the hell not. It's time I prove him wrong."

"You're kidding, right?"

"Don't tell me you're jealous."

"Jealousy has nothing to do with it, my friend. This is about the way this guy has treated you since who knows when and about your integrity."

At the same time, they could hear L.C. inquiring out for Orson's name once more; soon, the public joined him. They all called for Orson at the same time over and over again.

"You do remember that guy ruining your confidence as a musician. And now you're gonna go in there like you were best buddies? It's pathetic!"

"Watch what you say, son!"

"I've told you, don't call me that!"

"Then stop acting like a child."

"C'mon Babe, let's go home. I don't like that we're fighting again. We'll come back next week."

"Hey, Orson!" yelled the bouncer. "They want you in here!"

"Give me a minute, will you, Mick?" Orson replied.

"I'm leaving, dude," Jesse announced.

"C'mon Red, stay, please." He begged. "Just one song."

"Yeah, right. You go and play all night if you like, but I'm not staying, I'm sorry."

"Really, Red?" Orson turned his head to the door, and the crowd was getting louder calling out his name. "Don't do this."

"I'm too upset; I won't enjoy it."

"How are you getting home?"

"I'm calling a cab."

"Are you sure you don't wanna stay?" Orson started to walk a few steps backwards.

"I'll see you at home." Jesse just turned around and walked away.

"Are we cool, Jesse?"

"Yes, Babe, we're cool." Jesse lied to Orson for the first time.

It didn't take long for Jesse to hear the mob cheering for Orson as he returned to the bar. The guy reached out for his jeans back pocket, and the word "fuck" was yelled across the parking lot with only Mick to hear it. Jesse realized his pocket was empty, remembering he had left his cell phone charging at his home the night before. He wasn't about to go back to the bar, so he figured he'll walk a mile or so to the main road and flag a taxi home. In the worst-case scenario, he could come back to The Grasshopper's parking lot and stand by Abe until it was all over.

As he moved further into the road, he could still hear the music from the bar and distinguish Orson's piano, it all slowly faded away as he drew away at a steady pace. He made the first right, remembering the road they had taken earlier to get to the bar.

Half a mile away, Jesse began to slow down, thinking he might have overreacted, that maybe he wasn't being fair to Orson. Maybe L.C. had called Orson to the stage to finally make it up to him, Jesse thought. After all, the response from the audience to Orson was unmistakably favorable, and it was time for L.C. to acknowledge Orson's talent. Maybe L.C.

decided to give Orson the credit he deserved. 'Tonight is Orson's big night,' he thought, 'I should be there.' Jesse turned around and started heading back to the bar. Nearly 100 yards behind him, on the same stretch of road, the dark orange Camaro, driving slowly and with the headlights off, followed Jesse. Completely unaware of this, the guy had picked up his pace, not wanting to miss out on the rest of Orson's performance. He imagined himself emerging from the center of the crowd until Orson would spot him and greet him with a big smile and the gentle twinkle of his gold tooth. Jesse never made it back to The Grasshopper that night.

TWENTY-SIX

WHILE PUSHING WITH ONE HAND an empty shopping cart across the Piggly Wiggly parking lot, Orson checked his phone for the umpteenth time. He was heading back to the store after helping a young couple of newlyweds to their car with their first groceries. He realized his mind was somewhere else, mainly on Jesse, and hadn't been as attentive to the couple as he normally was. While he scrolled through his phone, he had hoped to find at least one text message or a missed call notice from Jesse. It had been three days since they had seen and talked to each other. Orson had been thinking about that night and the look of disappointment on Jesse's face when they parted ways. He had called him several times and texted him a few more without success. On Tuesday, Orson went by Jesse's house in the morning before going to work and saw his rental car parked in the driveway and thought about stopping unannounced, but pride got the worst of him, and he kept driving. The following day, Orson tried again and saw that the car was gone. He had enough time to stop and write a quick note that he slipped under the door as a peace offering.

Orson had just placed the kart back to its station and noticed he had a few dollar bills in his hand. The young former groom had given him a $13 tip, and he hadn't even realized it, so he figured he had been his usual self on automatic pilot. The sliding doors to the store parted, he had barely stepped in when his cell phone rang with Jesse's name beaming on the screen.

"Finally!" Orson answered in a cheerful tone as he walked out to the parking lot. "Where the hell have you been, Red?"

"Hi Orson, this is Lauren." The voice replied from the other end.

"Lauren . . . is Jesse OK?"

"No, he's been hurt." She tried not to cry. "Orson, I couldn't get to you sooner. I'm sorry."

"But what happened to Jesse?"

"He was viciously attacked, beat up by some . . ." Her voice cracked.

"Wait! What? Who?" He couldn't help it. He was almost yelling at Lauren.

"No one knows. The police don't know."

"But I drove by his house just this morning and his car . . . I don't understand." Orson could not finish a thought. "When did this happen?"

"Sunday night, most likely, they said." She paused for one second. "I just found your note under the door. I'm staying at—"

"How's Jesse, please?"

"Not good, Orson, not good. He's unconscious now, and we almost lost him."

"Which hospital is he in?" His hands began to tremble. "Please, I need to see him now!"

"At Methodist North Hospital, room 1001, do you know—"

"Yes, I'm on my way." Orson answered abruptly and hung up without saying goodbye.

Orson hurried to the manager's office to tell his boss about the emergency. Mr. Hucklebun made one of his many disapproving faces before saying yes; not that Orson cared about losing his job, he was going to see Jesse whether Mr. Hucklebun said yes or no. Orson quickly went to the locker room and grabbed his black helmet and leather gloves. He put on his jacket as he stepped out the door and ran out the back of the building to find his bike. Once he sat on it, he held the keys and realized his hands were still shaking. He figured there was no way he would arrive safely to the hospital the way he was feeling. He took his phone and called Ambar and asked her to pick him up to take him to the hospital.

About thirty minutes later, Orson and Ambar were walking down the hallway of the hospital on the 10th floor. Orson found it ironic how such a sterile place would display such cheesy Christmassy decorations. He always hated how corporate America pushed the next holiday barely three days after Thanksgiving weekend. Ambar escorted him all the way to the door 1001; it took Orson a few seconds to gather enough courage to finally knock. A tall man in his mid-50s that looked very much like Jesse opened the door, he shook hands with Orson and introduced himself as Kyle Santos, Jesse's dad. From the doorway, Orson saw a black lady sitting on a chair in front of the foot of the bed. Orson didn't feel brave enough to explain he was Jesse's boyfriend, lover, partner, or whatever they were because their status had never been completely defined by themselves. Orson stuck to "good friend." As he greeted Jesse's father, he realized right away where Jesse had got his good looks and the ability to make anyone feel welcome.

Kyle showed him in and introduced his wife as Dr. Patricia Douglas and also as Jesse's mom. All the while, Orson avoided looking at Jesse, he could hear the machines that kept his guy going, but currently, he was focused on the introductions, not wanting to face reality. In contrast to Jesse's father, Dr. Douglas did not show any kind of empathy for Orson. While they shook hands, he realized she had been observing him since he walked in the door; studying him from his shoes to the name tag on the work apron he forgot he was still wearing. He knew that judgmental look; one that he had seen a few times in his life.

Orson had had enough of her, and he finally turned to look at Jesse. At that instant, he felt as if a bucket of ice water had been thrown on him. He slowly walked to Jesse's side. It was hard to tell if that was really his boy. Jesse's face was swollen beyond recognition and with a spectrum of colors that ranged from red to purple. Strapped to his face and arms were all sorts of tubes and cables. His head was wrapped with a wide bandage that barely let a few of his curls sneak out.

Orson stood there staring at Jesse, trying to stay put, acting manly— for himself and the couple in the room. Alone with Jesse, he would have never done that, he would have wrapped his arms around him, to save him. A profound sense of sadness invaded Orson's soul. He put his hand over Jesse's gently but squeezed it tight. He could not bear seeing his Red so spiritless nor to be in that room for any longer. He then announced in a broken speech that he would be back later; without looking at anyone in the eyes, he walked out without saying goodbye.

Orson met Ambar outside the room; she was standing two steps away from the door. He approached her and virtually dropped his two big arms over her shoulders in a hug. He was numb, but embracing Ambar, he felt human, like blood was pumping through his veins. For he was questioning his own emotions; he wasn't crying for Jesse, although he was sad, drowning in sorrow but without a shred of pain on display. 'Maybe I'm in shock,' he thought, trying to make some sense, 'or just plain angry.' Their lives together seemed to finally head someplace, and what had just happened to Jesse was not part of that plan, even though there was no plan. So he had to stand strong, he figured; be on guard, almost alert in the moment, not really understanding why.

Ambar found herself supporting a man triple her weight, but she was the one sobbing in silence as though relieving her friend of his sorrow. She knew her friend would let it all out one day; she had to watch for the signs to see it coming and be there for Orson. He moved to her side and put his arm across Ambar's back, they leaned into each other, his head over hers, as they walked down the hallway towards the elevator. Before reaching the elevator, Ambar noticed a woman coming towards them. She was dressed in Bohemian-style clothing; in colors combining purple and olive green, she wore a bright orange scarf that almost identically matched her hair. So much color seemed out of place in a hospital, Ambar thought, too lively perhaps. She noticed the woman was carrying a to-go tray in one hand with four cups of coffee and a bag that came from a local bakery in the other. The women acknowledged each other with soft smiles as they passed each other. Orson didn't even notice her. Ambar and Orson made it to the elevator, and just as the doors were closing, she noticed the same woman from afar, empty-handed and seeming to rush towards them. Ambar and Orson, holding on to each other, were too far from the elevator panel to push the door open button.

Ambar and Orson exited the hospital and walked to the parking lot. At first, neither could recall where she had parked her car. They stopped to look for it when they were approached by the lady with the orange hair.

"Excuse me, Orson?" The woman said, nearly out of breath. "I'm Lauren."

"Hello!" Orson quickly turned to her and embraced her. Keeping his firm but gentle poise, he held on tightly to her for nearly a minute without saying anything.

"He'll be fine. Jesse will be fine." Lauren patted him in the back. "I'm glad to finally meet you, though I hate for it to be this way." She said as she pulled away. "When I saw you upstairs, it didn't register that it was you. I think I figured you would be by yourself." She turned to Ambar and extended her arm to her, "I'm Jesse's mother, you must be Amber," and shook her hand.

"It's Ambar." she responded with the same gesture. "What happened to Jesse?"

"Do the police know anything yet?" Orson interrupted.

"No one knows. A truck driver found him in the middle of nowhere, early Monday morning, it was still dark out, he said . . ."

"That was the night you played." Ambar said as she turned to Orson.

"It was probably after our fight." added Orson.

"The man called 911 after finding him by the side of the road. So the police really don't have much to go on . . . Wait! You guys had a fight?"

"They argued . . ." Ambar volunteered. "They had a disagreement Sunday night at my club, and Jesse left by himself." She turned to Orson again." I thought you said he took a cab home."

Orson didn't have an answer, or really couldn't think. All of a sudden, he was overcome by guilt.

"The police are waiting for Jesse to wake up to question him." Lauren continued.

"He's gonna be OK, right?" The man asked with a slight tremor in his voice. "What did the doctor say?"

"We'll be meeting Dr. Brennan any minute now," she turned to her bare wrist as an old habit. "So I need to get back." She pulled her phone and read the time. "Right now, Jesse's stable. Orson, why don't we meet later today, or better yet tomorrow? Tonight is my turn to spend the night with Jesse. Breakfast, lunch, dinner; whatever works for you."

"Sure, tomorrow is good, but would you please call me later and let me know what the doctor says?"

"Of course. I'll be staying at Jesse's house from now on. You can text me at his cell phone, I have it on me, just in case someone calls." Lauren turned slightly and took half a step to head back to the building. "Right now, I have to go." She then walked away in a hurry.

As he watched her leave, Orson realized Jesse never called a taxi that night. He recalled Red telling him the night before; he had left his phone charging at home and forgot to take it with him. He shared that with Ambar, feeling angry for not remembering that small detail. He would have never let Jesse go, but Orson knew better than to go into an 'I should have' mode. Actions have consequences, and he chose to stay at The Grasshopper and play regardless of how upset Jesse was at him. 'What's done is done, now deal with it.'

He and Ambar walked to the car. Not a word he spoke while she drove him back to work. She might have got a word or two from him, so she let him be. That night he did not get any sleep. He would toss and turn in bed watching the clock by his bed, counting the hours to meet Lauren for breakfast as he had texted her earlier.

Orson picked the Arcade Diner in downtown Memphis. He had been there for an hour or so, tired of being at home alone. He had been sitting with a cup of coffee trying to write music in the little yellow notebook Jesse had left for him, but nothing would come out of his pen. When he saw Lauren walk in, he stood up and waited for her by their table. Orson received her with a kiss on the cheek and a hug. It felt nice, even though he hardly knew Lauren, she was Jesse's biological mother, the closest kin to the man he loved.

They sat down and ordered breakfast. Lauren started by apologizing to Orson for just texting and not calling the night before. She explained that being with the Santoses for more than 24 hours in a row was not an easy task, especially under the circumstances. She shared with Orson how she learned about Jesse's assault. The police had called his father Kyle from the hospital, and he immediately called her. She was in the middle of dinner with friends when she got the call. About 7 hours later, all three parents were on a direct flight to Memphis. They went straight to the hospital from the airport, where they met with Dr. Brennan at his office on the 10th floor.

The prognosis was not all that optimistic. Jesse had suffered two broken ribs and a broken arm, he received a severe contusion in the head, likely from a metal object, probably a crowbar. At that point, the doctor was not certain if there was brain damage. To be on the safe side, the doctor decided to induce a coma to give Jesse a fighting chance. If everything went as to the doctor expected, Jesse would be in a controlled vegetative state for at least two weeks. It was agreed by all the parties concerned that Lauren would stay in Memphis for as long as needed. The Santoses, on the other hand, would head back to San Diego in a couple of days due to work. They would wait out Jesse's changes, if any, from their home.

Breakfast finally arrived: two OJs, hot oatmeal, fruit salad, scrambled eggs, bacon, hash browns, one hot coffee, and one hot tea. Orson thought it would be a good moment to tell Lauren what happened between Jesse and him on their last night at The Grasshopper. He mentioned to her that he had dealt with guilt in the past, and he wasn't willing to go down that road again. Still, part of him could not help but feel responsible for what happened to her son. That thought didn't even occur to Lauren, she said, who believed strongly that everything happened for a reason. Before changing the subject, she said she signed in Orson as a family member for hospital visiting privileges. The man, who was about to put a fork into his scrambled eggs, got a bit emotional.

"Thanks, Lauren." He said in a low voice. "That means a lot to me."

"You know, Orson, this is one of those rare times when I lose faith in humanity. I find myself many times defending the human race, in spite of what everyone says. But now I don't . . ." She placed her hand on Orson's and squeezed it for a few seconds. She reached for the napkin dispenser and took one that she used to dry her tears. She then opened the small package of tea and pulled out the bag, dropping it gently in hot water. "Orson, you don't know how thrilled I was when Jesse told me you guys made up on Thanksgiving." She started eating her fruit salad.

"Actually, I do know. I was there when you called Jesse the following morning, remember?" He slid his coffee closer to him. "That was just six days ago."

"That's right, but that coincidence . . . Wow! That is fate, my friend!"

'Fate?' Orson thought, 'really?' He didn't know how to respond to Lauren's remark, so he said nothing. He just looked at his coffee while he stirred it with a spoon. It felt as if life was playing a trick on him, trying to cheat him. At least this time, there was a sliver of hope; there was a fifty percent chance Jesse would come back, unlike the disgraceful day when Genna died in his arms. Lost in his own thoughts, Orson missed some of what Lauren had been saying, but he quickly caught up.

". . . and he went on and on how much fun you were having this past weekend."

"Isn't it funny, Lauren? When I split up with Jesse, I couldn't believe how much I missed him. It took some soul searching to realize I might have made a big mistake." He picked up his cup and drank from it. "The age difference was a big hurdle for me, never been much for much younger than me. The race thing also, maybe a bit; meeting his stepmother yesterday, I understand Jesse a little better. He never mentioned to me she was black."

"Do you wish he did?"

"I guess not." He put his coffee down and went back to his plate. "Also, getting used to the fact that Jesse's so handsome, feeling at times that I had won him on a game show or something. I can't help it, for a man my age. So you see there were a lot of drawbacks, or hang-ups if you will. And then when the Thanksgiving thing happened, all of that stuff vanished."

"Loves finds Andy Hardy."

"Yeah, at sixty-three," Orson completed. "He's just great, the way he just talks to anyone as if he knows them. His kindness, never judging, he cares for everyone."

"That's funny; he practically said the same thing about you. Jesse told me you know a lot of people." Lauren said as she squeezed the plastic bear and let the honey drip over her oatmeal. "But you see, Orson, Jesse's always been like that. Ever since he was little, he had the ability to see into the heart of people. You don't know how many times he would strike up a conversation with strangers, and he was just six or seven. Every single one would fall in love with Jesse." She said before taking a full spoon of oatmeal. "That's why I was so surprised when he hooked up with Steven. They were so different."

"Really?" Orson leaned forward to listen while he continued with his breakfast. "I thought . . ."

"Professionally, they were perfect for each other, but Steven wasn't easy. His mood swings . . . And his mother, oh, boy! What a piece of work. I could tell Jesse didn't like her, even though he never said anything bad about her. Well, except for that time she gave Jesse an address to a family plot instead of his husband's ashes."

"Yes, I know about Dottie."

"I hated how she took advantage of Jesse like that." Lauren retrieved the tea bag from her cup and placed it in the saucer. "He was feeling so vulnerable because of his husband's death, convincing him to fly Steven's body to New Orleans so she could have her way." Her face grew increasingly red. "Not to mention, not giving Jesse a chance to attend to his husband's burial affairs. It makes me furious."

"I was with him right after she gave him the news. He was crushed."

"That's right. That was the beginning for you guys."

Those few last words hit Orson a bit hard. Dosed by pain, he stopped looking at Lauren. He didn't want her to read the sadness in his eyes. He moved his fork and played with his eggs. "I can't imagine watching your partner succumb to drugs," was the first thing that popped in his head. "And then discover him OD'd in their home."

"Is that what Jesse told you?" Lauren said, holding her spoon, not ready to eat more oatmeal just yet. "That he found him OD'd at home?"

"Actually, he never really told me what happened. I just assumed he found . . . well, he would get all quiet about it, half-spoken." Orson had finished his eggs and left the hash browns for last, so he proceeded to salt and pepper them.

"When Steven died, he and Jesse were not doing well at all. The marriage was in shambles because of Steven's substance abuse."

"That I know, Jesse told me himself."

"Well, Jesse started going to a therapist-slash-acupuncturist; a friend of mine, actually. It took some convincing from my part—Jesse doesn't care for 'alternative therapies,' " She air quoted the last two words, "or what I do for a living, but he went anyway."

"I know, I gave him shi—a hard time about it once."

"You can say shit; I don't care."

"I'm sorry. I figured you being Jesse's mom and all." Said Orson as the waitress came over to the table and refilled his coffee. Anyway, I told him to have more respect for what you do."

"Thank you, Orson." Lauren asked the waitress for more hot water, and continued, "Where was I? Yes! Jesse was cleaning up his act. The only thing that kept him and Steven together was work, plus, the house, investments, bank accounts, you name it. Jesse was waiting for the therapy to kick in, so to speak, and decide whether to make it work between them or break up. But he and Steven were in different places emotionally by then. Jesse was kicking the bad habits; Steven was not even trying. In the middle of that, their five-year anniversary was coming up. Steven, who was sensing Jesse was slipping away from him slowly but surely, came up with the idea of a surprise anniversary party for Jesse. Nothing intimate nor small. The kind of party that Jesse was trying to stay away from. Well, I don't remember how Jesse found out about it, either someone talked, or he found something in the house. Oh, yes! The caterers called the house by mistake, and Jesse picked up. He then told Steven to call it off, that it wasn't the right time; that they would celebrate when the time came. Steven wasn't backing out, he had already invited about eighty people, but Jesse wasn't having any part of it. And if you know Jesse, he can be stubborn."

"I had a slight taste of it recently, yes," said Orson with a peal of short laughter.

"Anyway, Steven moved heaven and earth to convince Jesse to go to that party. He had friends calling him and try to convince him. One friend even offered Jesse money, just to get Steven off his back. Steven went so far as to threaten Jesse."

"Really? Wow!"

"I'm telling you; poor Steven was not well at all." The waitress finally came and poured hot water in Lauren's cup. "Jesse thought it would be wise to skip town. So he and his executive producer and friend, Denise. Oh, shoot! I should call her and tell her about Jesse." She interrupted herself. "Anyway, they took off and drove down to a spa in Palm Springs for the weekend. He did have the courtesy of telling Steven he was leaving town the day before the party."

"So I take it the party went on."

"Yes, it went on, took off, and exploded, for sure." Lauren recycled her tea bag and let it soak a bit. "It got out of hand. Lots of people, lots of drugs, and plenty to drink."

"I think I know where this is going."

"This is the sick part. Steven basically documented the entire party, recording everything on his cell phone. This ended up saving Jesse when the police got involved. He would shoot video and send it to Jesse in real-time, almost. Welcoming guests, mostly guys, people eating and drinking, and having a good time. At some point, people were skinny dipping in their swimming pool. There was even footage of people doing drugs, having sex, the works. All through this, Steven taped himself, or someone taped him, popping pills here and there. Jesse watched the first few clips, but he switched off the phone, he couldn't bear it." She got her tea ready, and picked up her cup, drove it to her lips and carefully sipped. "It was really creepy. No, no, it was sad, that's the right word. The following morning, Jesse found that Steven had sent about fifty videos. He skipped through most of them, but then he got to the most disturbing ones, around the point where you could tell the party was dying off."

"Did you see these videos?" Orson asked.

"No, Jesse told us about them, sparing us from some of the most graphic details. Well, in the last video, Steven had set up his phone in front of the bed. He was with some young stud, both naked or half-naked, I don't know. Very hurtful towards Jesse. They were doing cocaine or meth or something and making out. Steven wouldn't take his eyes off the camera, very sadistic-like. At some point, he took some pill and put it in his mouth and shared it with the young man while kissing; they did this a few times. After, Steven grabbed a bunch of more pills from the night table and swallowed them with vodka or gin. He moved over to the phone, looked into the camera and said: 'Happy Anniversary, Whiskers.' That's what Steven called Jesse. Steven then switched off the camera, and I guess that's when he sent it. That was the last message.

"When Jesse saw that, he phoned Steven right away. Since there was no answer, he immediately called nine-one-one from Palm Springs and headed back to LA. Denise drove as fast as she could while Jesse tried calling Steven over and over with no luck. It was too late. When he got home, the police were there. The ambulance had already left. There was nothing to do; Steven had already passed. The young man he was with made it."

"Man, poor Jesse," Orson said while he set aside his empty cup of coffee. "Now I understand why he would get all weird out when I asked about Stevie . . . Steven."

"Jesse fell apart, all those people who went to all those wonderful and fun parties disappeared out of sight. Just a few old friends stuck around; mostly Denise. But Jesse was so tormented by guilt. No one could console him. He really wanted to be alone. His mother prescribed some antidepressants. Well, you know that. You met him fresh from California."

"Jesse mentioned Steven's overdose, but I didn't want to push him. I know what it is like to lose a partner unexpectedly, but I didn't know it was actually suicide. When that happens, you're left with many unanswered questions; this is me talking as a war veteran. I've lost a couple of buddies of mine that way." Orson saw the waitress coming over with the coffee pot, but then he signaled her to bring the check before she got a chance to arrive at their table. "Lauren, what did you mean by the videos are what saved Jesse?"

"Oh, from criminal charges or a lawsuit from that boy who nearly died in their bed. It also helps to have a good lawyer."

The waitress brought the check, and Lauren asked her to call a taxi for her. Lauren and Orson almost had a friendly argument over the bill, until the man made a mother-and-son comparison that flattered Lauren enough to let him buy breakfast. She insisted on leaving a tip for the cab-calling request. They walked out of the restaurant, and Lauren's taxi had already arrived. As Lauren opened the door to the back seat, she remembered there was something in Jesse's house for Orson and told him she would bring it the next time they met. She got inside her car and waved goodbye. Orson watched the car drive away and wondered what on earth could Jesse have left for him? He then walked a block away got on his motorcycle, not knowing where to go. He put on his helmet, leather gloves, and his Ray-Bans, and drove off to see Jesse.

214

TWENTY-SEVEN

HELLO RED, I'm not gonna tell you that I am OK with coming to see you and talking to you with the hope that you might come out of your coma. Dr. Brennan said we don't have to do this now; that during an induced coma, us talking to you won't help much. But Lauren thinks it's better if you start getting used to hearing our voices now. She literally made me promise I would do it. How could anyone say no to her?

I'm not going to hide that I am scared shitless seeing you like this. Knowing there's only a 50 percent chance of getting you back. Man, don't I wish I had the spunk Lauren has! She's positively convinced you will come around before Christmas. That's less than three weeks away, and by the looks of you, I find it hard to believe. Things in life don't usually turn out the way one wants them to, but sometimes they do, so I'm going to put you in that place where I hope the possibilities work in my favor. But I'm telling you, Red, this is no way to be spending the holidays.

Lately, I've been thinking a lot about how you came into my life and how you turned my life upside down. You see, Red, when you met me, I was dormant, living in my comfort zone, working, sleeping, eating, and occasionally going out to hear live music. I have a modest but comfortable pension from the mechanic's shop and the military, so I was working to keep boredom away, partly, but also to help Hank and Angela with Gennie's education. Life and time were just passing me by. I was lonely and with a great sense of lack, not knowing what. I certainly wasn't looking for love, it had failed me, and so I had no interest in it.

Then you came along, basically, out of the blue; it wasn't planned, it wasn't sought after, and it took us both by surprise. We were like, "Aaahhhh!" I mean, we fell for each other at exactly the same time. Then you know . . . well, I got scared . . . I was so overwhelmed . . . I had to break it off. Heartaches at my age? I wouldn't have it.

The funny thing was, you left such an imprint on me then. I felt anxious and out of my normal self. As if my world had been recharged and all that energy inside needed to be released. One day, in the midst of my solitude, I was thinking about you again; missing you, deconstructing you, figuring you out. I remembered your go-getter attitude. You had an idea, and the next minute you were writing a story or getting involved in some big project. I admire that about you. I must have had some sort of epiphany because I felt encouraged, and I went and bought myself the Imperial, the bike I've always wanted.

But most importantly, I started playing again. Oh man, do I want to tell you about that. When I come back tomorrow or maybe the day after, when I have nothing to do afterward, I'd like to tell you about that day. In any case, I owe you so much for that gift. Jesse, if it wasn't for you . . .

The truth is, you are a strong force in my life, and I am counting on that same strength to wake yourself up; to come back to me. And please, love me . . . Still love me as much as you've said you do. At times, I have the awful sensation you'll wake up and snap out of me. So Red, if you can hear me, stay there, wherever you are, as long as you need to. But don't make me wait long. I'll go *loco* if you do because I've waited long enough already.

On a lighter note, well, I'm not so sure it's lighter, but I invited your three parents over for dinner at my house two nights ago. I can almost hear you saying, "Why the hell did you do that?" Yes, it was quite a stunt that not even Evel Knievel would have tried . . . never mind, you probably never heard of him. Anyway, I felt bad that they were eating every meal in restaurants and hospital cafeterias. I'm not going to lie to you. I also wanted to impress your folks with my homemade cooking, the way I did you with my mac and cheese.

Well, the night wasn't as bad as it could have been if it wasn't for Lauren. She saved the night. The gathering started with a lot of small talk, too much for my taste. Red, honestly, I don't think your parents were ready for a blue-collar, 63-year-old retired grandfather as a potential son-in-law. No matter, they had a hell of a meal, I'll tell you that! I made catfish with mashed sweet potatoes and cornbread. I also made your new favorite, a Banana Frost, in your honor—all of it from scratch. You couldn't get more Tennessean than that.

It wasn't really that bad, I guess, but I was expecting to see a lot more of you in them. I guess they were pretty tired and understandably too worried about you to be relaxed enough to have a good time. Anyway, both your parents left this morning for San Diego, as you may already know.

Oh! I almost forgot. Hank is coming back to see you today. Man, he got so angry when he found out about your assault. When I told him about what happened, he came to see you that very day. He wanted to know who did this to you. The police have no clue. Now they're not sure whether they hit you with a metal tube or a bat. Sometimes I think it could have been those two boys in the orange Camaro, but I have no way of knowing that for sure. If I've only made a note of their license plate. I could call my old buddies at the police department . . . Anyway, Hank told his students about what happened to you. He said they all wanted to come and see you. They want to continue with the series just to show you they can do it. They're determined to come up with four more complete episodes to show you when you wake up. Hank thinks they are being too ambitious, but they are working so hard to prove him wrong. They even want to write your beating into the story, with a different character, that's what I understood.

The other day, I had to pick Hank up at Tom Lee Park. I still haven't gone to their house to fix his car. Anyway, he and the kids were shooting a scene there, and when they saw Abe, they were blown away. I was feeling all flattered and proud until they asked me if they could shoot one quick scene with it. Hank gave me an 'it isn't my idea' and an 'it's your call' kind of look. Naturally, I thought of you and the kick you would have gotten from their request. And that's probably why I let the kids twist my arm. In any case, it was a short scene where Hank played the role of a father picking up his teenage son in the parking lot. I can't wait to see what they came up with.

Red, you'll like this. Ambar called me today to ask about you, and she told me that people at the bar have been asking when am I going to play again. Imagine that; I think it's pretty funny. I won't be going back any time soon, not until you get better. Right now, I don't feel like it. Ambar also said that L.C. is still trying to get a hold of me. He complained to her that I took off right after our performance together, which is true. I was dying to get to you. I drove straight home that night, risking a DUI. Little did I know I wouldn't find you. Anyway, I still don't want to see that motherfucker. He's bad news.

Hold on, my phone's buzzing . . . Red, I have to take this . . . I'll be right back.

OK, I'm back. That was Angela. We just had our talk. A very long talk that is, down in the cafeteria. Hank told her you were here and that I would be coming here a lot. He told me that she had been going on and on about us ever since she found you at my house wearing my slippers. Hank's stuck to his "you two need to talk" line every time she brought it up.

She came here out of solidarity and with the best intentions. But, as usual, when she and I start talking, everything goes south. Anyway, I told her that you and I are indeed together. Oh man, I hate when she makes that incredulous face, I always wondered where she got that from; do I do that? She was curious about how I went gay all of a sudden. All this time she blamed you, even though she knew that it didn't make sense. I brought up Uncle L.C., and when we met in Vietnam—not in great detail—but I reminded her how suddenly he stopped coming around. I had to tell her the story of how L.C. and I met in the army, and how it was in 1973 that I realized I liked sleeping with men.

Angela also wanted to know whether her mother knew about me. I told her she never knew. Angela judged me and accused me of being unfaithful to her mother for all those years. Oh, Jesse, I was so tempted to tell her the whole story about Genna's death, but that would have only caused more pain and resentment and possibly would have severed our relationship for good. Right then, I decided to keep this part of the story buried in the vault for good.

She also wanted to know why I had kept it a secret from her for so long. I really didn't have a reason other than I just don't care to discuss this with anyone, as I'd even told you once. She was surprised, maybe a bit shocked. She asked if many people know about me and if you and I use protection and other more intimate questions that a father wouldn't normally share with his daughter.

You want me to tell you the truth, Red? Our conversation made me feel that she was more concerned about what other people think than about my happiness. That made me a bit sad. To make matters worse, she said she needs time to process this information and that if I still want to see my granddaughter, it would be best to call Hank first, so that we could meet when Angela isn't around. It's a drastic move, even for her. I'm not too worried about it because I'm sure Hank will work on her so that she can lift off her own personal curfew before Christmas. Which reminds me, I promised Gennie Santa would get her a puppy. I was hoping that maybe you and I could go and . . .

Red, I meant to tell you this past weekend that I regretted breaking up with you, I really did. How many nights I stared at that bottle, the half a bottle of Jack Daniels we brought back from New Orleans . . .

I thought about calling you, but I would have hated to ask you to take me back, only to find myself with my old insecurities again and making you go through that again? I don't think so. The truth is that I was lonely...

I'm so tired of feeling lonely...

Jesse, you don't know how many times I dro. . . Hold on, the phone again...

"Hello? Yes . . . Man, I was just talking about you a few—a little while ago . . . No, surprisingly, it was not bad . . . How did you get my number? . . . I figured . . . Yeah, she told you about that, too? . . . He's stable, thanks for asking, brother . . . L.C., I really don't think it's such a good idea . . . I don't have time . . . Frankly, man, I don't want to see you . . . Yeah, man . . . No, man . . . I know . . . Last Sunday night, you put me on the spot, literally . . . Yes, and I thank you, you know what I'm saying? . . . I hear you . . . I really have nothing else to say to you . . . Hey L.C., there is nothing to fix. You and I are good the way we are right now . . . I feel you, I feel you . . . Yeah . . . I know, goodbye, L.C."

Guess who that was?

Where was I?

Yeah! I drove by your house a few times. One night I even parked right in front, looking at your house, even knowing you weren't there. I remember I fell asleep in the car, and then you woke me when you drove by. Luckily, you didn't see me. I could definitely see you coming out of the car, looking fine, as always.

For a minute there, I wanted to call out to you, talk to you. Instead, I put my hand on the door handle, deciding whether I would come out or not. It quickly reminded me of that movie I saw where leading lady got a good grip on the handle for a while, but she never left the fucking car. I was so close to opening it when Hank called. I think it was about Thanksgiving dinner. But—

Jesse! How long have you been doing that?

Yes! Blink again, son! Shit! Love, yes, keep blinking! Let me fetch the nurse. Hang in there, Red. I'll be right back!

TWENTY-EIGHT

ORSON HAD JUST HUNG UP the phone with Lauren. He had been sitting peacefully at his kitchen table reading the paper, having his usual oatmeal and raisins, with milk and a touch of cinnamon, and enjoying the sound of the rain outside. The coffee brewing in the background was filling the room with a sweet noise and rich aroma. He was thinking about what news he would share with Jesse that afternoon. Lauren's phone call had shattered his restful morning reverie. She started with useless chit chat before asking him to meet her at the hospital in an hour, though she did not specify why. She kept saying everything is OK and not to worry, so Orson had to take her word for it. He hated it when people said that over the phone because it usually meant the opposite. And regarding Jesse, he wasn't willing to wait. He couldn't even finish his breakfast. He called the hospital right then to find out if there were any changes in Jesse's condition. He was put on hold for an endless 10 minutes, which made him all the more anxious. To both his relief and to that of his digestion, Jesse was still in a coma with no change for the worse. The previous week, when Jesse blinked, Dr. Brennan said that was definitely a good sign. Orson and Lauren felt they deserved credit for his improvement, so now both, along with Hank, agreed to take turns visiting Jesse. Hank would normally come twice a week and read to him the screenplay his students wrote for the next episode of the web series. Whenever possible, Hank would play video recordings of his students encouraging Jesse to get well soon. Lauren requested the mornings so that she could do some writing the rest of the day. She would read out loud to her son from whatever she thought would be interesting to him, mostly about the goings-on in Hollywood, usually from *Variety*. Every visit included an hour session of

221

Reiki therapy. Orson's visits in the afternoons were different. He would sit next to Jesse and talk to him as if they were having an ordinary conversation. Orson would tell him about his day or relate some anecdote from a long time ago, or not so long ago, or simply revisit moments they had together to remind Jesse of their story. He often asked Jesse questions. Even though he was not expecting an answer, he figured this would get Jesse's attention and hopefully result in a reaction. Sometimes, depending on which nurse was on the floor, he would play blues recorded on his phone as background to his conversations with Jesse.

Orson had already lost his appetite, so he flushed the remains of his breakfast down the garbage disposal. He looked at the clock above the door in the kitchen and figured he had some time to be alone with Jesse before Lauren got there. He cleared the table, did the dishes, grabbed the keys to the Imperial and his sunglasses from the counter, and walked out the back door to get to the garage. As he stepped outside, he nearly tripped over an old army footlocker sitting just outside his back door. The wide wooden box certainly looked familiar. It had a sticker in the center; it read "Private Orson Davis" in handwriting that he also recognized. He looked at it for a little while before he tried the box for weight. He picked it up from the handles on each side and took it inside the house. He carried it through the kitchen all the way to the living room and placed it on the floor between the coffee table and the fireplace. He grabbed the nearest chair and put it in front of the trunk. He sat down in front of it and unlatched the two clasps on each side; then, he released the one in the center.

He opened the lid and cried, "Oh shit!". Part of his forgotten past had just slapped him in the face. His last memento from Vietnam. His old big wooden trunk that until this moment, he thought, was lost. The first thing he saw clearly was a legal-size white envelope carefully placed in the center of the removable tray, his name was written on it in L.C.'s handwriting. He picked it up and looked at it for a few seconds, hesitant to open it, then he put it back right where he found it.

On the same top tray, in the right compartment, there was a manila envelope with a white label, also with his name and his last name typewritten on it. It looked like it contained quite a few papers. He had

222

no intention of opening it either, so he put it on top of the smaller envelope. In the left compartment, there were several old Kodak yellow and black envelopes; he hadn't seen those in years. And though he was more than a little more curious about their contents, he remembered Jesse and Lauren, whom he had to meet in about an hour.

Nevertheless, he found himself lifting the tray to see what was underneath it. He placed the tray on the floor to his right. Inside the bottom of the footlocker, he found about ten old LPs. He fingered through them quickly and knew then who had them all these years. He thought he'd lost them, so he replaced most of them in CD format, but he always felt it didn't have the same feeling or sound. There were his old-time favorites: Mississippi Fred McDowell's *I Do Not Play No Rock 'n' Roll* and *At the Gate of Horn* by Memphis Slim. Orson had completely forgotten about those two albums. There were other blues albums, plus a few Jazz albums including a Chet Baker, an Oscar Peterson, and a Sarah Vaughan. There were a couple of soundtracks by Henry Mancini as well. Behind these LPs was another manila envelope with worn-out corners. This one was thicker than the other one. He pulled it out and saw that it read in big red letters, "ORSON'S MUSIC." He was definitely curious about this one, so he opened it. He found sheet music filled out in his own handwriting. A mixture of anger and joy hit him in a flash. He thought these pieces that were written in Vietnam for the Out of the Blues band were long gone. It turned out L.C. had them all this time. Orson had asked him about them years ago, and his ex-lover denied having them or knowing anything about them. He thumbed through the music sheets realizing there were more songs than he recalled ever writing. He put the songs back in the envelope, 'Can't wait to tell Jesse,' he almost said out loud as he laid it on his coffee table.

Next to the records there was his old uniform folded neatly on top of a thin box covered in black leather—he recognized it immediately—and it read "BRONZE STAR" in gold capital letters. He took it in his hands and opened it. It revealed his beautiful bronze medal, a five-point golden star hanging from a red ribbon with a blue stripe in the middle and rimmed by a narrow white stripe on each side, and right in the center of the blue stripe was a small bronze letter "V" for valor. He recalled the day

223

he received this medal with pride. He was glad to be reunited with this significant piece of his past he thought was also lost.

He closed the small box and held it in his left hand. He reached out to the uniform with his right and touched it lightly with his fingertips and caressed the tag with his last name with his thumb.

Orson suddenly had enough of this sentimental journey, so he put back everything the way it was, except for the white envelope that was addressed by L.C . . . He left the case with his medal and the envelope along with his songs on his coffee table. He closed the footlocker's lid and got up. He turned to the clock on the small table by the sofa and saw he had to leave at once. He looked at the envelope in his hand and, for a second, was tempted to toss it in the fireplace as kindling for the next fire. Instead, he walked to the mantel and left the letter sitting on it. He quickly walked through the kitchen's swinging door. A gust of wind caused by the swaying of the door made the letter fly off the mantel and land inside the fireplace, just as Orson had contemplated doing moments before.

"Lauren, what was so important that you needed to tell me?" Orson asked as he got inside Abe and shut the car door.

"I just told you before we left Jesse. I need you to take me to the airport," she said as she put on her seat belt. She just figured out what was different in Orson. "I like the beard; it's very becoming."

"You think?" He took a quick look at himself in the rearview mirror. "I thought I'd surprise Jesse, and try to look dignified for his return."

"Are you trying to catch up with him? I've never seen my son with a beard until now."

"Me neither. I thought about shaving him, but I like his beard."

"I like yours too. You look very gentlemanly, if I may say so."

He chuckled out loud with real humor. "Yes, you may."

"This is the first time I've seen you laugh. Jesse told me it was priceless. He was right."

Orson, who was feeling a bit on the spot, quickly changed the subject. "Have you talked to Dr. Brennan this morning?"

"Yes, right after I talked to you on the phone. He came in to check on Jesse and told me that whatever we're doing seems to be working. To keep up with the visits and the talking, which is what I really wanted to see you about, and which is why you are taking me to the airport instead of a taxi. This way, I'll have a bit more time to talk to you. I was wondering if you could cover my visiting shifts this weekend. I remember Jesse saying you have flexible hours at work, and you can take off whenever needed."

"There shouldn't be a problem; it's the weekend. Are you going back home?"

"No, I have been asked to give a series of talks on Remote Viewing at a conference in Boston. It was a last-minute thing. And I owe these people a favor . . ."

"Remote viewing . . . that's ESP, right?"

"Yes, that what we call ESP nowadays."

"When are you coming back?"

"Monday night." She turned around and pointed at the back seat. "There are movie magazines in that green paper bag. Read them to Jesse. I tell him what shows are hot, what movies are coming out, and things like that. That way, he'll be up to date when he wakes up."

Orson didn't have a problem reading for Jesse, but he had a hard time believing his boy would remember any of it. "Is that all? That's the important thing you wanted to tell me? I thought it was something bad like you were taking him back to California or something."

"Actually, I wanted to talk to you about that also. But we haven't made a final decision, The Santoses and I were talking last night about Jesse possibly coming home after the holidays."

"But that's less than two weeks away!" He turned his head to look at Lauren in the eyes for a second.

"I know Orson, the Santoses wanted him back for Christmas, but I told them the doctor ordered us not to move him for at least two weeks; that way, I was able to buy you a little more time." She felt bad for Orson, who was speechless for the next mile or two. "I'm sorry Orson. Patricia has been talking to her friends at UCLA's Medical Center, and we all agreed that it is the best place for Jesse until he gets back on his feet."

"I understand. I'm really nothing to him. We've only dated for how long? A week tops? Not even that."

"Listen, you can fly to LA. I have lots of miles with Delta, I'll give you my miles. It won't be long until he comes back anyways. I feel it. Mothers know."

"Thanks, Lauren," he replied, not sure he believed her.

"Listen, this decision was made late last night. The Santoses and I, we're are all scared, and we are acting on what we think is best."

Orson took the exit to Memphis International Airport and heard Lauren suddenly say, "Oh!" From the corner of his eye, he noticed she was looking for something in her large purple and green handbag. While she was doing this, he realized that of all the times he had seen her in the past week or so, she never wore any other colors, apart from the occasional orange accessory, as in the day they met for the first time. He saw her as she finally pulled something out. He turned quickly to look at what it was.

"Aha!" She exclaimed, "Here's Jesse's cell phone, just in case he wakes up before I get back. I know he can't live without it—" she realized what she just said, too late to take it back. She handed the phone to Orson, who took it and dropped it in his shirt pocket. She went back to look in her bag one more time, she then retrieved a brown cardboard tube, 12 inches long and 3 in diameter.

"What's that?" Orson asked, barely keeping his eyes on the road.

"I told you about this." She tapped one of the ends of the tube, partially pushing out what was hidden inside the tube. "He left it for you at his house," She pulled out a rolled piece of white paper tied with a red ribbon and small card hanging from it. "But you have to wait till Christmas to open it."

"What?!" Orson turned to get a quick glance at it. "What is it?"

"I don't know. It was sitting on top of the dining room table."

Orson started seeing the different airport terminal signs, "Lauren, which airline?"

"Oh! United . . . There." She pointed at the sign, and Orson veered to the right to get to terminal 7. "Wow! It's so busy. This is crazy. It must be the holidays. I'm glad that at least it stopped raining."

Orson hadn't been listening to her, "Why do I have to wait till Christmas to open it?"

"It's written here." She picked up the hanging tab and showed it to the driver. " 'To Orson: Do not open 'til Christmas.' But you do whatever you want, I won't tell."

Orson pulled over his Lincoln Continental in front of the terminal and parked it. He quickly got out to get Lauren's small suitcase. He met her at the back of his car, opened the trunk, pulled out her luggage, and handed it to her. They hugged for a few long seconds without speaking. When they parted, they each noticed that the other had watery eyes and acknowledged it to one another with a warm grin.

"Goodbye, Orson."

"See you in a few days," he said, watching her turning away and taking a few steps before she stopped and turned around and walked back to him.

"Oh! I almost forgot. I heard your songs. I remembered that Jesse told me they were on his phone. I couldn't resist. I must say, Jesse was right, you are one talented musician. Keep it up!"

"That's the plan."

"You should play them for Jesse."

"I do it already. Some days I play music in the background while I talk to him."

"Your songs?"

"No."

"Get some headphones and play him your songs. He'll love that."

They said their goodbyes once again, but then Lauren remembered something else and came back. She asked Orson to pose with her for a selfie with his phone. She complained that her arms were too short, besides her phone was buried in her bag somewhere. Lauren wanted photographic evidence to show her friends at the conference of her most likely future son-in-law. Just the way she said it tickled him. He took his phone out of his pants pocket, pulled Lauren into a side hug, stretched his arm out, and shot the photo.

After many demands, Orson promised her he would send the photo right away and said goodbye one final time. He watched her walk into the terminal building, making sure her absent-mindedness wasn't going to bring her back. He got in his car and was about to send the selfie to Lauren when he looked in the rearview mirror and spotted a policeman walking towards Abe. Orson quickly put the car in gear and drove away.

Orson's mission then was to find a place to park and keep his promise, so he pulled into the first strip mall he found. The parking lot was full, and while he drove around looking for a spot, he was getting annoyed by the Christmas carol playing over the shopping center parking lot. It wasn't the song itself, for he liked "O Little Town of Bethlehem," but the sound system and how loud it was. To him, it sounded like the music was coming from a can. In fact, it reminded him of the speakers in the camp, back in Vietnam. He finally saw an empty spot and went for it fast. After he parked, he looked up and saw a pole with a round neon sign on top in red, yellow, and black. He could not believe his eyes; it was Gibson's Donuts. This is where Jesse bought their to-go breakfast for their road trip to New Orleans. What a perfect spot to send the selfie from, he thought. He switched off the engine and picked up his phone, which he had left on the car seat. He hit the photo gallery icon and ran through the thumbnails with his index finger. He noticed one that had Jesse's face on it he couldn't recall ever seeing; it had a play video icon in the corner of the screen. He sent the selfie to Lauren to be done with that promise. With trembling promise fingers, he clicked on the video, and it started. It showed Jesse shooting a selfie video lying in bed next to him sleeping. Red was about to say something when Orson stopped playing the clip. He needed to catch his breath to continue. Once he did, he restarted the video. Jesse was trying hard to whisper while wearing a big smile:

"Hey Babe, you are just about an hour and a half away from your big night. You've been rehearsing all day. We've just made delicious love and look at you, sleeping like a big teddy next to me. It can't get any better than this. By the time you watch this, my prediction will have been a reality. You were great and knocked the socks off everyone at The Grasshopper. I'm so sure of it that I can say this to your face: I told you so! I love you, Mr. Nipples." Jesse blew a kiss to the camera and stopped it.

Orson felt his heart imploding, shattering like laminated glass, broken but with all its pieces remaining in place. His eyelids began twitching, and his eyes began to burn. His lower lip trembled uncontrollably. He knew this was coming since the day he first saw Jesse lying in that hospital bed. He didn't know where or when, but it was coming close, very close. His hands started to shake, and the phone fell in his lap. He reached for the steering wheel, something he could grab on to, and he held it as tightly as he could. There was no use trying to keep his grief in any longer . . . He exploded.

A loud cry came out of his mouth, and the tears finally drained out of those rusty pipes in his eyes. He dropped his head on the wheel between his hands. He cried and cried some more. If anyone outside had knocked on his car window, he would not have noticed. He was only aware of the tinny music that kept playing without mercy, but even that no longer bothered him. He was somewhere else. He was all to himself in this private moment of missing Jesse; more than he could have ever imagined possible. He sat inside his car, this large all-American metallic aqua shelter, for who knows how long.

Eventually, Orson pulled himself together the best way he could. He reached out to the glove compartment hoping there would be tissue or something that would do the trick. He opened the small door and found a stack of white napkins. He pulled out the first two or three on the top, and before he blew his nose, he noticed the logo printed on them. It was from Gibson's Donuts; probably from one of the many late nights he and Jesse ate at the very spot Orson was parked on. After fixing up his face, he figured he would feel better, but no, he had never experienced such heartache. But this was a different kind of heartache; it was clean and honest. With no regrets because he knew that what he had with Jesse was real. Maybe one regret, he stopped to think. 'All that time we were apart after New Orleans . . . What the hell I was thinking, not trusting him?' He lamented. 'Why was it so hard for me to believe Jesse, there was no reason to mistrust him. . . All that time wasted when we could've . . . Damn you, L.C., for messing with my heart, and making me feel insecure about everyone else after.'

He shut the glove compartment harder than it deserved, then started his car, realizing it was useless to have feelings of regret or even blame at this point in his life. 'Now is now.' He reminded himself as he backed up his car. 'You know better than this. You've got this.' He put Abe into drive, not totally convinced by the words in his head. 'C'mon, Jesse's waiting.'

He slowly pressed on the gas pedal and made the necessary turns to exit the strip mall. The light turned green, and Orson made a left turn; a twenty-minute drive would take him straight to Methodist North. He needed to hold his boy Red's hand for as long as it took to get his heart back into gear and return to feeling whole.

TWENTY-NINE

IT WAS PARTICULARLY QUIET that night in the ICU. There were only two nurses on the floor and two interns on shift. At least, that's what the nurse at the front desk told Orson. The clock on his phone displayed 22 minutes 'til midnight, and he was anxious for Christmas day to start; mainly because he wanted so badly to open the present Jesse left for him and because he wanted to prove his best friend wrong. Before leaving for Saint Louis to see her father for the holidays, Ambar bet $50 that Orson wouldn't be able to resist the command to wait; that he would cave in and open Jesse's gift before Christmas. Perhaps she was right to think that. Orson thought she knew him better than anyone, but what he felt for Jesse could overcome any temptation. He loved and respected the guy too much.

Another reason he was desperate to make it to midnight was to put behind that particular day, for he had been through quite the ordeal. Orson had begun to wonder if he should have spared Jesse of some details of this day because the telling him about it seemed to drag as much as the day itself. For starters, that morning was probably the busiest he could ever recall since he started working at the Piggly Wiggly two years before. To top it off, three of his work colleagues called in sick with the flu. As a result, he had been running around the store performing duties he never signed up for. "It's payback time," said Mr. Hucklebun late that morning, referring to all of those extra hours Orson had taken off in recent days. That meant he would have to stay until 3:00 p.m., which would be cutting it very close to be on time for picking up Lauren at the airport. But his immediate concern was Knookie, Gennie's gift from Santa. The poor puppy was probably annoying the hell out of the neighbors, howling away

231

from loneliness in Orson's house and most likely pooping all over his basement. It was a good thing he put Angela's old boxes to good use, finally. He created a corral around a big enough space for the puppy to be comfortable.

In the middle of the work crisis, Hank called, so Orson promised to get back to him on his next break. He stood outside by the backdoor of the supermarket where he could talk without being distracted by constant "hellos" he was not in the mood for. His son-in-law had bad news. Their annual Christmas Eve dinner was canceled, something about Angela falling ill. Orson could tell by the tone in the young man's voice that he was lying—possibly against his will—to avoid a three-day silent treatment from his wife. It was so obvious to Orson this was all Angela's doing; she thought of her own father as deceitful, and she couldn't possibly have him join them for a picture-perfect family holiday dinner. At some point in their conversation, Orson politely confronted Hank, saying he knew exactly what was going on in the Emerson household. Without malice, Orson asked Hank if Angela was right nearby him. From that point on, Hank's answers were monosyllabic to the father-in-law's carefully phrased questions, hoping this would prevent a confrontation with the wife. Before hanging up, Hank did assure Dad they would see each other the following day. As every year, the family would come over to Grandpa's house on Christmas day for lunch and to open the gifts Santa had left for little Gennie. For obvious reasons, Angela wouldn't be coming over this year, nor would there be lunch. Normally, Orson would spend the day before Christmas preparing food for as many people as needed, usually, the same Thanksgiving gang and the occasional extra. But having Jesse at the hospital did not inspire Orson to buy a Christmas tree nor decorate his house, and much less prepare a big meal for guests. That's why he deliberately volunteered to work that morning at the Piggly Wiggly, so he wouldn't have to give any excuses for not having it.

Barely hanging up from Hank, Lauren called. Good thing Orson was still on his break. With much regret, she said she was definitely not going to make it back to Memphis in time for Christmas. She had tried for the second day in a row to get back, but due to heavy snowstorms in the Northeast, it was impossible to get a flight out of Boston. She was being very apologetic about it, but Orson was secretly glad he did not have to explain to her why they had been uninvited to Christmas Eve dinner.

But that wasn't the worst part of his day, Orson recalled as he looked at his phone again, reading there were 14 more minutes to go until he could open his little rolled up gift.

It was past five o'clock when he finally got off work. He certainly paid his dues to Mr. Hucklebun; he owed him nothing from then on. It was raining hard, and Orson had to run to his car wearing just a plastic bag over his head for protection, so by the time he reached Abe, he was soaking wet.

On his way home, he had to make a quick stop at a pet shop to get a leash he had forgotten to buy for Knookie. He drove to a busy shopping mall, and naturally it was hard to find parking space, and the way his day was going, finding the furthest spot possible seemed just about perfect. Fortunately, he had his iconic yellow umbrella in the car, and luckily, the pet shop was near the main entrance, so he didn't have to fight the Holiday Spirit mob. Orson entered the pet shop and bought the first leash he found, there was no line to pay, and he was out of there. He walked to his car, thinking it was too good to be true that he had accomplished the task in less than 8 minutes. He couldn't wait to go home and unwind a bit with the help of some weed. He would then shower, have a quick improvised dinner, and head to Methodist North to welcome Christmas with Jesse.

He sat inside his Lincoln Continental, put the keys in the ignition, and the car wouldn't start. "Fuck" came out of his mouth several times in a row. The rain was still coming down hard, and he wasn't about to investigate what was wrong with his car. He called AAA immediately, but they said it would take them a couple of hours to assist Abe due to the festivities. He found himself with two choices: staying inside his car for two hours or go inside the mall and watch merry shoppers running about, something he had been successfully avoiding every Holiday season for the last 15 or so years.

Sitting with his present in hand, Orson looked over at Jesse lying still on that hospital bed with his eyes closed. He wondered where the young man he liked to call his boy, could be. His phone read five more minutes to Christmas. Why was time ticking by so slowly? His thoughts went back to that parking lot, sitting inside Abe while it rained only a few hours ago.

He could have stayed in his car, writing some music while he waited for AAA, but he had left his last notebook at home on the piano. For the last few days, he had been recording a lot, preparing his Christmas gift for Jesse, a playlist with what Orson considered his best material. This included many of the completed songs from the music sheets he recovered from L.C., plus some of the ones he had finished recently. He kept looking at the Cartier clock on the dashboard, getting more and more impatient. He still could not believe he had to wait two whole hours at least to get his car serviced when usually he could fix the car himself. 'I'm wet already,' he considered for a brief second. 'But hey, I pay monthly for a service, I might as well get my money's worth.' He took a long breath and then another. It seemed that his frustration diminished a bit, and then the background sound of the rain hitting the roof of his car caught his attention. The rain was much softer this time. He turned the key in the ignition halfway and switched on the windshield wipers for a few seconds. He looked up, and the sky seemed to be clearing. The gentle dripping of the rain made him think of Jesse more and more, and he wondered why he wasn't with him already.

Desperation kicked in, so Orson pulled out his keys and got out of the car and walked across the parking without the bright yellow umbrella. He went inside the mall, mostly in search of a newsstand to buy a new small notebook and a pen. Again, he wanted to be out of there quickly, so indiscriminately, he picked out the two items he needed and went straight to the register. As he was waiting for his change, Orson looked down at the newspapers that were laid right below in front of him; all the local ones read basically the same thing. The news stopped him cold. The first one read: "BLUES LEGEND PASSES Leroy 'Lazy' Cooper dies of cancer at 67." Orson got his change back and, losing his manners momentarily, he walked out of the store without thanking the cashier or saying goodbye. He got a hold of his phone and called Ambar while he walked to his car.

"So, did I win my bet already?" Ambar answered.

"L.C. died, I just read it," Orson said without greeting her. "You knew he was dying, didn't you?"

"Yes, I knew, I'm sorry."

"Is that why he wanted to talk to me?"

"Among other things, yes. When did he pass?"

"I don't know; I assume he died yesterday," Orson replied. "Do you know he left a box at my house with my old stuff, stuff I thought I'd lost."

"I know that too, L.C. told me he would do that."

"You sure kept it all a secret."

"He said not to tell anyone, not even you. He didn't want anybody to feel sorry for him or treat him differently, or give him shit about not getting treatment."

"Fool! What a damned fool. That son of a bitch, it's so like him, he always hated hospitals. It was all that blood and guts he saw in Nam. But I can relate now. I'm beginning to hate hospitals too."

"Are you with Jesse now?"

"No, I haven't made it yet."

"But I thought . . ."

"Long story," he interrupted, "but I'll be there as soon as I can. Are they holding a service for L.C. in Atlanta?"

"I don't know; probably, I haven't read the paper yet."

He talked to Ambar for a few minutes longer. Hanging up, Orson remembered the letter L.C. had enclosed in the footlocker and wondered why he hadn't read it yet. L.C. was so far gone from his mind that he simply had forgotten all about it. He only now remembered thinking he would throw the letter away; maybe he did.

Eventually, AAA showed up, 'At least they were punctual,' Orson thought when he saw them park behind Abe, just as he finished writing a song. About thirty minutes later, he was dropped off at home, but his precious Lincoln Continental didn't come along. With much regret, he saw Abe at the mall being lifted onto a flatbed to be taken to his old shop, the same one he sold to his previous employees, just like Mr. Andrews did with him. Abe would probably not be ready until after New Year's. That was fine. He had other things on his mind. He could get around on his new motorbike or with Ambar's car if he needed to.

Orson had spent the next 45 minutes cleaning up after Knookie, feeding him, playing with him, and, hopefully, leaving him to rest peacefully in the basement. He then collapsed his butt and the rest of himself on the sofa, he let a long gush of air out of his lungs and stared at the window in front of him. Not fixing on anything in particular, his vision eventually became blurry out of pure weariness. He noticed a white spot on the lower right side of his visual field. He turned his head a bit and saw L.C.'s envelope, resting beside the logs inside the fireplace. Orson got up and walked to the mantel and kneeled down to retrieve the envelope. He dusted off the ashes and returned to the sofa and sat down in the same spot and the same manner as a moment ago. He opened the envelope and pulled out the letter inside and read.

L.C. started off with "Davis," just as he had always called him. He wrote about his memories of their first meeting when Orson auditioned for The Out of the Blues band. Also, about when they made love in the jungle for the very first time, all the way throughout the end of the war; their brief assignment to Germany and finally, their first eight months living together in Memphis when L.C. convinced Orson to leave New Orleans to move in with him. Both made their way into the blues music scene by playing in jam sessions at joints around town. They had agreed that Orson would get a steady day job to help pay the bills, while L.C. concentrated on music with his voice and guitar. They never counted on L.C.'s career taking off so quickly and much less imagined it to skyrocket the way it did. It wasn't long before the lovers started having problems due to L.C.'s drinking and constant infidelities, with men and women. Fed up with the fights, L.C. eventually kicked Orson out of their place.

Orson remembered those days with pain and resentment. He had been working as a mechanic's assistant, thanks to his experience in the service. When L.C. gave him the boot, he had no place to go, and he considered going back to New Orleans. Lucky for him, Mr. Andrews, his boss, and his wife took Orson in with the condition that he go to church with them every Sunday. He had no problem with their request. He needed a home and, honestly, some guidance. He was feeling insecure and a bit confused about his feelings. He had never thought of himself as gay. He was a large, black man with a very masculine persona that didn't fit his idea of what he or anyone considered gay at the time.

The neighborhood church welcomed young Orson with open arms. He joined their choir as a pianist and found himself setting his true feelings aside, at least temporarily. He eventually sent for Genna. She had been on hold since he left for Vietnam. Through Orson's occasional and ambiguous letters and phone calls, he kept the flame going. Mr. Andrews and his wife had a lot to do with this decision to call for his bride. Now that Orson had some money saved, they encouraged him to find a home big enough for two or three and get married and settle down there. Orson and Genna got married in a small ceremony, mostly with members of the congregation. Orson's parents, sister, and brother-in-law drove all the way down from Chicago, and his grandmother and his future sister and mother-in-law, plus a few more relatives, all came from Louisiana for the occasion.

With L.C.'s letter still in his hands, he pondered about those years with him, thinking how lost he really was, living through other people's expectations and none of his true emotions. It took a major event such as Genna's death for his pretend life to collapse. Orson found no consolation in the church after the tragedy. There were only repetitive affirmations and platitudes that did nothing for him. Booze and weed did, however, but he ended up neglecting his daughter, who conveniently preferred spending more time with Ambar than with her own father.

Orson had always felt he owed Ambar a debt for playing such a big role in getting his act together. She suggested he needed to find a therapist who could help him accept his sexuality, release the guilt for his wife's death, and forgive himself for deceiving Genna and the people he loved.

L.C.'s writing continued by finally admitting that fame had changed him, recognizing how inconsiderate, selfish and cruel he could sometimes be, throughout all their years together. He expressed regret for missing out on Orson, the only man—L.C. admitted in writing—he ever loved. He closed his letter by apologizing and hoping Orson would find room in his heart to forgive him. To try to make up for all the heartache, L.C. granted Orson the royalties from all his recordings, which were many. Thirty-eight years of music on two different labels; the legal papers were inside the footlocker, all he had to do was sign them and give them to

L.C.'s lawyer. He ended the letter by wishing for Jesse's full recovery, wishing him and Orson a happy life together, and finishing by signing his full name: Leroy Charlton Cooper.

Orson had no idea Leroy had a middle name, that was his first thought before realizing L.C. had set him up for life. He leaned back on the sofa again, resting his head on the top pillow, releasing the letter from his fingers and letting it float away to the floor. He gazed into space, thinking about what would be next in a day such as this one. He dozed off for a few minutes. When he came to, it was nearly ten o'clock. He had to rush to meet Jesse. He opened the coat closet and grabbed a red wool scarf and his thick black leather jacket and gloves, got the keys to his bike, and left for the hospital with two Christmas gifts inside his backpack, Jesse's and his.

Seated next to Jesse's bed, Orson kept staring at his phone, toying with his present, holding the scroll by its ribbon and spinning it like a suspended propeller while the last infinite seconds came to an end. When the clock hit 0:00, he thought he would unroll that sucker off, but instead, he set it right on the bed and went straight for his backpack, pulling out Jesse's gift: a pearl-colored, gift-wrapped box tied up with a fat red ribbon with golden edges. He placed it on Jesse's lap.

"Hey, Red, I hope you weren't too bored by me bitching about my day just now, but I just had to let it out. I don't know why, but I sense you can hear me. Maybe it is just wishful thinking. Now, being with you is all I need, you and me here alone. Our first Christmas together. It is not how I pictured it, the little that I allowed myself to fantasize. I was convinced Lauren was right and you would be back by now, and we would be out and about at who knows where, your house, my house. I'm just glad you're sticking around, and I get to hold your hand and feel your touch that I love so much." Orson got up from his chair and stood by Jesse and started caressing the guy's hair above the forehead. He reached for the pearl-colored gift box and started unwrapping, revealing a brown box with red and white lettering, he opened the box and pulled out a set of new matte black headsets. "Here, Red," Orson said. "I've already linked . . . I mean, paired it to your phone where the real gift is. You should thank YouTube for teaching me how to get this done. You should be proud of your man.

Merry Christmas, Jesse." The man placed the headphones on Jesse's ears, kissed him on the forehead, and then hit play on the guy's phone. Orson then sat back on the chair and took the scroll in his hands. He slid the ribbon off and unrolled the scroll open from top to bottom. Orson read two words on the top that served as the title in silence and then exclaimed, "You did it, Red!" then read the next two sentences. "You, son of a gun." The man began to tear. "You sneaky, clever, adorable bastard, and right on time for Christmas, just like I asked you to." He leaned back in his chair and read.

GENTLE RAIN
Music by Orson Davis
Lyrics by Jesse Santos

Awaken by the sound of sweet gentle rain
I'm watching soft blue light sneak through my window pane
Feels like I'm still dreaming, you're still by my side
With your arms around me, all troubles set aside

Mister sun is trying hard to make himself show
But the clouds are determined to make him lay low
Let my room stay like this, all tinted blue
So when you finally wake up I can share it with you

As sure as I love you I want time to be still
Us here close together, there is no bigger thrill
Right now I'm in heaven and feeling no pain
I need nothing other than you and the gentle rain
Just you and the gentle rain

Familiar fingers caressed the tiny dark and silver curls in Orson's beard. The gentle touch made the man blink his eyes open a few times. Seated in his chair, he had cried himself to sleep on Jesse's chest, resting his head on his own crossed arms, still holding on to the piece of paper Jesse gave him for Christmas. The familiar hand then rested on that side of his face and made Orson blink his eyes closed again. It felt warm and smooth, just

239

like he remembered. 'I don't want this dream to end,' the man said to himself. Part of him wanted to lift his head and turn to look at Jesse, but Orson was having a moment of bliss. Just Jesse and him alone, like that early morning in the hotel in New Orleans, when the street lights went out and their room became tinted in blue.

Orson blinked a few more times, thinking that the state he was in— somewhere between dream and reality—was becoming more tangible by the second. 'This dream stage does not usually last this long,' he thought. Nonetheless, he had a sudden urge to spread his arms and try to get a hold of Jesse in this way, just in case it was a dream. But he needed to know, by looking into those green eyes, if the sparkle was still in them and Orson could see with his very own throughout Jesse's soul and know if his boy still loved him.

THIRTY

'IT FELT SO REAL,' Jesse remembers while holding his heavy mug of coffee and staring at the other half of his burger on the plate. Entering into a huge pitch-black empty hangar by himself and feeling excited. He and a large crew had just finished a big production, and the wrap-up party would be taking place at that large empty space, but no one had arrived yet, and to him, that was totally OK. There was a spotlight on him, and whenever and wherever he walked, the circular glow followed, but he didn't seem to care or notice. The soundtrack for the film was playing in the background even though he knew it had not been written yet. He recalls being exhausted but with a great sense of accomplishment for finishing the movie. A big, epic, larger than life movie that he wrote, produced, and directed. One of those World War II epics of Hollywood's yesteryears with plenty of Nazis, allies, spies, soldiers, pilots, paratroopers, victims, orphans, and heroes. The name of the movie still escapes him; he remembers the crew wearing the t-shirt with the logo, but in his memory, he had never been able to read the title. So when he finally did write the script in the real world, he had to name it something else. Looking back, making such a movie seemed very much out of his range at the time, but now, almost twelve years later, it's almost part of his everyday life. But to make a movie of that magnitude for the duration of his coma is still impossible.

To this day, Jesse is not clear on the sequence of events during his induced dream state; it all seemed to happen at the same time, he had mentioned to Lauren. She suggested he write down everything he could remember, and once it was all on paper, he could probably find a timeline. One thing he was certain of, stepping inside that hangar was definitely the last event during his coma.

He and Orson talked about it soon after he woke up, and what Jesse thought to be the soundtrack for his film, was actually what was playing on the headphones he had just got from Orson for Christmas. The same occurred with other instances; happenings from real life that blended into his dream state. He recalls having conversations with Orson, Lauren, and Hank that coincide with whatever they said or read to him during his coma, even though, in reality it was a one-way communication. Jesse recalled things the nurses and doctors said when in the room. That's why when he finally snapped out of it, he didn't panic at the sight of those machines, tubes, and wires hooked up to him.

He remembers vividly waiting under the spotlight for the wrap-up party to start. When suddenly, what Jesse recognized as the main theme for the movie started in the background. While the song played on, the spotlight on him grew larger and larger, and the gigantic space got brighter and brighter until there was no more darkness; with the total absence of shadows, it was as if Jesse was floating in mid-air. Thinking back, he later realized it was "Gentle Rain" that brought him back. The next thing he remembers was Orson sobbing right next to him at the hospital, immediately recognizing the sheet of paper the man was holding in this hand. Jesse doesn't have a memory of how long it took him to gather enough strength to reach out to Orson's face to caress it. Surprised to find there was no smooth skin to touch, but a full-grown beard Jesse needed to explore. That feeling was eclipsed by the expanding warmth of Orson's arms, wrapping him with love. Jesse was overwhelmed by a deep sense of surrendering, very much like their first-ever kiss. When they finally locked eyes onto each other, all the emotions they had ever lived coalesced into one single moment. No words were needed, although he longed to hear the man speak. When Orson finally did say his name, Jesse could not contain the commotion in his heart, making the monitor pick up on it. It didn't take long for the nurses on duty to burst into the room.

He now takes the last drink of his coffee and glances at his empty plate with the Waffle House logo on it and can't believe he just gobbled up Orson's favorite, the Double Bacon Cheeseburger. He stares at the small plate with the side order of hash-browns and finally accepts that it was not a good idea to have ordered them because he won't be able to even take a bite of them. He and Orson had stopped eating fatty foods about a year into Orson's big leap to California. They would make an occasional exception for a specific craving, but generally, they kept to a healthy diet—LA style. Jesse could almost hear Orson now giving him shit about wasting food; now, he longs for it. He then takes the heavy mug and wonders if he should ask for a free refill. He looks over the cup and sees little Gennie, no longer little, walking through the door looking around for him. For an instant, and many others like it, he wishes Orson was there with him to witness how beautiful she looks, all dressed up for the big occasion. He admires how the yellow of her slim dress accentuates her vivaciousness. Jesse watches as she finally spots him. He gets up, looks at the tab, and leaves $16 on the table. Jesse and Gennie meet halfway, in the middle of the aisle, sided by booths where other customers are having lunch.

"Grampa Jess!" Gennie greets him as they embrace.

He then holds her by the shoulders and looks at her and compliments her on how beautiful she looks every time. As usual, she's modest about it; she's very self-conscious. She discreetly looks around to see if people are staring at them, then lowers her head a bit with a timid smile.

"What did you just call me? Grampa Jess? I thought we'd talked about this."

"Sorry, I can't help it."

"What did we agree on?"

"Sorry, Grampa Red."

"That's better."

He hugs her again for a few seconds. Unlike the last time they embraced each other goodbye five months ago at LAX airport. It was much longer and far more emotional.

"Is your dad outside?" Jesse asked.

"Yes, he and Cindy are in the car, they're talking to Mom on the phone."

"How's that going?" Jesse gestured for her to lead the way out.

"Much better. Now Mom and Daddy only fight when I come down to visit. But she adores Cindy. Mom says Cindy keeps him on his toes."

"Glad to hear that."

"When I go back to Syracuse in a couple of days, they'll stop arguing until I come back again."

Gennie and Jesse walked out of the restaurant to find Hank and his new 11th-month girlfriend waiting by his SUV. The two men greet each other as usual, with a shake with elbows down and half a hug with a soft bump. They comment on the respective ties they're wearing and then laugh about it. Jesse is officially introduced to Cindy, whom he had only met by video call. They chat for a little bit before getting in the car, glad it had stopped raining and that the sky was finally clearing out. The men sat in front. They wanted to catch up in person, even though they've been talking on the phone a lot lately.

"I read the article on Dad from *Esquire* you sent me . . . and Man!" said Hank, slightly swinging his head to the side. "Wow!" He then starts the car.

"I thought it was a beautiful tribute." Replied Jesse as he buckled.

"That's exactly what Angela said, all teary-eyed."

"Really? Angela?"

"I'm telling you, man, us splitting up was the best thing . . ." Taking advantage that his daughter and girlfriend are wrapped in a conversation behind them, Hank continues, "How are you holding up, buddy?" Turning his head to look at Jesse as he drives off.

"Better than the last time we talked," Jesse replies, he doesn't turn to Hank so as to avoid crying. "Sorry about that, buddy." Referring to the last time they spoke two days before, when Jesse lost it over the phone.

"Nothing to apologize about. I completely understand. It's only been . . . five months? I miss Dad, too, we all do. I'm just glad we got to see him all those times he came down here."

"Well, that's what killed him, all that work. If only I . . ." Jesse couldn't finish his sentence.

"I feel you, man, but it was his time," Hank replied. Both men were quiet for a minute or so, while Cindy and Gennie kept talking.

"It's the mornings, Hank." Jesse flicked the visor mirror to check if he was looking good. "Mornings are hard sometimes. I was so used to his early morning joy. Not knowing how he was going to tease me that day, the singing, the grabbing . . . but by night, it's not that bad. I'm so tired from work that I just fall asleep immediately." Jesse feels around all his pockets with his hands looking for something. He finally pulls out a folded piece of paper from his pants back pocket and whispers in relief. "Good." He unfolds it into a letter-size sheet with printed sentences.

"Is that your speech?" Hank asks.

"Uh-huh"

"Is Lauren coming?" Says Gennie from the back seat.

"She wouldn't miss this for the world," Jesse replies.

"Good, she's so cool," she then turned to Cindy. "Wait till you meet her."

"She's probably there already," Jesse added.

"Are you ready for it?" Hank questions.

"I don't know. I figured if I've learned it by heart, I wouldn't have to think about the words and I can avoid the waterworks."

"Do you mean like giving your speech on automatic pilot?" Cindy asks.

"Well, yes. That's it. But I just can't seem to learn it; maybe I'm just too nervous. I hate those speakers that read their speeches. I may have to do just that. I don't know how actors memorize whole scripts. That's why I could never be one."

"Dad, can I take a selfie of all of us?" Gennie pulls her phone from her purse. "I want it to be part of the event to post it."

"Suki, we can't be late for the inauguration, besides I don't want to get a ticket."

"There," Jesse pointed outside. "She can take it at that stop sign."

"Thanks, buddy," Hank replied with irony. "You know how much I hate selfies."

"Oh yeah, I forgot."

Hank makes the requested stop, and Gennie quickly unbuckles and gets between her father and step-grandfather; Cindy poses right behind her. The young woman then stretches her arm and takes the selfie. Hank then starts the car again and takes the route Jesse knows by heart. They cruise by a very busy Graceland and turn at the next corner. When they arrive, Jesse can hardly recognize the old house, although he had looked at photos, architectural drawings, and plans, even videos Hank had been sending him during renovations.

Hank pulls into the new parking lot across the street. He recalls how it took some maneuvering and many lawyers for Orson and Jesse to acquire that property; the owner was reluctant to sell. Still, the couple's persistence and money literally paid off. He parks the SUV, and he's excited to see the parking lot was already half full as they drove in.

Jesse gets out of the car ahead of the others and stares from across the street at what used to be Steven's grandparent's house. The truth is that the place is unrecognizable, and although the new trees in front of it are still young, it easy for Jesse to envision how it all will look like eventually.

Until now, he has been hesitant to check the time. Twenty-one minutes to go before his speech, Jesse realizes after finally looking at his phone. "How did I get myself into this?" He says loud enough for himself only, thinking about delivering his speech in front of a bunch of strangers. Before crossing the street, Jesse takes a long breath and says softly enough for Orson, "Miss you, Babe."

Jesse joins Suki and the adults crossing to the other side of the street, where Angela is standing on the sidewalk by the driveway. He admires how Angie is all dressed up as he has never seen her before, not even at her father's funeral in LA. She is smiling, not showing all her teeth, though, but she's smiling and happy to see him. 'She looks good,' Jesse thinks, less tense and friendlier than he ever remembers. She greets them, and they all talk for a while.

Jesse has a little moment of patting himself in the back. It took some doing on his part to get Orson and Angela to bury the hatchet they left out in the open to rust for years. On the other hand, Hank's back was worthy of extra patting too. It was through him that Angie eventually accepted her father's sexuality, not that she had a problem with homosexuals. It was the fact that her father had concealed it from her and everyone in the family for so long. She liked Jesse right from the beginning, back when Hank used to brag about how dedicated the screenwriter was to his students. But father and daughter still had their differences over the years, but much less as time went by. They eventually and willingly developed a bond that had been missing since Angela was a child. A thin line held only by love and the admiration they had for one another's integrity, which is why she got involved in her father's new life project, mainly to work on the legal aspects of the music school they are inaugurating today. It was Hank who suggested Angie should give the presentation speech and to introduce Jesse for his. People kept coming in, even some of Hank's all-grown-up students that worked on the web series years before came to say hello to Jesse. And of course, most of Orson's veteran friends from the Pig Pickin' who, through Jesse's invitation, came to pay their respects.

Before entering the building, Jesse took a few steps back and looked over the entrance, reading ORSON DAVIS INSTITUTE OF MUSIC chiseled in stone. The chill this gives Jesse results in a severe case of the goosebumps and fills his bursting heart with great pride. As the crowd passes him by to go in, Jesse recalls the night they came up with the idea for a music school for underprivileged individuals. It was late one night—he and Orson had been living in Franklin Hills in Los Angeles for more than nine years, and married for five—and they were driving back home from an award show. One for which Orson had been nominated for his score for *Broken Truths*, a mini-series produced by Netflix, his first project in which Jesse was not involved. Red was driving, and Orson had been quieter than usual on their way home. The guy figured his husband must have been disappointed for not winning, so he held his hand silently from time to time as he drove. When they got home, Orson finally opened up.

He explained to Jesse that he was moved by Gary Sinise, an actor they shared their table with. The man had recognized the actor from playing a Vietnam veteran in the movie *Forest Gump*, and at some point, Orson felt brave enough to approach him. He broke the ice by calling him Lieutenant Dan, the role the actor, now also a director, had played in the movie. Naturally, the Vietnam War became their subject of conversation, which led to Mr. Sinise's charity work with veterans from that very war and his involvement in other causes. Orson was impressed by his philosophy and his sense of compassion and felt inspired by his humanitarian work. This brief encounter put Orson's wheels in motion, deep in his heart he had always wanted to do something for people in need, but never had enough of anything to give away. With the last eleven years of film score composing, six complete soundtracks, two Emmy award nominations, and a very solid safety net under his belt—thanks to L.C.—Orson decided this was his moment of truth.

Jesse loved the fire that had been ignited in Orson that night, and the idea of his husband wanting to start on a charity project. Pumped up by enthusiasm, both men pulled an all-nighter sitting in bed proposing all kinds of possibilities on how this could go about. A school of music, mainly for kids from low-income families in Memphis, was decided when dawn came peeping into their bedroom. The next step was to wait for Hank to get off work and ask him if he wanted to take part as the second man on board.

This was Orson's baby, and Jesse's only involvement and contribution was the house he inherited from Steven. It had been vacant for the last few months after being rented, ever since Jesse and Orson moved to the west coast. During the video call to Memphis, Hank's response could not have been more positive. He wanted at all costs to be part of Orson's music school. The son-in-law felt honored by the offer to take part in the new dream of the most important man in the teacher's life.

That was nearly two years ago, and all the time between then and five months ago Orson had given his heart and soul to his new life project. He wisely turned down a couple of movie soundtrack offers due to the time invested in the new music school, which at the time still didn't have a definite name. Orson toyed with the idea of L.C.'s name for the institute in his head, but opted for it to stay there for Jesse would have most likely hit the roof.

Orson flew back and forth between Memphis and LA a few times for meetings with architects, constructors, suppliers, donors, and lawyers. That's when Angela came on board. Then there were fundraisers, city council meetings, and plenty of red tape. Taking advantage of Orson Davis' recent notoriety in the film industry, it was much easier to open doors.

Although Orson had plenty of help and people he could delegate to, the work put a strain on his health. It was during a flight back home to

California that the man suffered a mild stroke. Orson took it lightly, thinking it was only fatigue, therefore failing to mention it to his husband. One week later, Orson was in an ambulance due to a second stroke that occurred during dinner with Jesse at a restaurant. There was not much to do, Orson passed away on the way to the hospital, literally dying in Jesse's arms.

The guy makes a sudden and harsh effort to erase away those memories, otherwise he'll crumble right there, at the entrance of the institute in front of everyone, and what would Orson say? He thought, now that he'd made it this far without the slightest shade of a whimper.

Everyone is already in the building, waiting inside the Leroy "Lazy" Cooper Auditorium. A semi-circular space that now hosts about two hundred and fifty people in attendance for the opening ceremony, which began with an introduction by the Memphis Symphony Orchestra. Jesse is seated in the front row between his mothers and Kyle Santos next to his wife. Ambar has Lauren on her left and Gennie, Hank, and Cindy on her right. Evelyn and Gladys are right behind them while Angela is in the center of the stage. She's in front of a podium, delivering her last few words before all the guests who want to be part of Orson's vision. Jesse is in disbelief. He turns around and takes a look at the audience's faces, sitting quietly and attentive to what was being said.

Jesse feels Orson is in the room standing right before him, waiting for his boy to go on stage, probably curious about what he has written, the guy thinks. Lauren recently said to him that his husband hasn't really left; that he is nearby. Even though Jesse is not completely keen on her beliefs, it's comforting to know that at least someone else thinks Orson is still that close. Jesse hears Angie calling his name, and that's his cue to give his speech. He gets up and hears the applause, and right before he takes his first step to go on stage, he whispers to himself and Orson, "Babe, we're on."

Jesse flips through the radio stations manually. He doesn't recall ever actually dialing a radio in his life, but he had seen how it is done in millions of movies, and by Orson, naturally. He's riding in Orson's Lincoln Continental, way past midnight, taking the longest way home, cruising on a lonely desert road near the end of Arizona. He finally picks something on the radio he likes: "Last Night" by Little Walter, a song he heard a few times before, but never really paid attention to until he heard Orson humming to it one morning.

It is one of those moonless nights where stars do their best to draw attention before the dark blue sky. Above the mountains in the background, clouds gather around the tiny sparkling lights creating scattered patches of blue competing against each another. At two or so in the morning, cars are very scarce on either side of the road, making his trip more intimate. Jesse loves that feeling of being the last human on the planet.

Abe left Ambar's garage two days ago. The poor fellow had been sitting abandoned in her garage for 12 years. That long ago, Orson was so afraid of driving it to LA that it just sat there while the man tried to make up his mind about what to do with it. Jesse had no trouble convincing Orson to send for the Imperial, which they eventually named Otis, to California. But Jesse knew better than to persuade Orson to ship Abe. Every time the guy brought up the subject, his husband would get defensive and argumentative, making the guy regretting ever mentioning it. Jesse never saw the end of it. That day, it occurred to him to suggest to Orson to sell the old Lincoln Continental. Orson said something like, 'it is one of a kind, you don't know what I went through to find it and how hard I worked to get it and fix it; the same every time the subject came up. Jesse decided to detach himself completely from that subject, eventually forgetting about the car altogether. It was at Orson's funeral in California that Ambar reminded him that Abe was still in her garage. She mentioned knowing several people who would be more than willing to get it off his hands.

Now, it was Jesse who wouldn't let go of Abe. Now, every few miles, he still wonders if it was such a good idea to drive the old car all the way to LA when it was easier and less nerve-wracking to have it shipped. But the auto mechanic assured him that after the $82,857 Jesse had spent on it, the vehicle was as good as new and would cruise smoothly all the way to LA.

The truth is that Jesse wants the alone time and what a better way to do so than driving cross country while having the feeling, which he often doubts himself, that his husband is by his side. Could it be that all that mumbo jumbo that Orson and Lauren loved talking about had finally rubbed off on him? At times, Jesse could swear that he senses the man nearby, and believes that he often catches himself saying one-liners to him.

As he approaches the border of California, he reflects on the speech he gave at the inauguration five days ago. He feels it went pretty well, in spite of the fact he had a knot in his throat that lasted all through his delivery. He thinks it was wise to avoid eye contact with any family members and friends present, for when he met them after his speech, there weren't enough tissues around to take care of the contagious crying. He's especially thankful to Hank and Angela for counting on him to talk about Orson and his dream for the center. It was true he had second thoughts about taking such an important part of the event, considering the fact that the creation of the institute is what actually killed his husband. But Jesse could easily see the big picture; the whole project and the effect that it would have for the community is large enough to eclipse whatever doubts he had.

Jesse has been having perfect weather so far, if he can call tornado warning while crossing Oklahoma a good forecast. All the way throughout the state, he watched for flying cows among the humongous white clouds painted in the solid blue sky over the beautiful and vast landscape. But now, a couple of miles away from Needles, he encounters a sudden storm so strong that he is forced to pull off the road due to bad visibility. That is just as well because he has been driving for nearly twelve hours today, with nearly four to go to reach LA, and he needs to rest. Right after he parks in a safe spot, he lays across the long seat and rests his head on his jacket against the passenger door. About 15 seconds later, he dozes off.

When the storm is nearly over, Jesse is awakened by the few heavy drops hitting hard on the roof of the car. He begins to move up until he is seated and resting his head on the door window, he closes his eyes and listens. The rhythmic sound above Abe immediately takes him to that

251

Thanksgiving night, nearly twelve years ago:

"Red," Jesse likes to remember Orson asking, "May I call you Red again?"

"God, yes," Jesse granted him with a smile. "Please, call me Red."

"Red, there is nothing more that I would like to do right now than to take you to my bed and stay there all weekend long."

"Is there enough food in the house?" Jesse asked.

"Thanksgiving leftovers."

"Sold!"

Orson laughed out loud. "God, Jesse, you don't know how I miss this." he moved his upright hands, unsynchronized back and forth. "Our thing, you know? Us, like this again."

"I sure know, I've been feeling just the same ever since New Orleans."

Orson paused for a few seconds, selecting his words. "I may be going on a limb here, but Jesse, I've missed you so much." Orson hesitated a bit but continued talking, fed up of holding back. "I'd like for us to go steady if that's still a thing."

"Go steady?" Jesse shook his head and blinked, surprised by the old-fashioned term he did not see coming aimed right at him. "Wow, I wasn't expecting that!" He then blurted out, "I'm in! If that's what it takes to convince you about me, I am definitely in."

"Red, I've been such a fool, being scared of us. Can you imagine? Me afraid of this? You are the most genuine soul I've ever met."

"Man, I can't get over this . . . what you're saying to me right now is more than I ever wanted." Jesse's voice began to break, "Orson, my feelings for you are strong as ever."

"I can't believe it has taken me till tonight to make this realization. Am I a fool or what? I don't know if I'm making any sense."

"Look at my hands." Jesse extended his arms with his palms upside down. "I have goosebumps on my hands, how is that possible?" He took his eyes off of his hands and looked at Orson. "And yes, you are making perfect sense."

Orson moved closer to Jesse, extended his arms, and placed each of his hands on Jesse's cheeks. With his fingertips slightly touching the back of the guy's neck, Orson pulled Jesse gently towards himself, making the center point above their foreheads meet. Jesse moved up his hands and held on to Orson's wrists. They looked at their unfocused faces for a few seconds and then closed all four eyes. They sat there still, sensing each other while emotions went back and forth. Orson slid his fingers towards the back of Jesse's head. The guy let go of his wrists and put his arms around the man, moving their heads next to each other. The man embraced him back. Time stood still as the rain gently synched with their hearts—using into one. Jesse can't recall now who let go first but remembers both of them settling back in their seats after a while. They stared at one another in silence trying to read what was on each other's mind. Jesse sure knows now.

Jesse reaches out his arm in hopes of finding Orson's hand to hold it tight. He lies there alone for a few more seconds and smiles, thinking of how fortunate he is for having loved so and getting so much more in return. He sits up and slowly slides over to the driver's side and hits the switch to open the car windows on his side. He invites in the wind and the few remaining raindrops and let them merge with his tears. "Let's go, Babe," he says out loud as he turns the key. Abe roars strong and mighty and gets back on the road. Jesse switches on the windshield wipers briefly, then contemplates the road ahead looked over by stars, each of them dispersed across a dawning horizon feathered from indigo to dark blue. He heads home; no need to rush because, with Orson in heart and spirit, Jesse is already there.

THE END

ABOUT THE AUTHOR

Mario Arturo was born in San Juan, Puerto Rico. He studied at the University of Georgia, USA. He began his professional life as a graphic designer in Puerto Rico where he lived until he moved to New York to work in editorial advertising. He moved to Barcelona, Spain where he currently lives and works as a book cover designer.

He is the author of *Barcelona Tiles Designs*, *Havana Tile Designs* and *Puerto Rico Tile Designs* (Pepin Press, 2006, 2007 and 2010, respectively).

Gentle Rain is his first novel.

Spotify Playlist: Gentle Rain – Mario Arturo
https://tinyurl.com/mchfyp

Cover design: Mario Arturo
Cover photography: Freemind-Production / Lindsay Helms/Shutterstock
Back cover photography: Georgii Shipin / Shutterstock

Made in the USA
Middletown, DE
09 September 2021